THE VICTORIA VANISHES

www.rbooks.co.uk

Also by Christopher Fowler and featuring Bryant & May

FULL DARK HOUSE
THE WATER ROOM
SEVENTY-SEVEN CLOCKS
TEN-SECOND STAIRCASE
WHITE CORRIDOR

THE VICTORIA VANISHES

CHRISTOPHER FOWLER

Doubleday

LONDON • TORONTO • SYDNEY • AUCKLAND • JOHANNESBURG

TRANSWORLD PUBLISHERS
61–63 Uxbridge Road, London W5 5SA
A Random House Group Company
www.rbooks.co.uk

First published in Great Britain
in 2008 by Doubleday
an imprint of Transworld Publishers

A CIP catalogue record for this book
is available from the British Library.

ISBN 9780385610681

Addresses for Random House Group Ltd companies outside the UK
can be found at: www.randomhouse.co.uk
The Random House Group Reg. No. 954009

The Random House Group Limited supports The Forest Stewardship Council (FSC), the leading international forest-certification organization. All our titles that are printed on Greenpeace-approved FSC-certified paper carry the FSC logo. Our paper procurement policy can be found at www.rbooks.co.uk/environment

Typeset in 11/13pt Sabon by
Kestrel Data, Exeter, Devon
Printed and bound in Great Britain by
Clays Ltd, St Ives plc

2 4 6 8 10 9 7 5 3 1

For Steven, my brother and friend

ACKNOWLEDGEMENTS

My editor Simon Taylor has been with Bryant and May from the outset, and remains as tenacious as my sleuths, although he has the tougher job because he's not fictional. Likewise, my agent Mandy Little continues to venture forth into the twilight criminal world of publishing to fight evil-doers. Meg Davis, my film and TV agent, is soft of voice but firm in her resolve to find new fans of Bryant and May. Thanks, too, to Kate Samano, whose knowledge of the PCU is now probably greater than mine, and to Claire Ward for providing visuals to this world.

Special thanks go to Jan Briggs, for the knowledge of London she gained on the beat and has been so willing to share, to Michele Slung, who advised and accompanied me on the pub crawl in the book (sorry you got your purse nicked), to Simon Rennie, who knows a lot about Londoners from both sides of the bar, to Maggie Armitage, the nicest woman ever to be turned into a witch, to Sally Chapman, my great friend and spookily efficient PA, and to Pete Chapman, for pretty much everything else.

No mention of mysterious murder would be complete without the field experts, Mike Cane, Barry Forshaw and Ali Karim. Finally, thanks to all the bloggers, reviewers and readers who do it for the love of the game.

The Victoria Vanishes takes place in London's quirkiest public houses. Since writing the book, some of these have already been destroyed or badly converted by greedy developers. The remaining ones are worth visiting, but I could have filled another volume with equally interesting venues. For more information visit: www.christopherfowler.co.uk

'It is most absurdly said, in popular language, of any man, that he is disguised in liquor; for, on the contrary, most men are disguised by sobriety.'

Thomas de Quincey
Confessions of an English Opium-Eater

PECULIAR CRIMES UNIT

1b Hampstead Rd
London NW1 0JP

DUTY ROSTER FOR MONDAY 26th FEBRUARY

Raymond Land, *Acting Temporary Unit Chief*

Arthur Bryant, *Senior Detective*

John May, *Senior Detective*

Janice Longbright, *Detective Sergeant*

Dan Banbury, *Crime Scene Manager/Information Technology*

Giles Kershaw, *Forensics/Pathology*

Meera Mangeshkar, *Detective Constable*

Colin Bimsley, *Detective Constable*

April May, *Office Manager/Liaison*

PLEASE NOTE THAT THE OFFICE WILL BE CLOSING AT 4.00 P.M. TODAY, IN ORDER TO ALLOW STAFF TO ATTEND THE FUNERAL OF OUR PATHOLOGIST, OSWALD ELIAS FINCH.

A NON-DENOMINATIONAL SERVICE WILL BE CONDUCTED AT ST PANCRAS OLD CHURCH AT 4.30 P.M.

DRINKS WILL BE SERVED UPSTAIRS AT THE DEVEREUX PUB, OFF ESSEX STREET, THE STRAND, FROM 6.00 P.M.

IN ACCORDANCE WITH MR FINCH'S WISHES, PLEASE DO NOT SEND FLOWERS TO THE CHURCH. INSTEAD, YOU CAN MAKE CONTRIBUTIONS TO:

C/O NHS Trust Ward ES
Psychiatric Unit
Broadhampton Hospital
Lavender Hill
London
SE5 8AZ

STAFF BULLETINS

We are in the process of clearing out the Bayham Street Morgue and refitting it as a Grade 4 'Secure Hygiene' area, so personal items may no longer be kept here. This notice especially applies to the person who left a box of Maynard's 'Olde Tyme' wine gums and a jar of Branston Pickle in one of the cadaver drawers.

Next Monday the PCU Film Club will be showing *It Always Rains on Sunday* with Googie Withers. This was Sergeant Longbright's choice, so all those who were expecting a screening of the new Martin Scorsese film should address their complaints to her.

Please read the new recommended guidelines on suspect searches and confiscation of property. Suspects have rights, apparently, even if you think they might have cut off someone's head and left it in their fridge. Don't blame me, I don't make the rules.

This Thursday's evening class, to be given by Raymond Land on 'Policework and the Power of Positive Thinking', has been cancelled due to lack of interest.

Please note that sardines in sunflower oil do not agree with Crippen, as the person who stacked their outgoing mail near his litter tray will discover to their disadvantage.

1

ASLEEP IN THE STARS

She had four and a half minutes left to live.

She sat alone at the cramped bar of the Seven Stars and stared forlornly into her third empty glass of the evening, feeling invisible.

The four-hundred-year-old public house was tucked behind the Royal Courts of Justice. It had been simply furnished with a few small tables, wooden settles and framed posters of old British courtroom movies. Miss Curtis had been coming here for years, ever since she had first become a legal secretary, but every time she walked through the door, she imagined her father's disapproval of her drinking alone in a London pub. It wasn't something a vicar's daughter should do.

Hemmed in by barristers and clerks, she could not help wondering if this was all that would be left for her now. She wanted to remain in employment, but companies had grown clever about making women of a certain age redundant. After her last pay-off, she had spent time working for a philosophical society instead of heading back into another large firm. Now she was waiting for

– what exactly? Someone to surprise her, someone to appreciate her, someone –

She stared back into the melting ice cubes.

Her name was Naomi, but her colleagues called her Miss Curtis. What was the point of having an exotic name if nobody used it? She was sturdy-beamed and rather plain, with thick arms and a straight fringe of greying hair, so perhaps Curtis suited her better. If she had married, perhaps she would have gained a more appealing surname. She regretted having nothing to show for the past except the passing marks of time.

She checked the message on her mobile again. It was brief and unsigned, but casual acquaintances sometimes called and suggested a drink, then failed to turn up; the legal profession was like that. Looking around the bar, she saw no one she recognized. Friends usually knew where to find her.

'Give me another Gordon's, darling. Better make it a double.'

Adorable boy, she thought. The barman was impossibly slim, probably not much older than twenty-one, and didn't regard her with pity, just gave her the same friendly smile he bestowed on everyone else. Probably Polish; the ones who worked in bars now were quick to show pleasure, and had a rather old-fashioned politeness about them that she admired.

She touched her hair back into place and watched him at work. She would never eat alone in a restaurant, but taking a drink by herself in a pub was different. Nobody knew her past here, or cared. There were no tourists in for once, just the Friday-night after-office crowd jammed into the tiny narrow rooms and spread out across the pavement on an unnaturally warm winter night. It would have to be a lot colder than this to stop the city boys from drinking outside.

When she noticed him, it seemed he had been standing at her side for a while, trying to get served. 'Here,' she said, pushing back her stool. 'Get in while you can.'

'Thanks.' He had a nice profile, but quickly turned his head from her, probably through shyness. He was a lot younger than she was, slightly built, with long brown hair that fell across his face. There was something distantly recognizable about him. 'Can I get you one while I'm here?' he asked.

Rather a common voice, she thought. *South London. But familiar in the way that certain men belong in pubs. Someone I've talked to after a few gins?*

'Go on, then, I'll have another Gordon's, plenty of ice.'

He slid the drink over to her, looking around. 'I wonder if it's always this crowded.'

'Pretty much. Don't even think about finding your way to the toilets, they're up those stairs.' She pointed to the steep wooden passageway where a pair of tall prosecutors were making a meal out of having to squeeze past each other.

He muttered something, but it was lost in a burst of raucous laughter behind them.

'I'm sorry, what did you say?' she asked.

'I said it feels like home in here.' He turned to her. She tried not to stare.

'My home was never like this.'

'You know what I mean. Cosy. Warm. Sort of friendly.'

Is he just being friendly, she thought, *or is it something else?* He was standing rather too close to her, and even though it was nice to feel the heat of his arm against her shoulder, it was not what she wanted. In a pub like this everyone's space was invaded; trespass was part of the attraction. But she did not want – was not looking for – anything else, other than another drink, and then another.

He showed no inclination to move away. Perhaps he was lonely, a stranger in town. He liked the pubs around here, he told her – Penderel's Oak, the Old Mitre, the Punch Tavern, the Crown and Sugarloaf.

'Seen the displays in the window outside this place?' he asked.

She turned and saw the swinging pub sign above the door: seven gold-painted stars arranged in a circle. The wind was rising. In the windows below, legal paraphernalia had been arranged in dusty tableaux.

'Wigs and gowns, dock briefs. All that stuff for defending criminals, nonces and grasses.' He spoke quickly, almost angrily. She couldn't help wondering if he'd had trouble with the police. 'I used to meet my girlfriend in pubs like this. After she left me I got depressed, thought of topping myself. That's why I keep this.' He dug in his pocket and showed her a slender alloy capsule, a shiny bullet with his name etched on to the side. 'A mate smuggled it in for me as a reminder. It's live ammunition. If things get too much I'd use it on myself, no problem. Only I haven't got a gun.' He'd soon finished his beer. 'Get you another?'

She wanted more gin but demurred, protested, pushing her stool back several inches. He seemed dangerous, unpredictable, in the wrong pub. He took her right arm by the elbow and guided it back on to the bar with a smile, but gripped so firmly that she had no choice. She looked around; most of the standing men and women had their backs to her, and were lost in their own conversations. Even the barman was facing away. A tiny, crowded pub, the safest place she could imagine, and yet she suddenly felt trapped.

'I really don't want another drink. In fact I think I have to – ' Was she raising her voice to him? If so, no one had noticed.

'This is a good place. Nice and busy. I think you should stay. I want you to stay.'

'Then you have to let go – ' But his grip tightened. She reached out with her left hand to attract the attention of the barman but he was moving further away.

'You have to let go – '

It was ridiculous, she was surrounded by people but the noise of laughter and conversation was drowning her out. The crush of customers made her even more invisible. He was hurting her now. She tried to squirm out of his grip.

Something stung her face hard. She brought her free hand to her cheek, but there was nothing. It felt like an angry wasp, trapped and maddened in the crowded room. Wasn't it too early in the year for such insects?

And then he released her arm, and she was dropping, through the beery friendship of the bar, away from the laughter and yeasty warmth of life, into a place of icy, infinite starlight.

Into death.

2

THE FIRST FAREWELL

Early Monday in Leicester Square. On a blue-grey morning like this the buildings looked heavier, more real somehow in rain than in sunlight. Drizzle drifted on a chill breeze from the north-east. The sky that smudged the rooftops looked so low you felt you could reach up and touch it.

John May, Senior Detective at the Peculiar Crimes Unit, looked around as he walked. He saw cloud fragments in lakes on broken pavements. Shop shutters rolling up. Squirrels lurking like ticket touts. Pigeons eating pasta. Office workers picking paths through roadworks as carefully as cats crossing cobblestones.

The doorways that once held homeless kids in sleeping bags now contained plastic sacks of empty champagne bottles, a sign of the city's spiralling wealth. Piccadilly Circus was once the hub of the universe, but today only tourists loitered beside Eros, trying to figure out how to cross the Haymarket without being run over.

Every city has its main attraction, May thought as he negotiated a route through the dining gutter-parrots in the square. *Rome has the Coliseum, Paris the Eiffel Tower, but for Londoners, Leicester Square is now the king. It seems to have wrested the capital's crown from Piccadilly Circus to become our new focal point.*

He skirted a great puddle, avoided a blank-faced boy handing out free newspapers, another offering samples of chocolate cake.

This is the only time of the day that Leicester Square is bearable, he thought. *I hate it at night. The sheer number of people standing around, what do they all wait here for? They come simply because it's Leicester Square. There's not even a chance they'll spot Tom Cruise and take his photo on their mobile phones, because everyone knows film premieres only take place on week nights. There's nothing to see other than a giant picture of – who is it this week? – Johnny Depp outside the Odeon cinema, plus a very small park, the cheap-ticket kiosk and those parlours selling carpet-tile pizzas that you could dry-stone a wall with. At least Trafalgar Square has Nelson.*

The scene before him was almost devoid of people, and could not reveal the diegesis of so many overlapping lives. The city was shaped by assembly, proximity and the need for companionship. *Lone wolves can live in the hills, but London is for the terminally sociable.*

May caught sight of himself in a shop window. On any other day, he would have been pleased to note how neatly he fitted his elegant suit. He had remained fit and attractive despite his advancing years. His hair had greyed, but his jaw and waist were impressively firm, his colouring healthy, his energy level consistently high. *All the more reason to be angry,* he thought. Today he had good reason to be ill-tempered. He had just come to the realization that he might very well be dying.

He tried not to think about the sinister manila envelope in his briefcase, about the X-rays, the Leicester

Square Clinic's referral letter, and what this meant to his future. For once he just wanted to enjoy London and think of nothing in particular, but the city wasn't letting him.

I remember when the square was different. Bigger and leafier, with cars slowly circling it and thousands of starlings fluttering darkly in the trees, that busker in a fez doing a sand-dance for coins outside the Empire. Look at the state of the place now. Kids need a purpose for coming here other than getting their iPods nicked. What will the next tawdry attraction be, I wonder? Celebrity mud-wrestling or the National Museum of Porn? At least I won't be here to witness the indignities thrust upon it. I'll be long gone. I used to drink mild and bitter in the Hand and Racquet with Arthur, then take a Guinness in the Green Man and French Horn over in St Martin's Lane. I wonder if we'll ever do that again? I always thought he would go first, but what if it's me? What on earth will Arthur do then?

Bryant and May. Their names went together like Hector and Lysander, like Burke and Hare, unimaginable in separation. May still felt young, although he was far from it. He still looked good and felt fit, but his companion in crime detection, Arthur Bryant, was growing old before his eyes. He had all his critical faculties, far more than most, but the physical demands of the job were wearing him down. May wondered whether to hide his news from his partner for fear of upsetting him.

Despite his dark thoughts, May was still at his happiest here, walking to work through the city on a rainy February morning. Being near the idealistic young was enough to provide him with the energy to survive. He tried to imagine how visitors felt, seeing these sights for the first time. Every year there were more nationalities, more languages, and the people who stayed on became

Londoners. It was an appealingly egalitarian notion. More than anything, he would miss all of this. Culinary terms were appropriate for the metropolis; it was a steaming stew, a broth, a great melting pot, momentarily levelling the richest and poorest as they rubbed shoulders on the streets.

Striding between the National Portrait Gallery and St Martin-in-the-Fields, he briefly stopped to reread the wording beneath the white stone statue of Dame Edith Cavell, the British nurse who faced a German firing squad for helping hundreds of soldiers escape from Belgium to the Netherlands. The inscription said: 'Patriotism is not enough. I must have no hatred or bitterness for anyone.' *If there's a more respectful creed by which to live*, he thought, *I can't imagine what it is*.

He put the blame squarely on London and the strange effect it had on people. If he hadn't come here as a young man and met Bryant, he would never have been infected with his partner's passion for the place. He wouldn't have stayed here all these years, unravelling the crimes deemed too abstract and bizarre to occupy the time of regular police forces. And even now, knowing that it might all come to an end, he could not entertain the thought of leaving.

Curiosity finally got the better of him, and he stopped in the middle of the pavement to take out the envelope and tear it open. He could feel the letter inside, but did he have the nerve to read it?

A good innings, some would say. Let the young have a go now. Time to turn the world over to them. To hell with it. With a catch in his heart, he pulled out the single sheet of paper, unfolded it and scanned the two short paragraphs.

A tumour attached to the wall of his heart . . . a recommendation for immediate surgery . . . a serious risk owing to past cardiovascular problems that had created a weakness possibly leading to embolism.

He took a deep breath and exhaled slowly. Worse than he had expected, or better? Did he need to start planning for the inevitable? Should he tell anyone at the unit, or would it get back to Arthur?

You can't go, old bean, Bryant would say when he found out, and find out he would because he always did. *Not without me. I'm coming with you. You're not going off to have the biggest adventure of all on your own.* He'd mean it, too. For all his appearance of frailty he was an extremely tough old man; he'd just recovered from wrestling a killer in a snowdrift, and all he'd suffered was a slight chest cold. But he wouldn't want to be left behind. You couldn't have one without the other, two old friends as comfortable as cardigans.

I'm not going without a fight, May thought, shoving the letter into his pocket and striding off through the blustering rain towards the Charing Cross Road.

3

END TIMES

Arthur Bryant blotted the single sheet of blue Basildon Bond paper, carefully folded it into three sections and slid it into a white business envelope. He pressed the adhesive edges together and turned it over, uncapping his marbled green Waterman fountain pen. Then, in spidery script, he wrote on the front:

> For the attention of:
> Raymond Land
> Acting Temporary Chief
> Peculiar Crimes Unit

Well, he said to himself, *you've really done it this time. You can still change your mind. It's not too late.*

Fanning the envelope until the ink was thoroughly dry, he slipped it into the top pocket of his ratty tweed jacket, checked that his desk was clear of work files and quietly left the office.

Passing along the gloomy corridor outside, he paused before Raymond Land's room and listened. The sound of light snoring told him that the unit's acting chief was at home. Usually Bryant would throw open the door with a bang, just to startle him, but today he entered on gentle tiptoe, creeping across the threadbare carpet to stand silently before his superior. Land was tipped back in his leather desk-chair with his mouth hanging open and his tongue half out, faintly gargling. The temptation to drop a Mint Imperial down his throat was overpowering, but instead, Bryant simply transferred his envelope to Land's top pocket and crept back out of the room.

The die is cast, he told himself. *There'll be fireworks after the funeral this afternoon, that's for sure.* Bryant was feeling fat, old and tired, and he was convinced he had started shrinking. Either that or John was getting taller. With each passing day he was becoming less like a man and more like a tortoise. At this rate he would soon be hibernating for half the year in a box full of straw. He needed to take more and more *stuff* with him wherever he went: walking stick, pills, hearing-aid batteries, pairs of glasses, teeth. Only his wide blue eyes remained youthful. *I'm doing the right thing*, he reminded himself. *It's time.*

'Do you think he ought to be standing on a table at his age?' asked the voluptuous tanned woman in the tight black dress, as she helped herself to another ladleful of lurid vermilion punch. 'He needs a haircut. Funny, considering he has hardly any hair.'

'I have a horrible feeling he's planning to make some kind of speech,' Raymond Land told Leanne Land, for the woman with the bleached straw tresses and cobalt eye make-up who stood beside him in the somewhat risqué outfit was indeed his wife.

'You've warned me about Mr Bryant's speeches before,' said Leanne. 'They tend to upset people, don't they?'

'He had members of the audience throwing plastic

chairs at each other during the last "Meet the Public" relationship-improving police initiative we conducted.'

They were discussing the uncanny ability of Land's colleague to stir up trouble whenever he appeared before a group of more than six people. Arthur Bryant, the most senior detective in residence at London's Peculiar Crimes Unit, was balanced unsteadily on a circular table in front of them, calling for silence.

As the room hushed, Raymond Land nudged his wife. 'I don't think your dress is entirely appropriate for the occasion,' he whispered. 'You're almost falling out of it.'

'My life-coach says I should be very proud of my breasts,' she countered. 'So why shouldn't I look good at a party?'

'Because it's a wake,' hissed Raymond. 'The host is dead.'

'Ladies and gentlemen,' Bryant bellowed so loudly that his hearing aid squealed with feedback. 'This was intended to be a celebration of our esteemed coroner's retirement, but instead it has become a night of sad farewells.'

The table wobbled alarmingly, and several hands shot out to steady the elderly detective. Bryant unfolded his spectacles, consulted a scrap of paper, then balled it and threw it over his shoulder. He had decided to speak from the heart, which was always dangerous.

'Oswald Finch worked with the Peculiar Crimes Unit from its inception, and planned to retire on this very night. Everyone had been looking forward to the bash. I had personally filled the morgue refrigerator with beer and sausage rolls, and we were planning a big send-off. Luckily, I was able to alter the icing inscription on his retirement cake, so it hasn't gone to waste. "*The funeral baked meats did aptly furnish forth the marriage tables*", only the other way around, and with retirement substituted for marriage.'

'What's he on about?' whispered Leanne.

'*Hamlet*,' said Land. 'I think.'

'Because instead of retiring, Oswald Finch died in tragic circumstances under his own examination table, and now he'll never get to enjoy his twilight years in that freezing, smelly fisherman's hut he'd bought for himself on the beach in Hastings. Now I know some of you will be thinking, "And bloody good riddance, you miserable old sod," because he could be a horrible old man, but I like to believe that Oswald was only bad-tempered because nobody liked him. He had dedicated his life to dead people, and now he's joined them.'

One of the stationhouse girls burst into tears. Bryant held up his hands for quiet. 'This afternoon, in a reflective mood, I sat at my desk and tried to remember all the good things about him. I couldn't come up with anything, I'm afraid, but the intention was there. I even tried phoning Oswald's oldest schoolfriend to ask him for amusing stories, but sadly he went mad some while back and now lives in a mental home in Wales.'

Bryant paused for a moment of contemplation. A mood of despondency settled over the room like a damp flannel. 'Oswald was a true professional. He was determined not to let his total lack of sociability get in the way of his career. True, he was depressing to be around, and everyone complained that he smelled funny, but that was because of the chemicals he used. And the flatulence. People said that he didn't enjoy a laugh, but it went deeper than that. In all the years I worked with him, I never once saw him crack a smile, even when we secretly attached electrodes to his dissecting tray and made his hair stand on end.' Bryant counted on his fingers. 'So, just to recap, Oswald Finch: no sense of humour, no charm, friendless, embittered, stone-faced and bloody miserable, on top of which he stank. Some folk can fill a room with joy just by entering it. Whereas being in Oswald's presence for a few minutes could make you long for the release that death might bring.'

He paused before the aghast, silenced crowd.

'But – and this is the most important thing – he was the most ingenious, humane and talented medical examiner I have ever had the great pleasure of working with. And because of his ability to absorb and adapt, to think instead of merely responding, Oswald's work will live on even though he doesn't, because it will provide a template for all those who come after. His fundamental understanding of the human condition taught us more about the lives and deaths of murder victims than any amount of computerized DNA testing. Oswald's intuitive genius will continue to shine a beacon of light into the darkest corners of the human soul. In short, his radiance will not dim, and can only illuminate us when we think of him, or study his methods, and for that I raise a glass to him tonight.'

'Blimey, he's finally learning to be gracious,' said Dan Banbury, the unit's stubby crime-scene manager. 'I've never heard him be nice about anyone before.'

'He must be pissed,' sniffed Raymond Land, jealously turning aside as the others helped Bryant from his wobbly table. He glanced down at the white-and-blue-iced fruit cake that stood in the middle of the pub's canapé display. The inscription had read: *Wishing You the Best of Luck in Hastings*, but *Hastings* had been partially picked off and replaced with a shakily mismatched *Heaven*. The iced fisherman's hut now had pearly gates around it, and the stick figure at its door had sprouted wings and a halo, picked out in hundreds and thousands.

'I hope the cake has more taste than the inscription,' muttered Land, shaking his head in despair.

Nobody had expected the retirement party for the

Peculiar Crime Unit's chief coroner to become a wake, but then life at the unit rarely turned out according to anyone's expectations. Oswald Finch had died, sadly and suddenly, in his own morgue, in what could only be described as extraordinary circumstances. Yet his death seemed entirely appropriate for someone who daily dealt with the deceased.

Raymond Land had never expected to stay on this long at the PCU. After all, he had joined the unit for a three-month tour in 1973, and was horrified to find himself still here.

Arthur Bryant and John May, the unit's longest-serving detectives, had been expected to rise through the ranks to senior-division desk jobs before quietly fading away, but were still out on the street beyond their retirement ages.

Detective Sergeant Janice Longbright had been expected to marry and leave the force, perhaps to eventually resume her old job as a night-club manager, but instead she had chosen her career over her husband and had stayed on.

The PCU itself should have been disbanded by now, but had successfully skated over every trap laid for it by the Home Office. Even Land had argued for the unit's closure behind his colleagues' backs, but had then surprised himself by fighting in order to preserve it.

Life, it seemed, was every bit as confusing and disorderly as the PCU's investigations.

Now, the annoyingly upper-class pathologist Giles Kershaw was to be promoted into Finch's position in charge of the Bayham Street morgue, which meant that the PCU was losing another member of staff. With grim inevitability, the Home Office would doubtless seek to use the loss as a method of controlling and closing them down. The oldest members of staff would be for the chop. Land had given up hope of ever finding a way to transfer out. He had nailed his colours to the unit's mast when he had reluctantly supported his own staff and attacked his superiors. Now, they would never find him a cushy detail in the suburbs where he could quietly wait out the remaining years to his retirement.

Land sighed and looked about the pub's upstairs room. Plenty of officers from Albany Street, West End Central and Savile Row nicks, even former ushers from Great Marlborough Street Magistrates Court had turned up for the wake, but the Home Office had chosen to show their disdain by staying away. Finch had upset them too many times in the past.

Sergeant Renfield, the ox-like desk officer from Albany Street, was watching everyone from his lonely vantage point near the toilets. Land headed over with two bottles of porter clutched between his fingers. 'Hello, Jack,' he said, refilling Renfield's beer glass with the malty liquid. 'I wondered if you'd show up to see Oswald off.'

'You bloody well knew I'd be here.' The sergeant regarded him with a baleful eye. 'After all, it's partly my fault that he's dead.'

'There's no point in being hard on yourself,' said Land. 'People working in close proximity to death face unusual hazards. It's part of the job.'

'Try telling that to this lot.' Renfield gestured at the room with his glass. 'I know they blame me for what happened.' The sergeant had made a procedural shortcut that had been revealed as a bad decision in the light of Finch's death. To be fair, it was the sort of mistake that often occurred when everyone was under pressure.

'Actually, Jack, today isn't about you. Besides, you'll get a chance to have your say.'

Renfield looked anxious. 'You haven't already told them, have you? Have you said something to Bryant and May?'

'Good God, no. Call me old-fashioned, but I thought we'd get Oswald into the incinerator before I gave them the good news. Come to think of it, perhaps you should be the one to make the announcement.' Land patted the sergeant on the shoulder and moved away. He wasn't alone in disliking Renfield, who was a Met man, as hard and earthy as the ground he walked on. Renfield had no time for the airy-fairy attitudes of the PCU staff, and didn't care who knew it. Left alone in the corner of the room once more, he decided to concentrate on fitting sausage rolls into his mouth between slugs of beer.

Over at the bar, Arthur Bryant adjusted his reading glasses, held up the aluminium funeral urn and turned it over to examine its base. 'Made in China,' he muttered. 'A lightweight wipe-clean screw-top final resting place. I suppose Oswald would have approved. But how quickly we sacrifice dignity for expedience, even in death.'

'Well, he didn't choose it for himself,' said John May. 'He'd have picked something less vulgar. He was always so thorough, and yet he decided to entrust his remains to you.'

'He knew I'd do the right thing,' said Bryant with a knowing smile.

'Which is?'

'I've been instructed to plant his ashes in a place that would annoy Raymond. I thought the little park behind Pratt Street would do nicely, because Land always goes there for a quiet smoke. I'm going to stick it right opposite the bench where he sits, so he'll have to keep looking at it. I've already had a word with the park keeper.'

'Do you think Oswald would want to be buried there?'

'Why not? It's handy for the office. He worked in the same place for fifty years. People don't like change, alive or dead.' Bryant lifted his rucksack from the floor to place the urn inside it, but changed his mind.

'One thing puzzles me, John. He didn't want floral tributes, but requested posthumous contributions for the Broadhampton Hospital. He never mentioned the place before. I thought it might be where his old school pal was kept, but no. Maybe he has a family friend staying in there, some kind of debt to be honoured. He probably wouldn't have wanted to discuss the matter in life. It's an asylum, after all.'

'No,' replied May indignantly, 'that's exactly what it's not. It's no longer a place of confinement. Nowadays it specializes in advanced treatment and research into mental-health care.'

'You know its sister hospital is the oldest psychiatric hospital in the world?' Bryant poked about among the canapés and thought about dipping a battered prawn. 'The Bethlem Royal was once known as Bedlam, famous for the ill-treatment of its patients. Visitors were given sticks so they could poke the loonies. Insanity was viewed as the result of moral lassitude, you know. Charlie Chaplin's mother and the artist Richard Dadd were both locked up in there. But I don't think Hogarth's ghastly engraving of the place is entirely to be believed. There were flowers and birdcages in its women's wards, and a few surprising instances of enlightened thinking on behalf of the doctors. It's been knocking around since the mid-thirteenth century and is still going strong, as part of the South London Trust.' Bryant removed a prawn-tail from his dentures and absently put it in his pocket. 'I don't trust this Mary Rose sauce, far too pink for my liking. Oswald told me he had no other living relatives. So why would he want us to leave money to a mental hospital?'

'I really have no idea.'

May was a poor liar and glanced uncomfortably at the floor. Bryant sensed there was something he had not yet been told about the deceased coroner.

4

BRINKMANSHIP

'Look out, here comes trouble.'

Bryant spoke from the side of his mouth and stuck out his little finger in the direction of Renfield, who was heading towards them. His comment might have been intended as a discreet aside, but came over as offensively loud and theatrical. Luckily, Renfield was as thick-skinned as a pub comic, and kept his course.

'Ah, Sergeant Renfield, given up flies for vol-au-vents?'

'What?' Renfield pushed a mouthful of pastry to one side of his teeth with a fat finger.

'Forget it, Renfield, Mr Bryant is making a joke,' said John May.

'I don't understand his sense of humour.' Renfield regarded them with the irritation of a perpetual outsider.

'Your name,' explained May. 'There's a character in Bram Stoker's *Dracula* called Renfield who lives in a madhouse and eats flies.'

'Perhaps your geriatric comrade will be laughing on the other side of his face when he hears my news.'

The sergeant talked over the top of Bryant's shiny bald head.

'Don't tell me you've decided to pursue a lifelong dream and join the South African police?'

'No, matey,' said Renfield with a smug smile. 'I've been kicked upstairs. I'm joining you lot. Just been appointed Duty Sergeant at the Peculiar Crimes Unit.'

Bryant was aghast. 'That's not possible,' he said. 'Raymond decides who comes and goes, and he only ever does what I tell him.'

'These are direct orders from the Home Office, chum.' Renfield's smile grew darker, like a portly cat moving in on a crow. 'I'm looking forward to a switch of scenery. I'll be going back to the manuals and doing things properly for a change. You can guarantee that I'll be putting a curb on some of your more illegal habits.'

'But you're not a detective,' May pointed out.

'I don't need to be, pal. It's about monitoring procedure and making sure there are no more of your famous breaches of conduct. You don't need to be a bloody detective to do that.'

So, this is the price of getting Giles Kershaw appointed as the new pathologist, thought May. The Home Office was planting Sergeant Renfield into the unit as a practical field man who would force them to play by the rules. The ministry officials had tried using Raymond Land to control the PCU, and that had failed. Now an alternative strategy had presented itself. He wished the unit could just get on with the business of solving crime, but instead it was mired in inter-departmental politics, despite the fact that it had been set up as an independent body to avoid government red tape. Its original purpose had been to deal with crimes that could cause civil unrest and political embarrassment, but over the decades (and under the guidance of Bryant and May) it had proven itself adept at cracking cases where even the most advanced technology failed to identify a culprit. No computer could replicate the sheer peculiarity of the PCU's techniques. England had a history of creating think-tanks where freedom of thought was more important than adherence to procedure.

Renfield is just another hurdle we'll have to find a way of leaping, he thought. *We've always managed in the past, and we'll do it again.* He was already imagining ways of defusing this latest strategy when Bryant dropped his bombshell.

'You're too late, Renfield,' Bryant told the sergeant. 'I'm not your chum, your pal or your mate. Rather, I have some news of my own that may surprise you. I've put in for official retirement. I stuck the envelope into Raymond Land's top pocket a few hours ago.'

May looked thunderstruck. Renfield's broad jaw fell open. Everyone knew that the day Bryant retired he would most likely drop dead.

'I know it's a shock,' said Bryant, 'and I know what you're thinking, retirement will probably kill me, but I've made up my mind. Actually, you're partially responsible for my decision.'

'Me?' Renfield distractedly set the remains of his mushroom vol-au-vent to one side. 'This is about our pathologist's death, isn't it?'

'Well of course,' said Bryant. 'Although I'm not really blaming you. Oswald Finch died because of the case you brought into his morgue, it's true. But it's not about what you did. You made me understand something in myself that I hadn't seen before. It's as you've always told me, I'm miles past my best. My powers of observation were at their peak thirty years ago. When Oswald died in such tragic circumstances, I was as much in the dark about the cause as everyone else. Oh, I understood at once *what* had happened to him, but not *why*. I couldn't appreciate the human origins behind the tragedy. When you lose that ability, you start putting others in danger.'

'But Arthur, you were out of town when it happened,' his partner reminded him. 'How could you be expected to fully comprehend a crime that had taken place hundreds of miles away? You couldn't conduct an investigation without any resources.'

'The point was that I thought I could,' said Bryant. 'I should have shared information instead of hogging the little knowledge I had. I failed to observe the most fundamental rules of crime detection. I wanted to test Janice and the others, to make them come to their own conclusions.'

'Jack, leave us alone for a minute,' May told Renfield. 'I need to speak with my partner.' He pushed Bryant away from the bemused sergeant.

'Outside, you. I'm not having this argument in front of our staff.'

Seizing Bryant by the shoulders of his absurdly baggy coat, he steered him down the steep nicotine-brown stairs of the Devereux public house and into the narrow courtyard that filled with bankers and lawyers on summer evenings.

'How on earth could you do this to me, Arthur? Could you not have had the decency to discuss it with me first?'

'What, and have you try to talk me out of it?' asked Bryant. 'Just look at me, John. I'm half-blind. I have to use four sets of spectacles: my reading glasses, my bifocals, my computer lenses and my distance-driving goggles. My observation skills are limited to noting whether or not it's raining. I wear a hearing aid. I take tablets twice a day. I use a walking stick, but might be better off with a spirit level. I'm older than Picasso's minotaur paintings. I can't remember my email address. My memory operates in an almost entirely arbitrary fashion. My sense of orientation is so poor that I'm lucky to find the front door of my house without the aid of an Ordnance Survey map. And on top of all that, I appear to be shrinking. How many more organs have to pack up before I accidentally cause somebody's death?'

'Look, I know Raymond said that your powers of observation were failing, but he was talking rubbish as usual, and I am absolutely not going to have this kind of self-pitying conversation with you,' May protested, holding up his hands. 'You're as tough as an ox. Your father was a weight-lifting champion, for God's sake. You told me his neck was the same size as Victoria Beckham's waist. Your dentist reckons you have the strongest tongue in London. He has to put you out just to clean your teeth. You know how you always exaggerate your faults. You're feeling guilty because you weren't here to save Oswald Finch, but there's no point in blaming yourself because you couldn't have done anything. A detective is someone whose life operates on a strict binary system, Arthur – you're either working flat out and fully committed or completely off the case. If you stop now, you'll really see how many parts of your body can start to fail. It's the job that keeps you supple in mind and spirit, can't you see that? I'm going to find Land and take that damned envelope away from him.'

'You'll do no such thing, John, not if you value our friendship.' Bryant looked up at him with an aqueous, azure gaze. 'Don't you see? It's important to know when the time has come to stop, and Oswald's death has made me realize that I've reached the point. Back in that pub there are younger, more energetic members of the PCU who can continue our legacy.'

'Wait a minute, what about me?' said May hotly. 'You may have decided that it's time to give up the ghost, but suppose I'm not ready to go yet? I'm younger than you—'

'Only by three years.'

' – And I'm certainly not ready to retire. We've been a team for as far back as I can remember. How am I supposed to survive without you? We can't just walk away from everything we've built, not now, not after all the battles we've fought.'

'We're not part of the Met any more, remember?' Bryant rarely raised his voice, but was close to doing so now. 'There's no one fighting for us, John. We're under the control of the Home Office, whether we like it or not. You've met that faceless little weasel Leslie Faraday. Worse, you've met his boss, the Phantom of Whitehall. They'll wear us down eventually.'

'So that's it? You just give up and walk away? What do you think you're going to do at home all day – thumb through your scrapbooks of past cases, stare vacantly out of the window jingling the change in your pockets? Or worse still, phone the office offering advice until nobody wants to take your calls any more? That's what happens when people retire, you know. Their colleagues tell them to keep in touch but they don't mean it. They'll just think you're too slow and out of the loop. They'll be too busy proving themselves to bother with you. You'll be nothing more than a nuisance to them. Ageism is the last real taboo.'

May knew he had to make his partner see the truth, even if it meant being cruel. 'If you leave now, you know what we'll have wasted? All those years spent showing that we could hold our own against overpaid young hotshots, the bean-counters brought in by government ministers eager to prove themselves. All our efforts to make Raymond understand why the unit needs to survive – ' Wait a minute – Raymond. Why hadn't the chief mentioned Bryant's resignation to him? Could it be that he hadn't had a chance to read the letter yet?

'Come with me.' Seizing Bryant by the arm, he dragged him back inside the crowded pub. Land was standing near the bar, talking to his wife. A thin band of white paper protruded from his top pocket. May could not tell from this distance if it had been opened. 'You are going to get that letter back right now,' he told his partner.

'I most certainly am not.' Bryant stood his ground. 'And kindly take your arm off me. I am still quite capable of perambulating around a room, thank you.'

'Then stay here while I get it and tear the damned thing up.' May pushed his way through the clusters of officers until he found himself standing beside Raymond Land's wife.

'Well, hello stranger. Where have you been?' Leanne's eyes were half closed and her lipstick was smudged, but she was sending out signals to her favourite detective. For many years she had held not so much a torch for John May as a smugglers' lantern, but his ship had never been tempted to ground upon her rocks.

'Hello, Leanne. I'm afraid Arthur was a little overcome after his speech and needed some fresh air.' He smiled while surreptitiously checking Land's top pocket.

'Ha, he'll be hard pressed to find anything fresh round here.' Leanne laughed, a tad commonly. 'Tell me.' She leaned in so closely that he could smell Tia Maria on her breath. 'How do you manage to work with Mr Bryant without losing your temper? My husband wants to wring his neck most days.'

'I never said that, Leanne,' Land bristled.

'Oh, Raymond and I have our ways of dealing with Arthur, don't we?' May smiled awkwardly as he casually placed his hand on Land's shoulder. He tried moving it around to the envelope in his top pocket and would have succeeded, but Leanne suddenly pulled him to one side.

'You know, John, I have a long-felt want that needs taking care of.' She made it sound like a furniture-restoration project. 'You awaken something in me that Raymond can't handle. He's too busy with his golf. I've no one to talk to. I live the life of a spinster.' In moments of desperation, Leanne's Morecambe accent surfaced. 'Can't we go out for a quiet drink one evening?'

'You're my boss's wife,' May reminded her, knowing that she never forgot. 'It's a matter of protocol.'

Staring over her shoulder, he realized he had drawn attention to the letter, which Land was now pulling from his pocket in curiosity.

'Raymond, don't read it,' he begged.

Land studied the envelope. 'This is Bryant's handwriting. What's he doing sending me letters?' His forefinger drifted towards the poorly adhered corner.

'Please, Raymond. Don't open it and I'll do a deal with you.' He thought fast. 'Leave it sealed until the weekend. Arthur didn't know what he was doing.'

'Another note criticizing my ability to manage the unit, I suppose.'

'Something like that. He wasn't thinking clearly. He'd just had one of his blue pills. If I can't get him to retract the contents, you can open it at this time on Saturday afternoon, how about that?'

'I don't understand,' said Land, who so rarely did. 'I don't like it when he insults me. Why should I hold off? What's in it for me?'

'Actually it's a secret, but I'll cut you in on the deal,' said May, thinking on his feet and lying through his teeth. 'Arthur insisted that your impatience would always get the better of you, and bet me fifty pounds that you couldn't keep your hands off that envelope until Saturday.

So if you prove him wrong and leave it unopened until then, I'll split the winnings with you.'

'I don't know.' Land thought for a minute. 'Why do I feel there's something fishy going on here?' He re-examined the envelope suspiciously, but finally returned it to his pocket undisturbed.

I can't believe I got away with that, thought May as he headed back over towards Bryant. *I've bought myself a little time, now all I have to do is convince Arthur to rescind his offer. I'm such a hypocrite, telling him off about his envelope when I can't bring myself to show him the contents of mine. It's no good, I'll have to get it off my chest. My God, I need a drink.*

He ordered himself a fresh pint, then prepared for the worst.

5

MORTALITY

'Arthur, I passed the statue of Edith Cavell the other evening.' It was an opening gambit in his bid to explain his fears about the forthcoming operation. May had just told his partner about the clinic's letter.

'Did you know there are memorials to her all around the world?' Bryant interrupted, sipping his London Pride bitter. 'There's even a mountain on Venus bearing her name, and of course Edith Piaf was named after her. Cavell said she was proud to die for her country. You don't hear that very often nowadays, which is probably a good thing.'

'Arthur, did you hear what I said? I'm rather afraid I'm going to die.'

'Rubbish! A blur on an X-ray. They'll get you in and whip it out like a rogue tonsil. It's a bit late to be having intimations of mortality. Hatch, match, dispatch; there's no dignity in life. We wet the bed when we're born and when we leave. You'll be fine so long as they don't leave a swab inside you or accidentally dose you with MRSA.'

'This thing growing inside me is the size of a conker. It's going to be a dangerous operation.'

'Oh, doctors always say that. It's a way of covering themselves. Nobody likes to admit their job is easier than it looks. Patients think heart attacks are caused by stress because the first thing doctors ask them is, "Have you been working hard?" Nobody in their right mind is going to say, "No, I've been winging it for quite a while now, but the boss hasn't noticed." Stop worrying so much.'

'Arthur, just for once try and take something seriously. I want you to be prepared for the worst.'

'If you go I won't stay around. It stands to reason. Wouldn't be much fun here without you.' He attempted to smooth his fringe of unruly white hair down. 'Anyway, we can't bow out yet. I need a few juicy final cases with which to conclude my memoirs. There's still the matter of the Deptford Demon – '

'You're the one who just handed in his resignation.'

'Yes, but I thought I'd get a bit more work under my belt before they pack me off with a pitifully small cheque and an engraved carriage clock. It'll take them months just to sort out the paperwork.'

'It feels like the end of times,' said May with a weary sigh. 'There are so many things to be put in order. If anything happens to me, someone has to take care of April. And who'll look after Crippen?'

'Oh, this is sheer morbidity. When are they taking you in?'

'I'm booked into University College Hospital at the beginning of next month.'

'You see? They can't be worried or they'd have strapped you on to a trolley the moment they saw the X-rays. I'll come in with you, even though it means standing outside with all the dressing-gown people every time I want a snout.'

'It's a quarter past ten,' said Raymond Land to Giles Kershaw. 'Bryant and May are still over there in the corner conspiring about something. What on earth have they been talking about for the last five and three-quarter hours?'

'You're being paranoid, old sausage,' said the plum-voiced forensic scientist who was taking over from their ill-fated coroner. 'They're not talking about you, they're discussing old cases.'

'You can show me a little more respect, young man,' warned Land. 'I know how you landed your new job.'

'What do you mean?' asked Kershaw, genuinely surprised.

'Come off it, sunshine. You're married to the Home Secretary's sister-in-law, or something like that. Bryant told me ages ago.'

'I once went out with a girl who worked in PR at the Home Office, but I certainly never married her. I'm afraid Mr Bryant was playing a trick on you.'

Land wearily passed a hand over his sweating face. 'Well, there'll be no more tricks now that Renfield is joining them. We'll finally get a little order around here.'

The wake was starting to break up. Two of the duty officers from the Albany Street cop shop were bombarding each other with the remains of a party-sized Swiss roll, and even Finch's farewell cake had been reduced to a controlled explosion of icing and sultanas.

Bryant set his glass down on the beer-stained paper tablecloth and buttoned his overcoat. 'I have to go home, my head is swimming,' he told his partner.

'We haven't finished discussing your resignation yet.'

'Don't be angry with me, John. Leave it to sink in for a few days. You'll see I was right in the end.' Bryant settled a squashed navy homburg on to his head so that the hat pressed down on the tips of his ears, knotted his mauve scarf under his chin so that his neck disappeared, and turned up the collar of his voluminous overcoat. He looked like a music hall comic preparing for an Arctic trek.

'Do you want to share a cab?' May called as the elderly detective tapped his walking stick to his hat brim in a farewell gesture and stumped off towards the exit.

'No thanks, the walk will do me good. I need a blast of whatever passes for clean air around here.'

'All the way to Mornington Crescent? It's uphill, you know.'

'Don't worry, I have my good shoes on and I'm quite capable of finding a taxi when I get tired. You have to learn to stop worrying about me.' Bryant pushed out of the door and was gone.

I've got one week to make him change his mind, May told himself. *It's not an unfeasible task*. But he knew it was almost impossible to alter Bryant's course once it was set.

6

OBSERVATION

Arthur Bryant cursed himself. *I should have handled the matter of my resignation better,* he thought. *After all these years of working with John, I should at least have taken him into my confidence first.*

But John May had always been able to talk him out of making sudden foolhardy decisions. His was the healing voice of reason, a counterbalance to the maddening pandemonium of Bryant's mind. John might protest, but he could survive perfectly well on his own. People enjoyed his company and opened up to him, because he didn't do anything that made them nervous. Right from the outset of their partnership, when the pair had launched a murder investigation at the Palace Theatre and solved the Shepherd's Market diamond robbery, Bryant had been upsetting applecarts and overturning the status quo while his partner followed behind, smoothing raised hackles and restoring order. Across the years, from the tracking of the Deptford Demon to the final unmasking of the Leicester Square Vampire, this out-of-kilter relationship had allowed them to resolve a thousand cases great and small. But everything came to an end, and knowing when to leave was crucial.

Now Oswald Finch was gone, and soon they too would pass into oblivion, to be faintly recalled as members of the old school of police work, a pair of *characters*, representatives of a classic style of investigation that had since become obsolete. Would anything about them be remembered, other than a few oft-told anecdotes, funny stories to be trotted out wherever old men gathered in pubs? Had they really achieved anything at all, changed any laws, improved the lot of Londoners? Or would they soon be as forgotten as old music-hall stars, the pair of them described as the Flanagan and Allen of the Met?

Bryant raised his head from his scarf and looked about. He was passing along the cream stucco edge of Coram Fields, the seven-acre park on the site of the old Foundling Hospital in Bloomsbury which no adult could enter unless in the company of a child. The wind was rising, clattering the leaves of the high oaks and plane trees above him. At ten forty p.m. Bloomsbury was almost deserted, but even during the day there was hardly anyone around. The area between Gower Street and Gray's Inn Road remained reticent and dignified, seemingly trapped in an earlier era between world wars. There were still a few indifferent second-hand bookshops housed in its mansion buildings, barber shops and fish bars left over from the 1930s, corner pubs that faded back from the street in a deliberate attempt to shun passing trade.

He crossed the top of Marchmont Street into Tavistock Place, feeling his legs twinge in protest as he climbed the kerb. There would be plenty of cabs on Euston Road. Cutting across the pavement in the direction of Judd Street, he found himself in a road he did not know, little more than an alley that opened out into a dog-leg. The sound of traffic had all but disappeared. There was only the wind in the trees, and the distant twitter of birds who had mistaken the perpetually sulphurous skies for dawn.

The effect of the alcohol in his system was starting to evaporate. Untangling his distance spectacles from the other pairs that rattled loose in his pocket, he wrapped the flexible metal arms around his ears and examined the street ahead.

So Raymond Land thought he had failing powers of observation, did he? He squinted at the narrow pavement with its high red-brick wall, the rustling cherry trees, the old-fashioned gas lamps that had been wired to hold electric bulbs. The jaundiced lighting gave the street an air of melancholy neglect, like a yellowing newspaper photograph found beneath the floorboards of a derelict house.

Note what you see, he told himself. *Remember how you used to do it when you were a young man.*

OK, the street had been severed at the far end by a grim granite office building, the other side of which presumably faced the hellish traffic of Euston Road. Several houses had been pulled down – they had probably survived wartime bomb damage to last for another two or three decades – and replaced with council flats. Their windows clumsily referenced the design of the surrounding Victorian terraces, but everything about the newer properties was cheaper and smaller.

A single original house, number 6A, had been left behind. Tall and narrow, gapped on either side, it had been stranded alone in the present day like an elderly aunt at a funeral.

A slender street to the left: Argyle Walk. An alleyway leading off to the right, with black bollards raised through its centre, copies of a traditional design; once, the city had found new lives for its naval gun barrels, upending them in the streets and inserting red cannonballs in the mouths to form bollards.

Above and behind the buildings, the sallow, ghostly clock on the gothic tower of St Pancras Station floated like a second moon.

What else could he discern?

A pale keystone over a door, initials entwined in a county badge, a concave shell-hood above another entrance, a feature used by early Georgians to provide protection from inclement weather, although this one was an Edwardian copy.

A carved blind window, created to provide balance for other openings in the side wall of the terrace. Or perhaps it had been bricked in because of William III's window tax.

A black-painted fresh-air inlet with a grating on its top, like a ship's periscope, designed to prevent vacuums occurring in the sewage system below the street.

The fragile lacework of a wrought-iron ornamental balcony, complete with a curving zinc hood.

A square iron lid recessed into the flagstones that read PATENT AIR-TIGHT FLAP, the cover plate for a coal-hole which would have been converted into a basement after the arrival of central heating.

A cast-iron railing of daisies and ivy leaves, one which had survived the mass removal of ironwork during the Second World War. Britons had been told that their railings, along with their saucepans, would be melted down 'for the war effort' in what was largely a propaganda exercise.

What else?

A door-knocker consisting of a hand holding a wreath, painted over so many times that the form had been all but lost. Carpenters, metal-workers and battalions of servants would have ensured that these domestic items remained in perfect condition. Now no one had the skills, and so they were scoured into oblivion by successive tenants.

A pair of small stone lions stood on a balustrade. Once, the lion could have been regarded as the architectural symbol of London, the leonine essence distorted into decorative devices throughout the metropolis, sprawled in sunlight on the Embankment side of Somerset House, winged and majestic at Holborn Viaduct.

A corner pub, The Victoria Cross, with a sign above it depicting its namesake, the highest recognition for bravery in the face of the enemy that could be awarded to any member of the British and Commonwealth armed forces. The decoration took the form of a cross pattée, bearing a crown surmounted by a lion and the inscription 'FOR VALOUR'. Beneath the sign were opaque lower windows, gold letters in a spotted mirror panel establishing the types of beers served and the foundation date. A deserted bar unit, mirrored and shelved, where bottles of whisky and gin remained in places they had doubtless occupied for decades. Above, an old clock was set at the wrong time, two minutes past eleven.

One expected to find untouched areas like this in Kensington and Chelsea, where old money had preserved past features that the poor were resigned to lose, but Bryant was surprised to see that parts of Bloomsbury, the West End's shabbily genteel cousin, were still so complete. *That's my trouble*, he thought. *I always see things, not people.*

A single pedestrian coasted the corner ahead of him. Bryant narrowed his eyes and conducted the same observational survey on her. She was between forty-five and fifty, and would once have seemed old, branded invisible and treated brusquely by the inhabitants of the Victorian buildings around them. 'She could very well pass for forty-three in the dusk with the light behind her,' W. S. Gilbert had written of an attorney's daughter in *Trial by Jury*. An unmemorable face, rounded and fattened by time, lined a little by care, or what was now termed stress. Mousy hair cropped close to her jaw-line, make-up a little too thick, small eyes downcast, head lost in thought. Her raincoat had seen better days, but her shoes were polished and of good quality. The heels suggested that she was conscious of her height, for she was small and broad-hipped. She looked like a council official. A bag on her shoulder, brown and shapeless, bulging with – what did women take with them these days? Documents, most likely, if she was returning from working late in an office. A drink after work, or rather drinks, for she appeared a little unsteady on those heels. Somebody's leaving party, a birthday celebration. A mother, a wife, going home late and alone after a hard week, heading in the wrong direction for King's Cross station.

Bryant watched as she stopped and looked up at the pub sign, then negotiated the kerb to the entrance. He slowed to watch through the window as she headed to the counter and a barman emerged to greet her, appearing like an actor taking his cue on a stage set.

There was nothing more to be noted here. Could it be that he was becoming less observant because there was less of interest to see in London these days? He needed the lights and noise of the station, where one could witness meetings and farewells, the discovered, the lost and the confounded. That was the best way to check whether his powers were truly waning. But he was tired, and as he passed into the covered alley that led out on to Euston Road, he decided to find a cab. It had been a long exhausting day, one that marked an end, and a new beginning that would not involve him. Appointments, resignations, speeches and arguments. And on top of all this, he had been entrusted with the ashes of his old colleague.

The ashes. Only now did he realize that he had no idea what had happened to the aluminium urn containing the remains of Oswald Finch.

7

RELIQUARY

'Christ's blood,' said Dr Harold Masters testily, making the phrase sound like an oath. 'Be honest with me, that's what you're looking for, isn't it? You're after information on some new pet hobby of yours. What was it last time – the whereabouts of some Egyptian sacrificial urn you thought was still floating about in the London canal system?'

Arthur Bryant had not expected the doctor to discern his purpose quite so quickly. 'Could you slow down a bit? I'm not a marathon runner,' he begged, hopping along beside the impossibly tall academic as they climbed the steps of the British Museum.

'I lecture on ancient mythologies these days, Arthur, I'm not in haematology any more, unless you count the Athenian. Christ's blood is one of those things like the Ark of the Covenant. It's largely a Judeo-Christian habit, you know, venerating bits of wood and stains on cloths. Henry VIII supposedly owned the left leg of St George. I don't suppose you'd catch Buddhists flogging each other bits of Gautama Buddha's sandals in order to assuage their suffering.'

'I have a good reason for asking,' said Bryant. 'I thought if anybody knew, you would. Your arcane knowledge is more far-reaching than any other academic's. We've known each other for so long, and yet I never really get to sound out your knowledge.'

'That's because you don't pay me.'

The grease-grey, soaking rain prevented students from sitting on the staircase, and the forecourt had the forlorn air of an abandoned temple. Only the man turning hot dogs on a griddle outside the museum gates seemed unfazed by the lousy weather. Masters was about to give a lecture on early London household gods, and was running late. He lowered his great emerald-panelled golfing umbrella to encompass Bryant.

'It's nothing new, you know, the attempt to trace the Scarlet Thread, the idea that man can only be brought into a covenant with God through the shedding of blood. My knowledge of haematology is of little help in such endeavours,' he said hotly, as if defending himself. 'Ever since all those books about the Knights Templars came out, I've been besieged by students with crackpot theories.' The lanky lecturer tore off his tortoiseshell glasses with his free hand and wagged them at Bryant. 'I tell them, "You think you're the first person to go searching for hidden treasures in London? Why, you're just the latest in a long line of would-be plunderers armed with an Ordnance Survey map and a few scraps of historically inaccurate data." Really, Arthur, I would have expected something better from you.' He stopped so suddenly that Bryant ran into him. 'Do you know, I still have Bunthorne?'

'Bunthorne?' repeated Bryant, taken aback.

'Don't you remember? You came round to my house with a ginger kitten in your overcoat pocket, said you'd found him on Battersea Bridge and that his name was

Bunthorne. You left him with me and never returned to pick him up. Popping in for half an hour, you said.'

'My dear chap, I'm so frightfully sorry, I forgot all about—'

'Oh, don't worry.' Masters waved the thought away with long pale fingers. 'He's been a great comfort to me since my wife died.'

'Oh, I didn't know . . .'

'Well, how could you? Honestly, this rain, hold on.' He flapped the great umbrella as he closed it, showering them both. 'I'm incredibly late. Want to sit in on my talk about Mithras and the Romans? Oh.' He stopped suddenly again. This time he had been brought up short by a mounted sign at the top of the steps that read, 'TODAY'S LECTURES HAVE BEEN CANCELLED'. Apparently a burst water pipe in the gents' toilets had caused Camden's Health and Safety Department to close the public-speaking room until further notice. 'Well, it looks as though you have me all to yourself,' said Masters. 'What is it you want to know about the blood of Christ?'

They queued for tea beneath the astonishing glass canopy of the Great Courtyard and seated themselves in a quiet, shadowed corner. Bryant dug into his overcoat and produced a sheaf of wrinkled paperwork.

Dr Masters was the one man he knew who might be able to answer his questions. The ambitious academic belonged to a group of intellectual misfits who went by the nickname of the Insomnia Squad. They regularly stayed up all night arguing about everything from Arthurian fellowships and Islamic mythology to the semiotics of old *Superman* comics. Most of them were barely able to hold down regular jobs, and tended to drift away from their target research like wisps of autumn smoke, but Masters was driven by obsessive curiosity and the desire to improve and repair the world, even if it killed everyone in the process. Academics could be so blind sometimes.

'I was recently researching the city's social panics and outbreaks of mass hysteria, you know,' he told Bryant. 'I'm surprised you didn't come to me when you were searching for the Highwayman. I'd have been able to give you some pointers.' A few months earlier, the Peculiar Crimes Unit had conducted a search for a killer dressed in a tricorn hat and riding boots who had caught the public's imagination.

'Actually, it was while we were conducting that investigation that I came across references to a local street gang known as the Saladins,' Bryant explained, sipping his tea. 'Extraordinary that a bunch of uneducated kids could name themselves after a nine-hundred-year-old legend.' Over the years, Bryant had become an accidental expert on the arcane history of London.

'So you know that after Saladin retook Jerusalem in 1187, his Knights Hospitallers survived in the district of Clerkenwell?'

'I've been reading about it, yes. I presume the kids we interviewed had accidentally stumbled across some local history.'

'I don't know how you find the time to study this sort of thing when you've got a full-time job in the police. Well, the knights were stripped of their properties and income by Henry VIII, during the dissolution of the monasteries. But they stayed in the area. They based themselves near the gothic arch of St John's Gate, a place of profound religious mystery. At the hospital and priory church of St John of Jerusalem, to be precise, where injured crusaders were cared for. You still find cafés and bars in Clerkenwell bearing their name.'

Bryant unfurled his paperwork with a flourish. 'I did a little research. Listen to this. On October the third,

1247, the leader of the Knights Templars presented King Henry III with a six-inch-long lead-crystal pot marked with the symbol of the knights, a red-and-white cross-hilt, said to contain the blood of Christ, the ultimate relic of the crucifixion. Its authenticity was confirmed by a separate scroll holding the seals of the Patriarch of Jerusalem, signed by all the prelates of the Holy Land. The vial was held in a box carved with the chevron of the arms of the Prior Robert de Manneby, an ancient pattern taken from the priory window of St John, the first baron of England.'

'Yes, yes.' Masters coloured with impatience.

'And all of the other tantalizing snippets, like the letters XPISK marked on the container, and the supposed decanting of the vial that resulted in the deaths of five prelates. Who'd have thought that the true heart of the crusades would lie in Clerkenwell, just up the road? Would you like a biscuit?' Bryant produced a squashed packet of lemon puffs from his coat pocket and set it down between them.

'I didn't know they still made these,' Masters remarked, pulling one from the packet. 'It's all unverifiable stuff, you know. I've heard the story many times before. Some students came to me insisting that the vial was lodged beneath the floorboards of the Jerusalem Tavern, Farringdon, which would be all very well if the pub hadn't been built on the site of an eighteenth-century clockmaker's shop. I told them then that even if it did exist, it would probably contain germs that would be potentially fatal to the city's present-day citizens. I mean, good God, they had the Black Death back then. I'm not disputing the existence of a vial of blood, even if one ignores current thinking that suggests Jesus was most likely an invention of the Romans. Why are you so interested, anyway?'

'Oh, I hate loose ends.' It wasn't much of an explanation, but it was the best Bryant could muster. 'Sorry, I have a bit of a hangover. We laid our pathologist to rest yesterday. It's funny that so many of the cases we've been asked to handle lately have involved historical artefacts.'

'Of course, there was a time when you couldn't move for religious relics,' said Masters. 'The Prior Roger de Vere gave the church of Clerkenwell one of the six pots Christ used to turn water into wine. It supposedly had transformational properties. This is the point where religion crosses into magic.'

'There's something I don't understand about religious relics. I mean, there have been splinters and nails from the true cross knocking about for millennia, all of them fake. Even if the vial of blood had been "verified" – by what means we'll never know – what made it so much more special?'

Masters raised his bushy eyebrows knowingly. 'If you'll forgive the phrase, it's considered to be the holy grail of relics. John 6:53–54, "*Then Jesus said unto them, Verily, verily, I say unto you, Except ye eat the flesh of the Son of man, and drink his blood, ye have no life in you. Whoso eateth my flesh, and drinketh my blood, hath eternal life; and I will raise him up at the last day.*" The blood of Christ covers, cleanses and consecrates. It's nothing less than the gateway to the Kingdom of Heaven, the elixir to the realm of the everlasting. And I suppose you want to know whether this fabled prize might still exist.'

'Well, it would be rather interesting to find out, don't you think?' said Bryant, somewhat underestimating the case.

'I daresay it would,' Masters admitted, 'although I think I can save you a lot of unnecessary pain by stating categorically right now that it vanished long ago.'

'How can you be sure?'

'Please, my dear Arthur, the priories and monasteries were all burned to the ground and their contents destroyed. Their basements were dug up, their tombs desecrated until nothing more than dust was left, and even that was carted off to King's Cross for sale to the Russians. Don't you think we'd have heard about something like this?'

'London's greatest treasures have always been carefully hidden whenever the city has been placed under threat. We know that Catholicism survived dissolution, and surely an item such as this would have been protected by the most powerful holy men in the land.'

'You might as well conduct a search for Atlantis,' sighed Masters. 'When it comes to the lost icons of antiquity, you have a gullible buyers' market and plenty of unscrupulous salesmen willing to feed it. We all want to believe. Look at the experts' willingness to ignore the implausibilities in the forged diaries of Hitler and Jack the Ripper. These days it's easier to manufacture something more recent, like a missing session from a rock band or the diary of a dead celebrity. They won't add much to the comprehension of the human condition, but they'll make someone's fortune on the grey market. Trust me, Arthur, the trail has had eight centuries to grow cold. Ask yourself where such an item could have been kept without disturbance and you'll realize the absurdity of it. There are plenty of easier things to find in London than Christ's blood, and even if it did survive, it wouldn't still be in Clerkenwell.'

'Well, thanks for the advice,' said Bryant, pinching his hat from the table. 'I'd better go and find Oswald.'

'Call me sometime, we'll go out for a spot of lunch,' said Masters, who had become more reclusive since the death of his wife. 'There are all sorts of things we should talk about.'

Bryant gave a little wave as he stumped out of the Great Courtyard. In the long winter months of his retirement, there would be plenty of time for old men to sit and set the world to rights.

8

INTRODUCTIONS

Time Out Guide to London's Secret Buildings: Number 34
Peculiar Crimes Unit
Camden Road, North London

> *Housed behind the arched, scarlet-tiled windows above Mornington Crescent Tube station, this specialist murder investigation unit has been instrumental in solving many of the capital's most notorious crimes. Founded during the Second World War to handle cases that could prove embarrassing to the government, it has continued operation right up to the present day. The unit now falls under the jurisdiction of the Home Office, which is attempting to make it more publicly accountable, and so its days are probably numbered. The PCU's unorthodox operating methods were highlighted in a recent BBC documentary that criticized the conduct of its eccentric senior detectives for their willingness*

to use illegal information-gathering procedures in the preparation of their cases.

Detective Sergeant Janice Longbright threw the magazine on to her kitchen table. *More unwarranted publicity*, she thought. At least this time the journalist had not gone into detail about the kind of informants Mr Bryant sporadically pressed into service at the PCU. No mention of the pollen-readers and water-diviners, the necromancers and psychics, the conspiracy theorists and eco-warriors, the mentally estranged, socially disenfranchised, delusional, disturbed and merely very odd people he asked to help out on pet cases, which was a blessing. How many times had they been threatened with closure before? She realized now that instead of the axe suddenly falling, they were to be slowly strangled to death with red tape.

She tapped the keyboard wedged on the corner of her sunflower-laminate-topped breakfast table and stared gloomily at her computer's empty mailbox. A month ago, she had posted her profile on an internet dating website, but so far there had not been a single taker. She wondered if she had been too honest, her tastes too quirky. Surely there were others whose interests coincided with hers, men who liked criminology, burlesque and film stars of the 1950s? She bent down and scuffed Crippen behind his nicked, floppy ear. The little black-and-white cat purred, coughed, then hacked up a hairball. *Great*, Longbright thought, *everyone's a critic*. She only brought the unit's cat home when she was feeling particularly lonely, but this morning even Crippen's presence had not helped.

Going into the hall, she found her doormat similarly bare of letters. She thought someone might have remembered that it was her birthday, but it was half past ten, and the postman had been and gone. *This is the world*

I've created for myself, she thought, looking about the patchily painted Highgate flat. *Three rented rooms above a charity shop, overlooking a roundabout. No partner, no family still on speaking terms, hardly any friends, only a manky old cat that no one else wants to look after.* Her former boyfriend was about to get married to someone else, but for her there was no love interest even remotely on the horizon.

She knew what the trouble was: she had given her best years to the Peculiar Crimes Unit. While other women of her age were presumably still enjoying romantic dinners and illicit weekends, she was usually to be found working late at the offices above Mornington Crescent Tube station, correlating the case histories of violent killers. It wasn't very appealing to have to tell a date you'd meet him at the restaurant because you were waiting for fingerprints to come in from a severed hand. She sighed, pushing back a thick coil of bleached hair, and was heading for the kitchen to wash up her single breakfast dish when the doorbell rang.

The courier looked far too young to be allowed near a motorcycle, but he was holding the largest bunch of yellow roses she had ever seen. A silver-edged card read:

Happy birthday from your greatest admirers
– Arthur Bryant & John May

It was the first time the detectives had ever sent her something on her birthday. Her colleagues remained her oldest and closest friends. She smiled at the thought, but as she unwrapped the roses and placed them in water, a green thorn plucked at the flesh of her thumb, and a single crimson droplet fell on to a silky yellow petal.

* * *

Raymond Land had assembled them all in the unit's main briefing room. His staff were gathered before him in two untidy rows. Nobody wanted to sit on the garish orange Ikea sofa because Crippen had been sick on it, and the velour was still damp. Renfield stood beside his new boss like a Christian missionary waiting to deliver a sermon before a tribe of delinquent heathens.

'I thought we could take this opportunity of introducing ourselves to Sergeant Renfield,' said Land jovially. 'Perhaps each of us would like to say something in turn about who we are and what we do, just to break the ice.'

Bimsley turned a snort of derision into a wet cough.

'Starting with you, Colin. Stand up, please.' Land glared at him. Bimsley's pupils shrank at the prospect of conjuring something to say. As the silence lengthened, Meera poked him sharply below the ribs.

'Colin Bimsley,' said Colin Bimsley. 'Detective Constable, which means I do the heavy lifting around here. I requested the posting to the PCU because my dad was in the unit and taught me all about the place when I was a nipper. I've still got his old uniform. I also inherited his balance problem, which has now been diagnosed as DSA, that's Diminished Spatial Awareness, which means I occasionally misjudge distances and bash into things. Mr Bryant and Mr May offered me a desk job, but I didn't want to let them down.'

'So instead he falls down steps and off roofs, and runs into lampposts when he's chasing criminals,' said Meera, not without a hint of affection.

'I've got four major topics of conversation – law enforcement, football, amateur dramatics and science fiction. And that's me for you.' Bimsley sat back down.

'Mangeshkar, you're next.' Land's glare intensified.

'I grew up on the Peckham Estate back when it was

really a mess,' Meera told Renfield. 'I got into the force and was packed off to dumping grounds like Dagenham, Kilburn and Deptford. They figured I knew the territory, and I was as tough as anyone on the estates. It wasn't working with junkies and nutters that got to me so much as the endless self-deception. Kids who thought they were going to turn their lives around, parents who insisted their kids could do no wrong, social workers who completely misread situations. If I'd just wanted to work with the poor I'd have joined a charity organization. I wasn't there to change lives, I was a copper, not an evangelist. Does it make sense to say that I came here looking for a more productive form of police work?' She stared down at her hands, as if expecting to find the answer there. 'I thought I could learn more in criminal investigation. Maybe I am, I don't know.'

'Hmm.' Land had been hoping for more of a career précis, but now it felt as though he was taking confession. 'April, I hope you can explain what you do here, because I'm buggered if I know.'

April glanced guiltily at her boss. She was aware that her grandfather had petitioned Land to hire her, and despite showing great promise at the unit, still felt as though she did not belong among professional criminologists. 'Well,' she began softly, 'I'm just here to help out. I'm good at putting things together.'

'What does that mean?' asked Renfield. 'What field of expertise did you train in?'

'I have no formal training, but the Scarman Centre at Leicester University advocated the hiring of non-professionals in specialist criminology units, and Mr May asked me to join the PCU.'

'You mean your grandfather invited you in. Jobs for all the family, eh?'

'Give her a break, Renfield,' said Longbright. 'The girl

is bloody good. She collates information and assembles it together with forensic evidence, witness reports, timelines, data analysis and profiling strategies, and she does it instinctively. Could you do that?'

It was obvious to Renfield that the rest of the unit was prepared to defend May's grandchild. It was now common knowledge that her mother had been killed in the line of duty, and that April suffered intermittent bouts of agoraphobia as a result. She was thin and ethereally pale; she looked as if a strong wind might blow her away. Was this fragile woman really the kind of person a specialist crime unit should be employing?

'Let's move on to Mr Kershaw,' Land suggested hopefully.

'I suppose I'm the odd man out,' Kershaw began, thoughtfully tucking a lock of lank blond hair behind his right ear. 'Giles Kershaw, twenty-eight, single, can't imagine why, ha ha. I went to Eton, which left my parents as impoverished as church mice but granted them a sense of genetic superiority over the sturdy farming stock in their parish. The police force is no place for the well educated, let me tell you. I was studying to be a biochemist when I became fascinated with the morphology of death, which pretty much put my sex life on hold. I've been under the tutelage of Mr Bryant and Mr May for long enough to appreciate the uniqueness of this unit, and the utter foolishness of attempts by the Home Office to close us down. Oh, and I'm your new pathologist.'

'Mr Banbury?'

Dan Banbury had passed his formative years in an East End bedroom sprawled across a candlewick bedspread, angrily punching a laptop connected to several thousand pounds' worth of computer equipment. From this unprepossessing, cable-festooned site he penetrated enough security loopholes to bring himself to the attention of a forensic team specializing in hi-tech fraud. However, he escaped prosecution after citing the case of Onel de Guzman, the twenty-four-year-old Filipino student at AMA computer college who evaded prison despite having released the world's most destructive computer virus. The police were so impressed with his defence that they asked him to check their own security system, and Banbury found himself studying on the right side of the law. It was hard to imagine that anyone so bright could have so few communication skills.

'Dan Banbury, the unit's IT guy and crime-scene manager,' he said simply, stepping forward. 'I trained in technology forensics and photography, I've operated in major incident agencies sorting data recordings, and I've done a lot of on-site work. People think only planes have black boxes, but anything with a microprocessor will leave a data print, and these days that includes everything from trains to washing machines. But sometimes you just want to go to a murder scene and work out who knocked over a chair.'

'And of course you know . . .' Land waved his hand vaguely in the direction of Longbright.

'Detective Sergeant Janice Longbright. Mr Renfield knows me, sir. There's really nothing more to say.'

'Come, come, Janice. I'm sure there's a lot we can learn from each other.'

'You're right, sir. From studying Renfield's behaviour I learned how to cause a colleague's death through incompetence.'

A cold intake of breath passed through the room.

'I think that's a bit *ad hominem*, Janice, if you don't mind my saying so,' said John May. 'We've already been over this, and I know that Renfield feels very badly about the matter. He admitted acting wrongfully and is trying to put the events of last week behind him.' It seemed that the sergeant's failure to involve the hospital services after he discovered a body on the street would stay to haunt him.

'I'd like to suggest that coming here, to work among Oswald Finch's oldest friends, wasn't the smartest move he could have made.'

'I know how strongly you feel, Janice, but this unit will not survive if it is divided, so it's our duty—'

'I don't think you need to lecture me on duty, John,' said Longbright angrily.

'She's right,' said Kershaw. 'Everyone knows Renfield's appointment is a trade-off for my promotion, and I'd rather step down than cause divisions within the unit.'

'You're causing a division just by offering,' Mangeshkar pointed out.

'This is exactly the kind of thing I expected to find here,' said Renfield. 'I heard you lot couldn't organize a tug-of-war in a rope factory.'

Land could sense control sliding away from him, and raised his hands. 'There'll be plenty of time to get to know each other later,' he told them. 'So, Jack—'

'Nobody told me there was a meeting,' said Bryant, wandering in from the corridor billowing a bonfire-trail of acrid smoke from his pipe. 'What's going on? Did I miss a punch-up? Are there any doughnuts left?'

'You can't bring that filthy thing in here!' Land protested. 'I sent you an email about smoking this morning.'

'Well, there's your problem, old sausage, I never read them. Hello, Renfield. How are you getting on with your new team-mates? You can't expect an easy ride, you know. Not after what happened.'

'Where have you been?' asked May. 'You were supposed to be here an hour ago.'

'British Museum. Christ's blood,' said Bryant. 'I'd like to say their Earl Grey exceeded expectations, but I'd be lying.' He turned to address the group. 'Now look, we all know Renfield here is a humourless pain in the *derrière* who wouldn't notice an ironic remark if you tied it to a stick and poked him in the eye with it, but I think that's one of his strengths. You might also know that his father was Sergeant Leonard Renfield, an old enemy of mine at the Met, and like his father, Jack has been denied promotion several times, for which he seems to blame my reports. But he has no axe to grind with any of you, and nor should you with him. It's early days, so let's start by drawing a line under the past and at least withholding judgement until a later date when we can all gang up on him properly. Most of the trouble between us is because the sergeant doesn't understand what we do, so now's our chance to show him.'

'You didn't have to say that,' said Renfield sulkily as the meeting broke up around them. 'I'm capable of speaking for myself.'

'I know you are,' smiled Bryant, 'but least said soonest mended on this occasion, I think.'

'Well,' May marvelled as his partner ambled past in a cloud of Sweet Briar smoke. 'I see you've added diplomacy to your repertoire of talents. You know we need all the allies we can get, and that Renfield has a lot of friends in the Met. You think if we get him on our side, he'll eventually spread the word and give us more power against the Home Office. You sly old dog.'

'Perhaps this is one dog you can teach new tricks,' said Bryant, daintily pirouetting the tip of his walking stick as he danced from the room.

9

RANDOM ACTS OF SLAUGHTER

'Whose bright idea was it to bring Jack Renfield in here anyway?' asked Dan Banbury.

Giles Kershaw was packing the last of his belongings into a plastic crate, preparing for his move to the Bayham Street morgue, where he would take over Oswald Finch's old post. 'Land's, apparently,' he answered. 'Part of the trade-off for allowing me to take over as pathologist. They're playing politics upstairs, trying to set you against me and undermine the working structure of the unit at the same time. The most confounding thing you can do is make the new man welcome. If you express dissatisfaction, you'll be playing directly into their hands.'

'But what will happen to Janice? There's only room for one sergeant in this outfit, and she's got years of experience over him.'

'There's a difference. She's a DS. She'll work it out,' said Kershaw, tamping down the crate lid impatiently. 'As will you. He's going to be sitting right here, at my old desk. OK, I'm out of here. See you later, old sprout.' He threw Banbury a salute as he hoisted the final box on to his hip and backed awkwardly out of the door.

Banbury had once thought that he and Kershaw would become a team in the Bryant-and-May mould, their respective talents complementing each other, but now it was obvious that his former partner could not wait to take up his new position. Kershaw was coolly ambitious and openly contemptuous of those who stayed behind. With a sigh of regret Banbury woke his monitor to examine the Dead Diary, Kershaw's nickname for the daily files listing those who had died in unusual or suspicious circumstances in the central London area.

It was Dan's job to pass on any new cases which he felt required the attention of his seniors. Today, the very first one on the list caught his eye. Bryant always asked for print-outs, claiming that the computer screen hurt his eyes, so Banbury made a hard copy, collected the document and headed across the hall. As he did so, he collided with Bryant, who was carrying a full bowl of porridge.

'God, I'm sorry, sir.' Banbury brushed milk and oat flakes from his paperwork. 'I thought you'd want to see this.'

'Come into my office.' Bryant set down the bowl, took the papers from him and dug out his reading glasses, waving Banbury to the cankerous crimson-leather armchair he kept for visitors. 'Sit down before you do any more damage. What am I looking at? Don't answer, it's a rhetorical question. The Dead Diary for Monday 26th, a forty-six-year-old deceased woman named Carol Wynley, found at the corner of Whidbourne Street, Bloomsbury, died some time before midnight. And this is of interest because . . . ?'

'It's just that John told me you cut across Bloomsbury on the way home, and I wondered if you'd—'

'Added random acts of slaughter to my already controversial repertoire of activities?' Bryant completed. 'Sorry to disappoint you, Banbury, but no. Around thirteen thousand outbursts of violence occur outside pubs and clubs in the UK every week.' He threw the papers back. 'Wait, show me that again.' He snatched back the printed photograph and re-examined it. 'Talk to Renfield. He'll know where they've taken her. If she's gone to Bayham Street, Kershaw will be about to get his first case.'

'It probably won't come into our jurisdiction,' warned Banbury. 'Not unless there's something especially unusual about her death.'

'It rather depends on what you regard as unusual,' said Bryant. 'It's certainly a coincidence. I think I saw this woman just minutes before she was found dead. Sexual assault?'

'No mention of that in the report.'

'If it's the same person, she was drunk when I spotted her. Let me have a word with our leader.' He turned and swung into Raymond Land's office without knocking. Land was cleaning pencil shavings out of the back of his desk drawer when Bryant made him jump, causing him to empty the drawer's contents over his trousers.

'I do wish you'd learn to knock,' he muttered irritably, brushing down his seams.

'Look here, Raymondo, why on earth are we stranding Kershaw over at the morgue? There's no point in having him hovering about in Oswald's old room with no one to talk to. He's far more useful to the unit here.'

'There's no room here,' Land snapped. 'Look how much space you take up – boxes of musty old books you never read—'

'They're for reference.'

'Smelly old suitcases full of outmoded laboratory

instruments, endless unlabelled bottles of chemicals for which I only have your word that they're safe—'

'I think you'll find I never promised that.'

'Half the stuff in the evidence room isn't ours, and I've no idea where you got it from—'

'I can't remember why I borrowed safe-cracking equipment, if that's what you mean, or what I used it on, but I promise to return it when I do. There's plenty of room for us all here. So that's settled.' Bryant gave what he hoped was a pleasing grin, revealing his patently false teeth to an alarming degree, then left the room.

Land dug in his drawer for one of the miniature bottles of Glenfiddich he kept there and was about to down it when the door flew open again. 'Forgot to mention we've a suspicious death coming in, woman in her forties found in Bloomsbury last night. I say it's *our* case – what I mean is I want us to handle it because I saw her alive. We've nothing urgent pending at the moment, have we?'

'You can't just decide to take the case any more, Bryant, you need to talk to Renfield about it. What do you mean, you saw her alive?'

'Haven't bumped into Renfield yet – running late on his first day, not a very impressive start, is it? John and I will get off to the morgue, then. You can tell him for us, can't you? And if you're going to start drinking that stuff first thing in the morning, I reserve the right to continue smoking my Old Sailor's Full-Strength Rough-Cut Navy Shag in the office, just so you know. Pip pip.'

The slam of the door was Land's cue to snap off the cap of his miniature and down it neat.

'Well, well.' Detective Sergeant Jack Renfield leaned against the door jamb, studying his opposite number. 'I never thought we'd end up working together, did you?'

'It doesn't matter what I think,' said Janice Longbright.

'The decision has been made elsewhere and I have to make the best of it.'

'I don't suppose it's occurred to you that I'm not too happy about the situation, either? I enjoyed being at Albany Street nick. All my mates are there. Blokes I grew up with, some I even went to school with. I've never pretended to be an intellectual. The only college I ever attended was the police college in Hendon. I know you think I'm common. I sound common, I drop my aitches, I haven't got the further education that you lot have got. And yet I've been brought in here on an equal footing with you, so what am I doing right?'

'You were useful to the boys upstairs, that's all.'

'I'm a copper, not a politician or an academic. I've spent most of my working life dragging nonces off the street and locking them up until someone smarter tells me to let them go. But I know what the law stands for, where it begins and where it ends, and I make sure nobody on my shift oversteps the line. Raymond Land is like me, he came up the hard way. I'm not going to report to him behind your back, Longbright. I'm not out to grass anyone up, OK?'

'Then what are you here for?'

'I'm just planning to do my job and obey the rules, and make sure everyone else does the same. If you or your bosses step out of line, that places you on the outside, with the criminals. You can think what you like about me, love, it isn't going to make any difference.'

He pushed himself away from the door and headed out into the corridor. Longbright continued clearing her desk, but found herself shaking with anger. Renfield knew how to get under her skin.

'Hi, Janice. You look like you lost a shilling and found sixpence. What's the matter?'

Longbright looked up and found May in the doorway.

She was always pleased to see him. 'Oh, nothing, John, I'm fine.'

'If you say so, but I heard what Renfield said.' May buttoned his jacket. 'Don't let the new boy get you down. If Land asks where I've gone, let him know that I'm checking out a possible murder victim, and no, I didn't get permission from Renfield first.'

'He's already given me a warning about proper behaviour.'

'He's not a bad sort, just a bit abrasive. He stopped me from getting beaten up by a street gang not so long ago. He's a good man to have on the ground.'

'It's not just Renfield, it's – ' She stopped and thought for a moment. 'Maybe I've been here too long. I have no life, John. I don't know who I am any more. Perhaps I have to stop dressing like this, looking like this.' DS Longbright certainly had a style of her own, mostly modelled on movie stars of the past. She was a fulsomely sexy woman and the look suited her, although it was somewhat inappropriate for her job. 'You know, my make-up never gets any older, but underneath it I do. Sometimes I take it off at night, and have to stop and ask myself if there's still somebody there. All I ever do is work. I don't exist outside the office. Does anyone even notice me?'

May tapped the door-frame with his ring finger. 'Can we talk about this later, Janice? I've just realized the time. Arthur's already on his way to the Bayham Street morgue.' He thought for a moment. 'And check out something for me, will you? Carol Wynley had a mobile, but it wasn't on her body or in her effects. See if you can track it down.'

10

THE VICTORIA VANISHES

'That's her.'

Arthur Bryant peered more closely at the waxen face in the gun-grey zip bag before him. He could only recall the woman on the examination table of the Bayham Street morgue because he had made such a deliberate effort to observe her. There was nothing remotely memorable about her appearance. If asked to sum her up in a single word, he would have said, damningly, that she appeared 'respectable'.

'Are you absolutely sure?' asked May. 'It's just that it seems rather an odd coincidence, you being there.'

'Not really. I bumped into my butcher at the Royal Albert Hall last month,' said Bryant. 'I always see people I know, even when they're trying to avoid me. This is definitely the woman I passed. What happened to her?'

'At first glance I'd say she slipped off the kerb and bashed her head,' said Giles Kershaw. 'There's a contusion at the base of the skull consistent with her falling on to her back, although I've not found any bruising at the base of her spine. Mind you, she was wearing a thick grey woollen skirt and a thick coat which would probably have protected her.'

'Just a little cut, hardly seems anything.'

'The contusion is small, but the surrounding area is soft to the touch, and if we push in you can just see that the dura is ruptured. I removed a small bone fragment, little more than a splinter. The fracture was enough to expose her brain, causing clotting. The pupil of her right eye is unusually enlarged, which suggests a clot on that side. Any impact can ripple through the entire head, right down to the spinal cord, causing traumatic damage. The impact point showed up like a tiny black star on the X-ray, and I could see some swelling in the rear right cranial hemisphere. I also found a few drops of cerebrospinal fluid leaked from her right ear, which suggests some form of basal skull fracture. There are so many things that can go wrong at the base of the skull. If she'd had immediate neurosurgical intervention I imagine she would have lived. There are more than a billion neurons in the human brain and we damage them all the time, but once the tissue starts swelling the damage rate rises exponentially unless intervention can halt it. She had quite a lot of alcohol in her blood, which exacerbated the effect of the injury. No recent food in her stomach.'

'So you think she was plastered and missed the kerb?'

'No, funnily enough I don't.' Kershaw swept a lick of blond hair behind his ear. Like Finch before him, he seemed determined not to wear protective headgear in the morgue. He tipped his head, studying the dead woman's physiognomy. 'I think she fell, all right. The impact point is consistent with a kerb fall, a real jab of a blow.' He gestured with his knuckle. 'The sort of thing you'd get from tripping over something sharp-cornered in the way of pavement furniture, but you'd have to fall very heavily. Something wrong about that, I think. You put your hands out when you fall, even if you're drunk. Her palms were completely clean. So no, not just plastered.'

'Do you have an ID?'

'She was reported missing by her partner at around two a.m., and a local officer was told to keep a lookout. Carol Wynley, forty-six, divorced, kept her married name, did part-time secretarial work in Holborn. She'd told her fella she was going for a drink with colleagues after work. She'd often done it before and they usually went on until nine or ten, birthday bashes and leaving parties, that sort of thing, so he hadn't been worried. They live in Spitalfields.'

'So it wouldn't have taken her long to get home, even if she had trouble finding a cab.'

'Do you have any idea what time it was when you saw her?'

He remembered the darkened dog-leg, London planes and copper beeches rustling dusty leaves above a battered brick wall. The black-painted bollards, the rendered keystone, the wreath-shaped door knocker, the ornamental wrought-iron railing, the carved blind window. Pushing deeper into his recollections, he saw the figure of Carol Wynley weaving slightly as she moved towards him, almost stumbling on the edge of the kerb.

How close had she come to falling at that moment? In his mind's eye he saw the frosted lower windows of the public house on the corner, the beery amber glow surrounding the gold lettering on the clear glass that read THE VICTORY – no, THE VICTORIA CROSS. A date of establishment that he couldn't recall. He saw a few beer and spirit bottles on sparse shelves, the opening door as she pushed inside. He heard the rise of saloon chatter, somebody laughing too loudly, the clink of glasses. A youthful figure appeared through the darkened doorway behind the bar, coming out to serve a customer. He could not bring to mind a face. The barman was ahead of her, already starting to take the order. As if he had been waiting for her to walk through the door.

'I wasn't the last person to see her alive,' he said with finality.

'You're quite sure this is where she was?' John May asked for the second time as they walked through the alleyway towards the top of Whidbourne Street.

'Yes, but obviously I was coming from the other direction, heading up to the Euston Road,' said Bryant. 'Do you want half of my Mars Bar?'

'Bit mainstream for you, isn't it, a Mars Bar? I thought you'd be breaking out the aniseed balls, milk gums, sugar shrimps, or some other brand of confectionery not seen since the last war.'

'My supplier's been closed down,' said Bryant gloomily, sounding like a drug addict who had lost his connection. 'I suppose I could order them over the internet but it wouldn't be the same. And I've a sweet tooth, as you know.'

'Your teeth are false. Go on then, give me a bit.' May accepted a chunk and popped it in his mouth. He stopped at the corner of the pavement, removing the blue adhesive tape left for him by one of the Albany Street officers. 'Spot where she was found,' he said, poking a toecap against the kerb. 'Nothing much to be seen here. No sharp corners except that low wall, which I suppose would do it.' He indicated an area of broken brickwork. 'Dan will have taken a sample. No scuff marks, no signs of violence.' He glanced up at Bryant, who had suddenly turned pale. 'What's the matter?'

'No pub,' said Bryant in a small strangled voice.

11

MISTAKEN

The pair were standing at the dog-leg in what Bryant now saw was Whidbourne Street. They looked up at the corner, which was occupied by the Pricecutter Food & Wine Store, its yellow-and-green livery coated with dust, the window plastered with stickers for the unlocking of mobile phones and the arrangement of cheap calls to Ethiopian towns. It had clearly been there for a number of years.

May shot his partner a glance. 'This can't have been the right corner.'

'But it was, I'm positive,' said Bryant, although he didn't sound too sure. 'She went into an old boozer with its name, the Victoria Cross, picked out in gold lettering over the window.'

'Then you must have seen her on another street, before she reached this point.'

'No, it was here, because I remember the way the light from the saloon bar fell on the opposite wall and over the trees above it. The clocktower of St Pancras station was exactly in that position. She stopped right there,' he pointed to the edge of the pavement, 'then crossed the road and went inside.'

'The streets around here look very similar to each other.' May was trying to be kind.

'I'm not losing my mind, John. I remembered thinking that I didn't know this street. I thought I knew pretty much every route through central London, so I was surprised when I came across one I hadn't seen before. Have forensics been here?'

'Kershaw and Banbury were ahead of us, but I don't yet know if they found anything out of the ordinary. If you're not imagining things, someone in the shop might be able to shed some light on this.'

May led the way inside. An elderly Indian man was virtually invisible behind the counter, buried beneath racks of gum, mints and phone cards. May introduced himself as a police officer.

'They found some old lady in the street last night,' the shopkeeper told them. 'Dead, wasn't she?'

'I'm afraid so. What time did you arrive this morning?'

'I live in Enfield,' said the old man. 'This is my son-in-law's shop. We open at eight.'

'And last night?'

'Close at ten, same as always. It's nothing to do with us, what goes on over there.'

'What do you mean?'

'The estate, those boys hang around here at night causing trouble, we don't know what they get up to. That's why we've got steel shutters. I have to close them every night. I complain to the police but nothing happens. They never do anything.'

'Mind if we take a look around?' May led his partner away by the arm. 'Is it just possible you made a mistake, Arthur?' he asked. 'It was late and we'd been drinking for hours.'

'No,' Bryant insisted, but suddenly faltered, looking around at the shelves. 'Well, I don't think so. It occupied the same footprint as this building, with the door in the same place – but . . .'

'That's understandable. Areas like this would have been planned by a single architect, so most of the streets have the same-sized building plots. Why don't we take a walk around the neighbourhood, retrace your steps and see if we can find your pub elsewhere?'

Bryant allowed himself to be led between the racks of crisps and bottled drinks, but stopped by the front counter. 'Do you know a pub around here called the Victoria Cross?' he asked.

The old Indian shook his head without even stopping to think. 'Not around here. There's the Skinner's Arms, the Boot and Mabel's Tavern, but I don't drink so I wouldn't know. The pubs are all trouble, boys getting drunk and spray-painting their filth all over the shop.'

Outside, May pointed at Number 6A, the single remaining dwelling that stood at the end of the dog-leg, surveying the street like a sentinel. 'What about that house?' he asked. 'Maybe the owners saw something.'

They approached the front door and rang the single bell, but there was no answer. May peered through the letterbox and saw bills and flyers spread across the hall carpet. 'Looks like they've been away for some time.'

'All the lights were off,' Bryant recalled.

'All right, forget the name of the pub,' May told his partner, 'you might have got that wrong. Just concentrate on finding a place that looks like the one Mrs Wynley entered.'

The pair followed a rough ziggurat back along Bryant's route, passing half a dozen public houses on the way, but none of them seemed entirely right. It was as if parts of them had been incorporated into a single phantom composite.

'I'm not going mad,' said Bryant anxiously. 'I saw her go into the saloon bar and get served by the barman.'

'Wait, you sure it was the *saloon*? Arthur, pubs haven't been divided into public and saloon bars for years.'

'Oh, you know what I mean. It was old-world, not messed about with. No beeping fruit machines.'

'Can't you give me more descriptive detail than that?'

'Yes – no, I mean, perhaps I was a little drunk.' He rubbed his forehead, trying to recall the exact sequence of events. 'I don't remember as clearly as I thought. I'll have to sit and think.'

'Did it smell different, this alternative space-time continuum you ventured into?'

'Why should it smell different?'

'You know, Victorian smells. Horse dung, tobacco, sewage, hops.'

'I don't know, I can't remember. I don't suppose Victorian London smelled any worse than the corner of Tottenham Court Road and Oxford Street does during the present day.'

May didn't mention it, but he was reminded that hallucinations could often be accompanied by sharp changes in one's sense of smell. Savoury odours of leather and burning were common. 'Are you still taking your medication?'

'You mean have drink and drugs addled my brain, causing it to slip into the febrile desuetude of Alzheimer's? No, they have not and it has not, thank you so much.'

'Then let's go back to the unit and see what else we can uncover.'

At the PCU, John May's granddaughter came in and set several pages before them. 'There are eight public houses named after Queen Victoria in London,' she explained, 'plus the Victoria Park in Hackney, the Victoria and Albert in Marylebone and the Victoria Stakes in Muswell Hill. The nearest Victoria to Bloomsbury is just over the road, off Mornington Crescent. Actually, I think I've been there with you.'

'There you are, you see? You've muddled the memory of another pub with the one you passed,' said May soothingly.

'I did not muddle them!' Bryant all but shouted. 'Good God, do you think I can't tell the difference between Mornington Crescent and Bloomsbury? She went into the pub on that corner, and then left and died or was killed on the street outside.'

'We could settle this if you knew the exact time you passed each other,' said May. 'We know she was alive when you saw her, so if Kershaw can pinpoint the time of death we'll be able to see if there's a discrepancy.'

'I want an artist,' said Bryant stubbornly. 'I need someone who can draw what I saw.'

'I can draw,' April volunteered. It had been one of the many talents she had perfected during the flare-up of her agoraphobia, during which time she had rarely left her shuttered apartment in Stoke Newington.

'There are sketchpads and some pens in the evidence room,' said May. 'You'll have to get Renfield to unlock it for you. What else have we got on Carol Wynley's movements last night?'

'I was about to give you this,' said April. 'I've put together a timeline from statements volunteered by her partner and work colleagues. Wynley worked at the Swedenborg Society in Bloomsbury, but was meeting up with friends from a former workplace, a charity organization working with Médecins Sans Frontières. They had drinks in a pub called the Queen's Larder—'

Bryant perked up. 'I know that watering hole. It was named after Queen Charlotte, the wife of King George III. He was being treated for insanity at a doctor's house in Queen Square. The queen leased the cellar beneath the pub to keep the king's special foods there.'

'Wynley left the Queen's Larder some time after ten – no one's been able to pinpoint the exact time – and made her way up to the Euston Road, but then she doubled back into Bloomsbury, which suggests a deviation from simply returning home.'

'I told you so,' said Bryant. 'She had another destination in mind.'

'Then perhaps you made a mistake about the name of the pub,' May suggested.

'We'll soon see.' Bryant climbed the small stool behind his desk and reached up among his books, pulling down a green linen volume with untrimmed pages. 'Here we are, *The Secret History of London's Public Houses*.'

'Wait, when was that printed?'

Bryant checked the publisher's page. '1954. Not one of my more recent acquisitions.' He flicked to the index. 'Here you are. Going mad, am I? Look at this.' He turned the book around and held it up with the pages open.

The others found themselves looking at a photograph of a public house built on the corner of Whidbourne Street, Bloomsbury, but they did not seem pleased.

'What's the matter?' asked Bryant. 'I was right after all, wasn't I? We just overlooked it. Let's go back and—'

'Arthur, this can't be the place,' said May. 'This picture was taken two years before the pub was demolished, in 1925. It's been gone for over three-quarters of a century.'

12

ECDYSIAST

'What do you think you're doing?' asked DC Colin Bimsley. 'That belongs to Mr Bryant.'

'It's a marijuana plant,' said Renfield, dragging the great ceramic pot along the corridor towards the top of the stairs.

'It's for his rheumatism.'

'And it's illegal, or did nobody bother to point that out to him?' asked Renfield.

'Give him a break, Jack – he gets pains in his legs.'

'Then he should be retired and relaxing at home. He could be working as a consultant.'

'It's not your job to decide what he does.'

'It is if he can't do his job without the aid of psychoactive narcotics.'

'Wait, what else have you got there?' Bimsley pointed to the battered cardboard box Renfield had also dragged out of the office.

'Old books. They're everywhere, even blocking the fire exits. I'm stacking them by the rubbish. They can go to charity shops.'

'You can't do that, he's taken a lifetime to collect them.'

'Land has asked him to take them home dozens of times, but they're still here, so out they go.'

'But he needs them for research.'

'Really?' Renfield bent down and retrieved a stack of slender volumes. 'Let's see what he's been researching, shall we? *Yoruba Proverbs*; *The Anatomy of Melancholia*; *Embalming Under Lenin*; *Cormorant-Sexing for Beginners*; *The Apocalypsis Revelata, Volume Two*; *A Complete History of the Trouser-Press*; *Financial Accounts for the Swedish Mining Board, Years 1745–53*. I suppose the next time they bring a gunshot victim in from Pentonville, he'll be able to use these in his investigation.'

'You'd be surprised,' said Bimsley, 'how an intimate knowledge of the workings of the trouser-press might aid in the capture of a determined rapist.'

'Are you making fun of me?' asked Renfield suspiciously.

'You'll never know, will you?' Bimsley stood his ground.

'I say, what are you doing with Mr Bryant's books?' asked Giles Kershaw, who had found his path blocked upon entering the hall. 'He'll go bananas if he sees you've moved them. They're very useful.'

'Not you as well.' Renfield was starting to wonder if the senior detectives had brainwashed the unit staff. Kershaw raised his long legs in a spidery fashion to climb over the obstruction, and admitted himself into the detectives' office.

'I'm thinking the bash was incidental,' he began, throwing himself into the guest's armchair.

'I'm sorry, what are we talking about?' asked May.

'Mrs Wynley. There's an abnormality in the base of her skull. The bone is extremely thin. It wouldn't have taken much of a knock to damage it. But even so, I think it occurred as the result of something else.'

'Like what?' asked May.

Kershaw sucked his teeth pensively. 'Not entirely sure yet. Gut feeling. People don't usually keel over like fallen trees, with their arms at their sides. Not very scientific, I know, but there's something else. Midazolam – it's a fast-acting benzodiazepine with a short elimination half-life. A pretty potent water-soluble sedative, but the imbiber doesn't actually lose consciousness unless it's taken in overdose. I found a tiny trace of it inside her mouth. If you were to inject it between the gums and the inside of the cheek, it could enter the bloodstream immediately. She would have dropped like a log.'

Bryant wrinkled his face, thinking. He looked like a tortoise chewing a nettle. 'This is making less sense by the second,' he said. 'A woman walks into a pub – which, by the way, hasn't existed for the best part of a hundred years – gets injected in the face and leaves without complaint. She falls down outside, bashes her head, and is left for dead by everyone else who leaves the pub, including the staff. I don't suppose we have any suspects, either.'

'Her partner was just a couple of miles away, home alone watching TV – no witnesses, says he had several phone calls, but all on his mobile, none to their flat.'

'So they're traceable but don't prove he was there. Then we should bring him in,' said May.

'There's a problem with that,' April told her grandfather. 'He's in a wheelchair after suffering a stroke some while back, can't do much for himself at all.'

'She was a legal PA,' said Bryant, looking up from one of the books Renfield had tried to throw out, *Religious Philosophers of the Eighteenth Century*. 'At the Swedenborg Society, no less. Swedenborg was a Swedish philosopher famed throughout Europe for his contributions to science, technology and religion. When he got older, he supposedly experienced visions of the spirit world. Reckoned he visited both heaven and hell, where he held conversations with angels and devils. Upon his return, he wrote something called the *Apocalypsis Revelata*, or *Apocalypse Revealed*. He claimed he'd been directed by Christ himself to reveal the details of the second coming. Understandably, everyone thought he'd gone round the twist. Died in Clerkenwell in 1772. His home in Bloomsbury still houses the Swedenborg Society.'

'Your point being?' May wondered.

'What? Oh, nothing . . . it's just odd, that's all.' Bryant poked about in his jacket and produced the walnut bowl of his pipe. He peered into it wistfully. 'I don't suppose I might be allowed to—'

'No,' said May and his granddaughter in unison.

'It's just that the Swedenborg Society lost another of their legal secretaries at the beginning of the month,' he explained, screwing the pieces of his pipe together. 'I believe she was found dead in a London pub, the Seven Stars, just behind Lincoln's Inn Fields.'

'Why on earth would you remember that?' asked May, intrigued.

'Because it reminded me of the nun found unconscious in the Scots Flyer,' said Bryant, not really managing to answer the question.

'Wait, explain the part about the nun first,' April demanded.

'The Scots Flyer is one of the most disgustingly awful pubs in London,' said Bryant, 'a grubby little sewer of a King's Cross strip-joint, crammed for many years with the most unsavoury characters imaginable. But the lady in the wimple who passed out inside it was no ecdysiast, disrobing for a handful of coins collected in a beer mug.

When I saw the incident report, I naturally wondered what she was doing in such a place.'

'Ecdysiast?' April raised an eyebrow.

'She wasn't a stripper,' Bryant explained. 'I followed the case and made notes on it. I have them somewhere.'

He withdrew a drawer from his desk, removing a handful of pipe-cleaners, a Chairman Mao alarm clock, a collection of plastic snowstorms and a bottle of absinthe, before finally unearthing a small black book.

'Here, in my Letts Schoolboy Diary.' He held open a page filled with tiny drawings of flags. 'A full report of the case. Well, by the look of it I appear to have written up the salient facts in a code of Edwardian Naval signals, but you get the idea. Sister Geraldine Flannery from Our Lady of Eternal Suffering said she was in the pub to collect for charity and was overcome by the pressure of the crowd, but it turned out her robes had been specially constructed to hold wallets and handbags. She wasn't a nun at all but a dip, and not a very good one, obviously, otherwise she wouldn't have chosen to pickpocket some of the poorest punters in London. The point is – ' Bryant's raised index finger wavered in the air. 'I've forgotten the point.'

'The legal secretary from the Swedenborg Society,' April prompted. The old man really seemed to be losing it. 'The Seven Stars.'

'Ah yes. This time the face on the bar-room floor belonged to a respectable middle-aged lady named Naomi Curtis, the daughter of a clergyman. What had she been doing by herself in a pub?' Bryant popped the empty pipe into his mouth. 'Most people don't stray far from their natural habitat, and according to her father, Miss Curtis was a creature of habit. She liked a tipple, and had been drinking more heavily in the last couple of years, but rarely went to a pub without arranging to meet someone.

Suddenly she turns up dead one night in a Holborn boozer. I kept notes on her, too.'

The others looked at him blankly.

'Don't you see? When something's out of whack, when people don't match their locations, a little bell goes off inside my head. There was something else. One of the punters remembered Curtis checking her mobile at the bar, but by the time the ambulance arrived she had no phone on her. Land wouldn't allow me to investigate at the time, but he will now. Two women, two public houses, and an investigation involving drink, drugs, death and Swedish philosophy.'

'I assume this means you want to handle the case,' said May drily.

'Oh, don't worry, I will whether I'm allowed to or not. I'm far too old to start obeying the rules now.' Bryant made a hideous draining noise through his pipe stem. 'If anyone needs me, I shall be in the pub, conducting a little research.'

13

FORGETTING

'We can't take it on,' said Raymond Land. 'A case doesn't come under PCU jurisdiction just because you two have a funny feeling about it.'

'Giles and Dan agree with us,' said May. 'They think there's enough circumstantial evidence to link the two cases. The Naomi Curtis death was given an open verdict, although the coroner told relatives that she probably suffered heart failure following heat-stroke.'

'I don't know,' said Land, wiggling a finger in his ear and examining it. 'All you've got is the fact that they both worked for the same organization as legal secretaries.'

'Which meant that they probably knew each other. And they also died in a similar manner, in or near public houses,' May added.

'But they didn't, did they?' Land pointed out. 'This Wynley woman wasn't in a pub, unless Bryant somehow managed to cause a rift in the bloody space-time continuum and plunge himself back to Victorian England. He's gone to Bloomsbury for another look, hasn't he? It's not like him to miss coming in here and having a go at me.'

'He doesn't believe he could have made such a mistake.'

'Look, it was late, he was a bit plastered, the road was dark and, knowing Bryant, he was probably thinking about the history of the area. He'd read about the pub or seen a picture of it in one of his weird old books, and superimposed it over the scene. This wouldn't be the first time he's been wrong. He's not infallible, you know.'

May had an image of the retirement letter in Land's pocket. He would have transferred it to his desk by now, perhaps even left it at home. He suddenly saw a way to protect his partner. If they were given the case, Bryant would be presented with an opportunity to come up with a solution. It was the type of investigation at which he excelled. His confidence would be restored, the letter would be withdrawn and Land would be satisfied that his senior detectives were still on the ball. 'There's also the issue of undermining safety in public areas,' he added.

'What are you talking about?'

'If we imagine for a moment that there really is someone out there who has struck at two innocent women in crowded public places without anyone else even noticing their deaths, we have a real problem on our hands.' May knew that one of the less frequently invoked remits of the PCU was to 'ensure the maintenance of public comfort and confidence in the free and open areas of the city'. In other words, if someone dangerous was running loose in any building or public space to which the residents of London enjoyed open access, it could undermine their faith in the police, and ultimately the state, creating scenes of public disorder. It had happened many times before.

'You think the Home Office would come down on us?' asked Land, suddenly uncomfortable.

'Like a ton of bricks,' confirmed May. 'Leslie Faraday and his sinister boss Kasavian are still angry about us leaping their last hurdle.' The HO had booked a royal visit to the unit, hoping that the detectives would make fools of themselves by incurring the disapproval of a member of the monarchy. Instead, the detectives had seen off their common enemy and resoundingly silenced their critics.

'I'll make the recommendation,' Land sighed. 'You'd better brief the others so we can hit the ground running.'

'Whatever you think best, sir.' May left the room with an inward smile, thankful that Land had failed to effect a transfer from the unit.

'What do you mean, it's not here?' said Bryant with indignation. 'Where's it gone?'

'It was on the bar all evening, but I don't remember seeing it when we closed up,' said the barmaid of the Devereux.

'Good God, woman, it contained the poor man's corporeal remains. It was a cremation urn.'

'Oh. We thought you'd won it at bingo. Well, one of your lot must have taken it.'

'You opened the bar to the general public at ten, didn't you? It could have been anyone.'

'A roomful of police officers,' the barmaid sniffed. 'Not much of an advert, is it? Rather calls your observational skills into question.'

'Don't you start.' He threw her a card. 'You'd better call me if you hear anything.'

Back on the streets of Holborn, he reread his notes on Naomi Curtis and wondered if there was really much likelihood of the two cases being connected. The only reason he had filed a note on her was because she had died in the wrong place. It was inconceivable to imagine what had brought her from a vicarage in Sevenoaks to a smoky Holborn pub at the age of fifty-four unless she was in some kind of trouble, and had arranged to meet someone inside.

Similarly, Carol Wynley had been heading home to take care of her housebound partner when she had chosen to deviate from her route. Perhaps he had muddled the streets, and she had gone into a different pub – the Skinner's Arms on Judd Street was also on a corner and he must have passed it – but she had placed herself in a situation that led to a skull fracture.

A phone call to the Swedenborg Society confirmed both women's employment records. Carol Wynley had taken up her predecessor's position, but they had overlapped by a month. Bryant made notes – in his regular spindly handwriting this time – for Kershaw to check whether traces of sedative had also been found in Naomi Curtis's body, and for Longbright to check past Dead Diaries for any other cases with shared circumstances.

Most murders were committed without the involvement of logical reasoning. In one of his notebooks, Bryant had jotted down a quote from Gary Gilmore, the first man to be executed after the US Supreme Court reinstated the death penalty, who said that 'murder is just a thing of itself, a rage, and rage is not reason'. In his experience, he had found most murders to have been committed in states of rage, but the PCU had been created to investigate those cases which fell beyond the normal parameters of violent death.

A vague idea began to form in his brain, one requiring proof that Carol Wynley had entered the Victoria Cross public house alone on the night she met her death. He felt sure that May would be able to get an investigation launched, but had no clear idea of how to proceed, not while a question mark hung over his ability to recall events clearly. He needed to be positive that his deductive capability was not diminished.

* * *

The third thud dislodged a framed photograph of Colin Bimsley's father, sending it to the floor in a tinkle of glass. Bimsley reached down and gingerly removed shards from the monochrome portrait. The grim-faced young man who peered out of the picture between chinstrap and helmet peak seemed to belong to another era, possibly early Victorian. In fact, the photograph had been taken in 1958. The old police uniforms were cumbersome belted tunics with steel buttons and metal identification numbers on the epaulettes. The outfit commanded authority from the criminal fraternity because it linked directly to the past, reminding one of Sir Robert Peel, guards and dragoons and even a knight's armour, but my God, it must have been uncomfortable to wear.

'What on earth is he doing in there?' Bimsley asked.

'Putting up shelves,' said Meera, 'to house his collection of law-enforcement rulebooks. Renfield is planning to report all infringements the unit commits, no matter how minor.'

'Janice hates the idea of sharing her office with him. I think she's convinced he's got his own private agenda.' Bimsley carefully wrapped the broken glass with tape before placing it in the bin, but still managed to nick himself.

'I don't see why everyone's so down on Renfield,' said Meera hotly. 'He's only trying to bring a bit of old-school discipline to the unit.'

'I might have known you'd support him. Renfield hasn't the faintest understanding of how this place works. All he'll do is spy and sabotage and screw things up.'

The hammering recommenced. Bimsley peered over the top of a charge sheet at Mangeshkar. For months now he had made a fool of himself over her, and just as they were starting to find common ground, a fresh source of disagreement was appearing between them. When he thought of all the time he had wasted trying to win her over, he could have kicked himself.

Let her side with Renfield, he thought, *what the hell do I care? Why did I ever think she was even remotely interested? Since the day she swaggered in here ordering me about, I've gone out of my way to be as nice as possible. I've been barking up the wrong tree. There are plenty of decent women I could date. I'm all right, me.* Turning to the evening paper, his eye was taken by an advertisement for a speed-dating club, meeting tomorrow night. He threw her an angry glance and jotted down the details.

April looked at the picture she had drawn from Bryant's careful description. It showed a public house with cream tiles and a wrought-iron lantern over the only entrance, and a hanging sign with a depiction of a medal on it. The chipped brown paintwork of the double doors had been covered with brass hand-plates. The bar beyond the windows was shallow and high, with a large clock at the centre adorned with Roman numerals.

She glanced across at the image he had found in his book of public houses. The building was identical, down to the smallest detail, except that the original sign featuring a side portrait of Queen Victoria had been replaced.

What bothered her most, though, was the clock. She could read a single word on its face: *Newgate*. The hands were set at two minutes past eleven, the same time Bryant had given her from his memory of the night. After searching architectural websites, she had located several other maps and sketches, all from different angles, showing the saloon and public bars with different interiors, in different stages of its life, but not one of them showed the clock. The photograph in Bryant's possession was the only one to feature it, which suggested that he had previously noted the picture in the book and subconsciously copied it. April's grandfather had taught her to always trust his partner, even when Bryant's theories seemed maddeningly obscure, but for the first time doubt was starting to creep into her mind.

'Do you remember where you put your socks, Mr Bryant?' asked Alma Sorrowbridge. His Antiguan former landlady stood before him, blocking the way, her meaty hands placed on her broad hips.

Bryant eyed her warily over the top of his reading glasses. In matters of the home, a woman in a pinafore was not to be trifled with. 'I imagine they're in the laundry basket, where I place them at the end of each evening,' he answered with some care, knowing this could be a trick question.

'I ask because they were not, in fact, in the laundry basket. They were inside my oven, and I am seized with the urge to ponder what they might be doing there.'

Bryant thought for a moment. 'Are you sure?'

'On the top shelf above my cornbread, three navy-blue pairs.'

'I think I must have washed them, and wanted to dry them quickly.'

'So you grilled them. You've been getting very forgetful lately. You didn't tell me my sister called last night.'

'That's because I don't like her,' said Bryant. 'If I tell you she rings, you'll call and invite her over, and then I'll have to hide in my room for hours while you two bake and sing hymns. Do you really think I've been more forgetful lately?'

Alma detected a note of concern in her old tenant's voice. 'You've had a lot on your mind. And you're always stuffing your head with history from those old books you read. There's only so much room in a person's brain.'

'I saw a murder victim in a place that doesn't even exist any more,' he admitted miserably. 'And I lost our pathologist's ashes. I was entrusted with looking after them, but forgot to take them home with me at the end of the wake.'

'You run a unit full of detectives,' said Alma. 'John's granddaughter, she's a clever one. Give her the job of finding them.'

Bryant smiled. 'What would I do without you?' he asked.

'You'd be getting evicted by Camden's health and safety officers, and run out of this house by neighbours with burning torches, for all the experiments you've kept them awake with and the disgusting smells you've made,' Alma told him. 'Now stop feeling sorry for yourself and start solving something.'

'It's all very well for you,' Bryant wheedled, 'you remember every single thing that ever happened to you, particularly if it was my fault. You do it so you can bear the grudge for ever. But my brain cells aren't like yours, they're like footprints on wet sand. They only last for the length of a single tide. I need to improve my memory.'

Alma pushed past the overstuffed armchairs in their lounge and pulled a card from behind her Tyrolean letter-rack. 'Try calling this number,' she said. 'Mrs Mandeville is an old friend of mine from the church. She cured the late Mr Sorrowbridge's smoking habit, and replaced the springs in his ottoman.'

Bryant read the card:

Kiskaya Mandeville

Herbal Remedies – Organic Therapies –
Hypnotism – Sofas Repaired

'She sounds like my kind of woman,' he said, brightening up and reaching for the phone.

14

DISPOSAL

Just after ten o'clock on Tuesday evening, a chill drenching rain began to fall on Fleet Street. Once, the pavements would still have been crowded with couriers, journalists, printers, picture editors, typesetters, artists and accountants, and the lights of the buildings would have formed unbroken ribbons of luminescence from the Strand to St Paul's, but now the thoroughfare was almost deserted. The great rolls of paper that had been brought by barge up to the presses of Tudor Street had been moved to the eastern hinterland of the city.

Jocelyn Roquesby tilted the address she had printed out and tried to read it without her glasses. By doing so, she walked straight past her destination, and was forced to back up before the black-framed windows of the little Georgian house that housed the Old Bell tavern. The pub's rear door opened out into the courtyard of St Bride's Church. The cramped corners and angled nooks of its interior had barely changed in centuries. Mrs Roquesby's fingers itched to punch out a number on her mobile, at least to tell her daughter where she was going, but she had promised not to call anyone.

She scanned the front bar, then moved to the rear of the pub, wondering if she had somehow managed to miss her contact. She had been surprised to receive the text message, and would normally have suggested a morning coffee in the local Starbucks, especially now that she was trying to give up alcohol. However, a tone of anxiety in its phrasing had struck a chord, and she had replied with an agreement to meet in one of their former haunts.

She looked around the pub with a growing sense of disappointment. *This place used to be packed*, she thought. Now there were just a few lone drinkers at the bar, a couple of elderly tourists studying maps, a pair of snogging teenagers. She was a few minutes early, so she pulled up a barstool in the corner and ordered herself a vodka and tonic.

Arthur Bryant stood on the corner of Whidbourne Street and studied the supermarket opposite, kicking at the kerb with a scuffed Oxford toecap. The Victoria Cross had stood here for the best part of a hundred years, casting its welcoming saffron light on to the paving stones, its revellers wavering home to their wives at eleven – fewer women, and certainly no single ones of decent repute, would have been out drinking in the early years – or perhaps there had been a lock-in, with the heavy velvet drapes drawn tight to eliminate all light on the street. There the drinkers would have remained – so easy to forget the world outside – until the landlord decided they'd all had enough. 'Ain't you got no 'omes to go to?' he would have called jocularly. 'You're going to cop a right earful from your missus when you fall through the front door, Alf.'

Bryant remembered having to pull his father out of

virtually every pub in the East End, Bow, Whitechapel, Wapping and Canning Town. It had surprised no one when he died young. *Probably a blessing*, his mother had said when the old man passed on. *Your father was never a happy man.* But she had stood by him, despite the pleas from her side of the family to leave and take her son away. Parents rode out the most hellish storms for the sake of their children in those days.

He looked back at the corner, and the mental image of the public house faded to reveal the blank bright windows of the Pricecutter Food & Wine Store, its Indian proprietor staring dully at the sports pages of the *Sun*. Rain pattered against the glass, plastered with faded advertisements for Nivea moisturizing cream, Ernst and Julio Gallo wine, Thomson Holidays, Zippo's Circus. The past had realigned itself into the present, and nothing was in its rightful place.

The girl behind the bar had just called last orders. Mrs Roquesby sat back against the wall and listened to the song that was softly playing on the pub's CD deck. The Everly Brothers, wasn't it? 'All I Have To Do Is Dream'.

She wanted to sleep, but not dream. Dreams too easily turned into nightmares. Tired, she rested her head against the wall and listened to the lyrics. She had been stood up, but had at least found herself a drinking companion, although now he seemed to have disappeared, and she just wanted to let the night slide away into warm, wood-dark oblivion. *A bee-sting*, she thought, scratching at the back of her neck, *or an insect bite. Odd that they should be around so early in the year . . .*

When Mrs Roquesby began to slide majestically from her stool, Lenska, the barmaid, thought she would snap awake, but she kept going all the way to the carpet, landing hard on her knees. Running around from behind the counter, Lenska pulled at the lady, but was unable to wake her. Mrs Roquesby's head fell back and her wig slid off, revealing the sparse, wispy grey hair of a head that had undergone cancer therapy.

Lenska loosened the collar of her blouse and tried to find a heart beat. She looked around for help, but the bar had cleared since she had rung last orders. A thick yellow froth was leaking from the mouth of the woman in her arms. Lenska knew a little about first aid, but this was beyond her, so she laid the woman down and went to call for an ambulance.

Dan Banbury saw the world from a different perspective, usually starting at floor level. Gravity required everything to fall. Dust and skin flakes, hairs and sweat drops, everything sifted down through the atmosphere to land on the ground. Any movement stirred up the air, shifting molecules in swirls and eddies that resembled hurricane patterns on weather charts, and tumbling particles cascaded from one resting place to the next. You could track them if you were able to define the direction of the air current. Sometimes particle movement would lead you back towards the source of a disturbance; it was like hunting in reverse.

Banbury's long-suffering wife was all too aware of his enthusiasm for exploring the detritus of death, as it took the form of ruined trousers and jacket sleeves, and since he hated buying new clothes, she was forever racing to the dry cleaner's in her lunch break. Even now he was lying on the carpet of the Old Bell public house, pushing strips of sticky tape along the underside of the counter, which appeared not to have been cleaned since Boswell propped up the bar.

'I'm glad you managed to keep Bryant away for once,'

he muttered through clenched teeth, for he was holding a pencil torch in his mouth. 'It's a mystery how he always manages to make a mess of any crime scene.'

'He's gone to see someone about improving his memory,' John May explained. 'He forgot the urn containing Finch's ashes, and now he's feeling guilty. He got a crack on the noggin and lost the plot a while back. I'm wondering if he's suffered some kind of a relapse. Are you getting anything down there?'

'Far too much, that's the problem. It'll take chromatography to sort out the tangle of dead cells that have drifted down here. Forensically speaking, this sort of place is my worst nightmare. Dog hairs, crisps, meat pies, beer, mud flecks, skin, mites, a few mouse droppings, it's like Piccadilly Circus.'

'You're sure she was alone?' May asked the barmaid.

'She ordered a drink and sat in the corner,' said Lenska. 'I can show you the till receipt.'

'So she was here by herself for about forty minutes. Look like she was waiting for someone, did she?'

'Maybe, I don't know. I think I saw her check her watch a couple of times.'

'And she didn't speak to anyone else?'

'She was reading a copy of the *Metro* – actually, there was someone else. Some guy talked to her. He ordered two drinks, so I guess he bought her one.'

'What was he like?'

'I wasn't really paying attention. Early thirties, maybe, I didn't really take him in.'

'You wouldn't be able to recognize him again?'

'God, no. I didn't register his face at all – he was just one of those blokes you always get in a pub like this, sort of invisible.'

'You didn't see him leave?'

'No. I had to go downstairs to change barrels. When I

came back up he'd gone, and she was alone. Right after that she fell off her stool. I thought she was drunk.'

'If it's the same MO, Kershaw reckons he'll find traces of benzodiazepine again,' said May to Banbury. 'She had a red mark at the base of her skull like a sting, possibly from a needle. Whoever did this has found an effective method of disposal, and is probably planning to stick with it.'

'Interesting choice of phrase there,' said Banbury. 'Disposal. That's what it feels like, doesn't it? He can't be getting sexual gratification, and presumably he's not gaining anything financially from his victims, so why is he doing it? Plus, he's picked the worst possible place to get away with murder, acting inside a roomful of strangers. I'm no psychologist, but you don't think that's it, do you?'

'An act of exhibitionism, taking a risk in front of the punters? Possible, I suppose. Murder is an intensely revealing act, best performed in privacy. Seems a bit perverse to stage it as some kind of public performance. Besides, do people pay much attention to each other in pubs? You tend to concentrate on the friends you've come out with. I'm sure if Bryant was here he'd regale us with a potted history of public murder. She's roughly the same age as the other two. Is he looking to take revenge on a mother substitute? What were they doing drinking alone?'

'You always get one or two by themselves in London pubs. That's the difference between a pub and a bar,' Banbury explained. 'Pubs are about conviviality and community, meeting mates. Bars are for being alone in, or for meeting a stranger. So why would he pick his victims in the former? It doesn't add up.'

'Perhaps the killer has a mother or an older sister who was a drunk,' Kershaw suggested. 'If he's in his early thirties, she'd probably be in her fifties. Are the victims all similar physical types?'

'Not at all. Jocelyn Roquesby was fifty-six, a former copy typist and human resources officer, divorced, one daughter, no current partner, lived alone in a flat in Holloway. She had just finished a bout of treatment for breast cancer. According to the daughter she liked a drink, but never went into a pub alone unless she was meeting someone. Also, the chemotherapy made her sick if she drank. So who was she there to meet?'

Meanwhile, April had gone to the Devereux on the mission of locating Oswald Finch's remains.

'You were working behind the bar on the night of Mr Finch's wake, weren't you?' she reminded the barmaid in the upper bar. 'If you cashed up the till, you must have also cleared the counter, so you'd remember if there was something as odd as a funeral urn left behind on it.'

'I told your boss, there was nothing left behind,' said the girl, who regarded all men over thirty with narrow eyes and a cold heart. 'People leave their briefcases, umbrellas and handbags here all the time, but it stands to reason I'd have remembered an urn.'

'So someone took it with them.'

'And it had to be one of your lot, because you had the room to yourselves for most of the evening. Your Peculiar Crimes Unit have a reputation for being a bunch of practical jokers, you know. The manageress warned me. They've had parties here before. Somebody left an inflatable sheep in the ladies' toilet last time, frightened the life out of the cleaner.'

'Not much of a practical joke, is it,' said April, 'swiping the ashes of a dead colleague?'

'Depends on what they're going to do with them,' said the barmaid, with a disapproving sniff.

15

VISIBLE EVIL

Raymond Land tipped his armchair forward, cleared a steamed-up arc of glass and looked down into the street. Was there anything in the world more miserable, he wondered, than a wet Wednesday morning in Mornington Crescent? Especially when you felt you were no longer the captain of your destiny, more a third mate dragged in the undertow of someone else's foundering vessel?

'You and your partner like to work in a pincer movement, don't you?' he complained. 'First John creeps up on me with dire warnings, and now you. Three dead, at the very least! If the Home Office get wind that the proles think it's not safe to venture into a public house without risking death, our entire national fabric will collapse. The idea of a Britain without anyone in the boozers is unimaginable.'

Bryant lounged back on Land's sofa and felt about in his pocket. 'There's no doubt about it now, cheeky chops. Three murders in London pubs, all within a mile of each other. And this new woman, Roquesby, pushes the affair much further into the public arena because her former husband was security-cleared for some kind of government work. I think there's something really big going on here. Don't tell me we can't get the case prioritized now.'

'That's not an issue.' Land continued searching the street below, as if expecting to find the rest of his thought there. 'I just worry.'

'Good Lord, I know articulacy has never been your forte, Raymondo, but at least take a stab at piecing together an entire sentence.'

'I'm not sure the unit is up to handling something like this. It's a potential minefield.'

'What are you talking about?' Bryant dug a little silver box from his pocket and flicked it open. 'Don't worry, I haven't taken up cocaine. I thought I'd try snuff, seeing as nobody will allow me to light my pipe.'

'Well, suppose you fail to stop this lunatic, and in the process undermine national confidence in the security of public places?'

'You think you'll be given the order of the boot, don't you?' Bryant sniffed and sneezed abundantly. 'This is no time to start worrying about your frankly moribund career, old sausage, there are greater issues at stake. Suppose your wife was to walk into a public house by herself for a quiet drink and a gander at the papers?'

'Leanne would never do such a thing,' said Land indignantly.

'Far from what I've heard, but we'll let that pass. Imagine how much you'd worry for her safety, then magnify that a million times across the country – you see my point? When nobody feels protected, the economy simply starts to unravel. Look at the terrible side effects of past bombing campaigns against civilians. The public house is virtually the country's last unassailable place, now that so many churches lock their doors. For hundreds of years it has occupied a unique position in our culture. What's the one thing every pub is supposed to have?'

'I don't know.' Land scratched his chin. 'At least two brands of bad lager?'

'A welcoming hearth created by centuries of tradition. Wasn't it Hilaire Belloc who once said, "When you have lost your inns drown your empty selves, for you will have lost the last of England"?'

Land looked back blankly and shrugged.

'Pubs tend to stay constant because they're rebuilt on the same plot of land. The extraordinary thing is that brewers don't keep historical information on their own properties, so histories often only exist in the form of handed-down anecdotes. That's why pubs are different to any other type of building around us. The public houses of London are its keystones. Good Lord, the Romans brought them here two thousand years ago and put vine leaves outside to advertise their wares, no wonder they occupy such an important—'

'Look here, Bryant, don't give me one of your historical lectures on the subject of beer. I'm interested in catching a criminal, nothing else.'

'But that's my point, *vieux haricot*, you can't catch the criminal if you don't understand his milieu.'

'Yes, you can,' said Land, irritated. 'You can catch him by bringing in the victims' relatives and shouting at them in a windowless room for a few hours. And don't throw words like "milieu" at me. Renfield's going to be a breath of fresh air in this place. He won't stand for any of this nonsense, I can tell you. He's out there right now, tracking down contacts and conducting doorstep interviews. He *grills* people, makes the innocent feel miserable and uncomfortable until they provide him with accidental information.'

'General Pinochet did that, it's called torture and has nothing to do with police duties.'

'Listen, I know foot-slogging has become unfashionable, I know it's all computers and DNA matches now, but sometimes a bit of shoe leather and the odd threat of a slap is needed, and this is one of those times.'

'After all these years, you still don't understand how we operate, do you?' said Bryant. 'It's a complete mystery to you, isn't it?'

'Well no, not exactly,' stalled Land. 'I know you use various undesirables to give you information and that you wander off the beaten track a lot, that you won't stick to established procedures and once threw a sheep carcass out of the window of your old office at Bow Street to measure skull fractures. I know your methods are obscure, unsavoury and probably illegal, but somehow you seem to get the job done. But I don't know . . .' Land looked up and realized he was talking to himself. 'Where are you going?'

Bryant was attempting to pull a gabardine raincoat over a broad-stitched fisherman's sweater. 'To Mrs Mandeville's memory-improvement class,' he explained. 'I'd forgotten all about it. Later, I shall be employing a detection process photographers refer to as *Methodical Anticipation*. In this case it means catching the killer before he strikes again. I wrote a pamphlet on the subject in 1968. A casual browse through it may enlighten you.'

'Arthur, *please*.' Land felt uncomfortable using Bryant's first name, but was desperate. 'If you have anything at all that might constitute a lead, tell me. Whitehall is breathing down my neck. They're going to hang me out to dry.'

'All right. Ask yourself why all three victims were found without their mobile phones. We're waiting on their call records, but I think we'll find the killer has a rather novel method of contacting his victims, using each phone's address book to send a text message to the next victim in a sort of round-robin. Which means, of course, that all the victims knew each other. And the fact that Jocelyn Roquesby was found without her mobile suggests that he's going to do it again. Cheerio.'

Janice Longbright alighted on the Holloway Road and began checking the shop fronts. Mrs Roquesby's daughter Eleanor lived above a Thai takeaway, in a small flat that bore the marks of serial occupation. Hardly a room was finished; wallpaper ran out, rollered paint-marks fell short of the ceiling, units were missing doors, floorboards appeared beyond remnants of carpet. There was an overwhelming tang of damp in the air.

'You must be Sergeant Longbright. Sorry about the mess. I'm Eleanor Roquesby.' The ghost-faced girl held out her hand and forced a small smile. 'I always say mother must have been thinking of Eleanor Rigby – you know, the Beatles song?'

'I'm sorry to intrude upon you at a time like this. You have a lot to be upset about.'

'To be honest, I'm confused more than anything. I can't imagine why anyone would want to hurt her. Would you like tea?'

Longbright nodded with a certain amount of resignation. Copious tea-drinking was an occupational hazard because it was a comfort everyone knew how to provide, in the same way that people understood how to mend a plug but not a computer.

'She was such a kind woman,' Eleanor explained, placing mugs before them. 'She fostered children, ran playgroups, worked hard all her life, never had a bad word to say about anyone. I'm not her natural daughter, I was given up for adoption when I was two, and she raised me as her own daughter. I want to know how she could end up being murdered in a pub.' She looked over to the windows, her knuckle against her chin. 'You know, Jocelyn's own mother was old-fashioned. She used to tell me that women couldn't set foot inside a pub by themselves during the war without men thinking they were tarts. So we spent decades fighting for independence and equality, only to get attacked in a place that's now supposed to be safe.'

'I know it doesn't seem fair that she died, but we have to stop other women from risking the same fate,' said Longbright gently. 'In particular, I need to locate the man who bought her a drink last night. So far we haven't been able to track down anyone who remembers seeing him.'

'What about CCTV cameras?'

'There were none inside the pub, only outside. You say your mother never drank alone, so we must assume she had arranged to meet a friend who failed to turn up. The barmaid doesn't think the man who bought her a drink was her intended contact, because he had been at the bar for some time, while your mother was seated at the other end by herself. Do you have any idea who she might have been planning to meet?'

Eleanor thought for a minute. 'Not my father, because they don't keep in contact any more. Perhaps somebody from work?'

'We're looking into that possibility at the moment. Anyone else? Did she have any local friends who might have agreed to see her in town?'

'Not really. Her female friends around here are mostly married with kids, it's not the sort of thing they can do.'

'Did she belong to any clubs, societies, groups, see anyone who met regularly outside of the neighbourhood?'

'There was a sort of society she went to occasionally. She didn't mention it to her family because I think she was faintly embarrassed about it. I don't really think it had a name, although she called it the Conspirators' Club. She was interested in conspiracy theories – who killed Kennedy, crop circles, whether the moon landings were faked – just a fun thing really, something to do in the evenings. She read lots of books on the subject, but didn't take any of it very seriously. She just said it was a good way to make friends. They met in some pub once a month, I forget the name.'

'Could you try and dig it out for me?'

'I have her appointment book – I thought it might be useful to you.' She passed the sergeant a tiny dog-eared diary filled with what appeared to be the world's smallest handwriting. Longbright squinted at it. 'I haven't got my reading glasses.'

'Hold on. Here you are – upstairs at the Sutton Arms, Carthusian Street, near Smithfield Market, meetings every second and fourth Wednesday.'

'That would mean they're meeting tonight.'

'I guess so. Do you think this could have something to do with it? That she might have met somebody from the group?'

'There's one way to find out,' said Longbright.

April rubbed her eyes, then returned her stare to the screen, scrolling through the names in the Dead Diary. Based on the three known victims, she now had a set of correlating factors with which to match the Met's unsolved case histories; she was searching for professional women between the ages of thirty-five and fifty-five who had gone alone to public houses in the central London area. Unfortunately, the files only dated back to when the system was inaugurated, in March 1996, but she hoped that would be far enough to provide a more distinctive pattern.

She sensed that there had been alcohol issues in the

pasts of these three working women, all of whom had held positions of responsibility for some years. Was that why they drank, and perhaps were used to visiting pubs – was it the stress of maintaining their careers? So far as she could see, none had suffered mental-health issues, none had been designated as clinically depressed or suicidal. Many journalists would love to write about innocent victims like these because they fitted the white-middle-class demographic of their newspapers' readership. If they scented a failure on the part of the police, it wouldn't take them long to start running articles about how no woman was safe in the capital.

Her eye ran down the columns of names, matching and discarding until one name jumped out: Joanne Kellerman.

Her death pre-dated the other three, having occurred four days before Curtis's, but it fitted the pattern. She had succumbed in a tiny, crowded pub called the Old Dr Butler's Head, in Mason's Avenue, by London Wall. Last orders had been rung early, and as the drinkers thinned out, Mrs Kellerman had fallen to the floor in what appeared to be a faint. The barman had been unable to revive her, so he had called an ambulance, but she was pronounced dead on the way to the hospital.

A cocktail of narcoleptic drugs found in her system suggested that she had taken her own life, although why she had chosen to do it in a crowded pub remained a mystery – hence the coroner's decision to record an open verdict. There was no history of mental-health problems on record, although she apparently took prescription anti-depressants and sleeping pills. The Met had noted the death and uploaded her file to the Diary, even though they had chosen not to consider the case worthy of further investigation.

April ran her finger across the screen to the tabulated

comments from her next-of-kin, and noted that she had often enjoyed pub quizzes. Did all of the women regularly attend events in London pubs? If so, did their presence bring them to the attention of someone stalking victims in such an environment?

April's discovery of the death placed the women in a new running order: Kellerman, Curtis, Wynley, Roquesby. In a city where so many died in unexplained circumstances each day, each event occupied a slender borderline of visibility. Only when compiled together did they form some kind of new and alarming picture. This faint but discernible pattern had begun to coalesce from the mist of empirical data that blurred every death in the city. If no one agency possessed all the facts, there could be no resolution. This, she felt, was why the PCU existed. To transform a killer from smoke and shadows into flesh and bone. To make evil visible.

April began writing up her report for her bosses.

16

THE HEART OF LONDON

He was always watching the women.

Interesting how they were treated at different times of the day, in different places. In lunchtime city pubs they sat at their counters completely ignored, men reaching around them for beers and change as if they were mere obstacles. In the early evening they were engaged in conversation by men who used a cheerful, chatty manner with older women, as if talking to their mothers. Late at night, when the lights were lower, they became easy targets for leering drunks who felt sure they could never be rebuffed.

He felt sorry for the women, even when he had to take their lives.

The cavernous inns of the Strand, the narrow taverns of Holborn, the fake rural hostelries of Chelsea, the brash bars of Soho, each had their own tribes. The lotharios, the jobsworths, the brasses, the bosses, brash drunk kids, braying toffs, swearing workmen, all united by the desperate need for companionship. The single careerists were frightened to go back to their pristine apartments and sit on the ends of their beds, staring into the void of their dead lives. The ones in relationships delayed heading home to warm, sleeping bodies they could barely stand to touch.

He knew all about the power of pubs, and the invisible customers who kept them alive. The lonely matrons who drank a little too much, the ones with full, sensual bodies and sad old eyes that caught his gaze, holding it a moment too long in bar mirrors. He had been with them all his life.

He loved the women. As he prepared his poison, he prayed they would escape him.

'A little early in the day to be drinking, isn't it?' asked John May. 'It's only just gone noon.' Williamson's Tavern in Groveland Court was nearly empty, except for a pair of Asian IT managers playing a jittery fruit machine.

'Tomato juice, Worcestershire sauce, crushed celery, beetroot and horseradish sauce, John. No vodka, sadly.' Bryant held up his glass. 'Kiskaya Mandeville recommended it to sharpen my brain. She's prescribed a series of memory tests I must perform every day and put me on a juice diet. Reckons I'll quickly notice the results. I have to take three different types of fish oil tonight. My poor bowels will be positively peristaltic. This is Dr Harold Masters. Oddly, I don't think you've ever met.' He gestured at the curator/lecturer from the British Museum. May found himself facing an absurdly tall man with unsuitable tortoiseshell glasses and slightly mad grey hair.

Masters unleashed a great length of arm and shook May's hand vigorously. 'Not sure we've ever had the pleasure. But Mr Bryant has consulted me many times in the past.'

That figures, thought May. He ordered a half of Spitfire bitter. 'Let's hope this memory course of yours works,' he told Bryant. 'Perhaps you'll recall what happened to

Oswald's ashes.' He looked around at the sepia-tinted walls, the framed photographs and dust-gathering knick-knacks. 'What made you pick a pub in an alleyway off another alley? It was a bugger to find.'

'I wanted to make a particular point, and I find that sometimes, if I just talk to you, you sort of tune out.'

'That's because you have a habit of lecturing me,' said May.

'I most certainly do not. I try to direct your attention towards topics of interest.'

'Yes, and you used to tap me with a pointing stick until I broke the damned thing in half.'

'That was you, was it? Amongst other things, Dr Masters is an expert on the mythology and etymology of London. He's been helping me with a few ideas lately, and I thought it would be a good idea for the two of you to meet because he knows an awful lot about English pubs.'

My God, thought May, studying the academic, *we could all do with more women in our lives. This is what happens when men get lonely. They dry out.*

Dr Harold Masters knew far more about the dead than the living. Human beings were too emotional and messy. He had only been able to tolerate Jane, his wife, because she shared his arcane interests, and now she was gone. The awful truth was that her death allowed him to spend more time concentrating on his studies. He missed her, in the distant way that a man misses the regular arrival of dinner and fresh laundry, but relished the extra hours he could now spend among his research documents. Understanding the past was far more interesting than understanding people, especially women.

'Mine is a professional perspective, of course,' Masters snorted cheerfully. 'Take a look at this place. It looks quite unremarkable from the outside, doesn't it? But it was built from the ruins of the Great Fire.'

'Surely not. This bare-wood-and-ironwork-lamps look is 1930s, with a touch of last year chucked in.'

'The present-day building, perhaps, but it's been a tavern for centuries. In fact, it's constructed over Roman ruins that survive some five metres down. And it was once the official residence of the Mayor of London. William and Mary liked the place so much that they provided it with the iron gates outside. A gentleman called Robert Williamson turned it into a proper public house in 1739. And it has a ghost.'

'All London pubs say they have a ghost – it gets the tourists in.'

'Ah, but this one has something else,' Masters enthused. 'The heart of London. The bar is supposed to contain an ancient stone that marks the dead centre of the old city. The parade of historical characters through here has gone unrecorded and barely remarked upon. Why? Because the pubs of London are taken almost completely for granted by those who drink in them.' The doctor stabbed a long pale finger at the air. 'Every single one has a unique and extraordinary history.'

'That's true,' Bryant agreed with enthusiasm. 'Did you know that the basement of the Viaduct Tavern in Holborn contains cells from Newgate Jail? Its walls have absorbed the tortured cries of a thousand poor imprisoned souls. These places survived for reasons of geography. The Tipperary in Fleet Street used to be called the Boar's Head. It was built in 1605 with stones taken from the Whitefriar's Monastery, stones that allowed it to survive unharmed in the raging inferno of the Great Fire of London. And the Devereux, where we held Oswald's wake, is named after Robert Devereux, Earl of Essex, who was imprisoned in the Bloody Tower and beheaded. The point Harold is trying to make is that these places hold the key to our past, and therefore the present.

They're an unappreciated indication of who we are, and a sign of all we've lost and remember fondly, in which bracket I would include nurses' hats, single railway-carriage compartments, quality umbrellas, the concept of public embarrassment, correct pronunciation and the ability to tell a child off in the street without risking a stab-wound.'

'Pubs are just shops that sell booze, Arthur. What's more, they're dying at a rate of sixty-five a year in London because of property developers. You're over-egging the pudding as usual.'

'Not at all,' said Masters, jumping in eagerly. 'Walk the streets of London, and the only time you'll speak to strangers is when you apologize for stepping in their path. Public houses act, as their name implies, as homes for the general populace, where opposites can meet and confront each other without prejudice, on neutral territory. This is why the landlord is referred to as the host, and why rooms in pubs were always used to hold local inquests, to be sure of a fair and impartial verdict.'

'I think you'll find that the desire for alcohol also plays a part in their popularity,' said May.

'Obviously, but there's something more fundamental at the root of it. Walking into a pub alone is for many young people their first act of real independence. Such places have had a profound effect on our society throughout history, acting as every kind of salon and meeting place, from coffee-house pamphleteers to the cruelties of the gin palace. And of course, they reinvent themselves endlessly. Where political and philosophical meetings were once held, there are now karaoke and Jenga evenings, book readings and sexual-fantasy nights. And they come with an amazingly complex set of social codes, of course.'

'True, I suppose,' May admitted. 'There's nothing more embarrassing than finding that your pint-to-toilet cycle has become synchronized with that of a total stranger's.'

'Why, public houses have even influenced our language. Drinkers used to share the same mug, in which the level of ale was marked with a wooden peg, hence the expression "to take someone down a peg". The masons who built our churches were housed at inns, hence the Masonic connections of certain pubs, and of course, the Knights Templars had their own inns at Clerkenwell. When the polluted waters of London proved unpotable, everyone drank at ale houses. Pub names provide markers for all the historical events of England. The Red Lion, White Hart, Crown and Anchor, Royal Oak, Coach and Horses – each has its own convoluted meaning. We even find our way around by the location of public houses like the Green Man and the Sun in the Sands.'

'Think about it, John,' said Bryant. 'A couple of weeks ago, you and I had a drink at the Anchor, where others had sat drinking half a millennium before us, seeing the same view.'

'Do you realize that in the late-Victorian era there was a pub for every hundred people in the country?' asked Masters. 'We talk about the inner-city schools where pupils speak dozens of languages, but what about the melting pots that exist on almost every street corner?'

'And the history they hold, true or false as the case may be,' mused Bryant, drifting off the point, as he was wont to do. 'The Sherlock Holmes in Northumberland Avenue, presented as if Holmes was a real detective, and the Old Bank of England, a bar on Fleet Street touted by guides as the site of Sweeney Todd's shop, if you please. What complete and utter nonsense.'

'Whereas the pub in which I am to be found most evenings, in Smithfields, was once called the Path of Hope, because it stood on the route of condemned prisoners, like the Old King Lud at Ludgate Circus,' said Masters. 'Although it was always associated with St Bartholomew's Fair, the pub sign depicts a pair of stranded sailors. In Victorian times one often finds the idea of hope connected with the sea – hope of finding land or another ship. A popular maritime motto was "We anchor in hope", but by depicting sailors the sign-maker has misunderstood the meaning of the pub's name. You see? By decoding the tangled symbols of the past, we get close to the truths that history books miss.'

'What we're trying to say is that perhaps these places,' Bryant gestured around the bar, 'are as germane to the solution of a case like this as the identity of the victims. What if these unfortunate women met their deaths not just because of who they were, but where they were?'

'That's ridiculous,' said May hotly. 'It would mean they were selected from the population at random, and we have too many correlating factors to believe that.'

'Then imagine a man who, for reasons we cannot yet fathom, strikes only in public houses, and does so because of what they represent. By killing these women he is unstringing the very fabric of England.'

'It's true,' exclaimed Masters. 'If you wished to undermine everything we stand for as a people, you could do no better than damage the institution of the pub. You'd be striking at the heart of the nation.'

17

ASLEEP IN THE TREES

Sergeant Renfield was looming behind her, trying to read over her shoulder.

'Anything I can help you with, Jack?' asked Longbright pointedly.

'All a bit mundane, isn't it?' said Renfield with a disdaining sniff. 'People die in or outside pubs all the time, it just never gets reported. A little beneath you, this sort of thing. I thought the PCU was about tracking down lunatics in highwayman outfits and solving murders committed in ridiculous places.'

'When deaths occur outside pubs, the victims are never usually middle-aged career women who've been drinking alone,' Longbright replied. 'They're teenaged and in groups, drunk or stoned, and have been in fights with their peers over girls and loyalty and codes of respect. You've been there, Jack, you know that.'

'I ask because I'm trying to understand how this place works. You've got that girl April, who has no qualifications, trawling through cold cases looking for links to these dead women, and that's not logical. Procedure requires—'

'This unit doesn't operate according to the laws of logic,' said Longbright. 'Colin and Meera are searching for witnesses and conducting interviews as procedure requires, leaving us free to detect larger trends.'

'You mean there's no proper system in place here. It's like you've forgotten that you're working against the clock. Lives are at stake. Don't your bosses understand that others will die if they don't stop fannying around?'

'The system doesn't work within the normal structure of criminal investigation departments.'

'So what happens when a case comes in?'

'Raymond Land has to approve our involvement, but he gets overruled by Mr Bryant, who chooses the cases to which he thinks we're best suited. John usually backs him up. Then Land has to go cap in hand to the Home Office.'

'So what interests Bryant?'

'He's concerned with deaths that occur in circumstances too troubling for the Met to deal with. The detectives write up their notes – more themes and ideas, really. Then we spend the next few days hiding what we've discovered from anyone who might stop us.' Longbright was enjoying the look of creeping unease on Renfield's face.

'And where is everybody else this morning? I ask because I have to keep notes on you lot.'

'John and Mr Bryant are in a pub somewhere in Holborn consulting an expert in London mythology. April is calling the surviving relatives of Joanne Kellerman, and after work I'm getting my roots touched up before attending a society for conspiracy theorists. Raymond Land is probably in the Nun and Broken Compass playing darts with former officers from Bow Street station and slagging you off something rotten. Giles Kershaw will be running more tests on Jocelyn Roquesby, and Dan

Banbury is probably going over the crime scenes of the earlier victims. Happy?'

'And out of this farrago you honestly hope to find a murderer?' Renfield was staggered. He had expected an element of disorganization, but nothing on this scale. It would have been easier to predict the movement of cats.

'I don't know about that,' Longbright told him. 'Things have to get stranger first, or else Mr Bryant will lose interest.'

'And when do you suppose that might happen?' asked Renfield, fighting to keep his natural temperament under control.

'Oh, right around about now,' said Longbright with a sly smile. 'Come on, Jack, lighten up on us a bit. Our strike rate is more than double that of any other specialist unit. Find something positive to say.'

Renfield eyed her thoughtfully. 'You've got lovely legs on you, Janice,' he said at last.

Jasmina Sherwin checked her watch again. She had been waiting for her so-called boyfriend to turn up for nearly half an hour, but his mobile was turned off. She pulled her sheepskin coat more tightly around her, and looked out at the empty road. It was already starting to get dark. The trunks of the plane trees opposite were lost in shadows. Their uppermost branches stood out black against the dying sky. Nobody else was sitting on the benches in the front garden of the Albion, but she hated overheated rooms, and the saloon bar was unbearably warm.

The Barnsbury pub appeared to have been dropped down in the heart of the English countryside. Graceful Edwardian houses filled the backstreets between two busy thoroughfares. It was hard to imagine that the chaos of King's Cross was just a fifteen-minute walk from this spot.

A pair of crows sniped in the trees above her. A breeze rose, the shiver rippling along the street in a wave that caused the tops of the branches to gossip.

She knew she should never have agreed to meet him again, not after he had let her down the week before. What, she wondered, was the attraction of careless men? A car drifted past almost in silence, the driver insolently staring at her.

She looked over her shoulder, through the window of the pub. The barman had gone somewhere. The bar appeared to be deserted now, except for a small group of noisy fat men playing darts in the rear saloon, but she was sure someone had been standing close by her when she ordered her orange juice. She had seen him from the corner of her eye, just a dark shape really, but she'd had the sense of a heavy overcoat, a pale eye turned in her direction. Normally she was entirely at ease in pubs, but this one didn't feel as if it was even in the city.

Shiny dark birds cawing in the trees, the evening so quiet you could hear the breeze. Something was not right. Something . . .

He made her start, moving in to sit beside her without disturbing the air, so that she was sure he had not been there the moment before. She was strong, but he had the element of surprise. His grip was practised and complete. She felt the hot lance of the needle enter her neck, and knew at once that the time for escape had already passed. The freezing numbness flooded her body, like dental anaesthetic but much faster, more totally invasive, and she felt herself falling down into his waiting arms.

She heard his voice from far above, even though he could only be speaking in a whisper. 'Stay with me,' he told her. She tried to remain awake, sensing that if consciousness failed it would not return. She was young and mistrustful of men, so how could this be happening?

So unfair, she thought, *so stupid*. In that brief moment she felt as if all the evils in the world were there to be understood. Men were starving wolves who searched for weaknesses, and she had dropped her guard for the first – and only – time in her short life.

The Nun and Broken Compass had been shut for refurbishment, so Raymond Land's pals from the Met had suggested going a little further afield today, seeing as they were on short shifts, and Land could basically do as he pleased now that the Home Office called the shots for his unit. Land was still laughing at the superintendent's disgusting joke as they pocketed their dart sets and left the Albion. He didn't like Barnsbury – too many stuck-up north London politicians living here – but the Albion was a bit of a find, bucolic and becalmed, hidden behind artful undergrowth.

While they were discussing what would be the quickest way back, the superintendent noticed the girl. She was seated upright on the bench, her head hanging over her drink. Land had been about to make a remark about birds not being able to hold their booze, when one of the others realized that something was wrong with her.

In the deepening shadows, a young black girl had fallen asleep so soundly that she had died, her soul departing on respectful tiptoe, as quietly as the fading breeze.

18

PUB CRAWL

Thursday morning at the PCU dawned in a tangle of disbelief and recriminations.

'You were actually on the premises,' May accused his superior, pacing the latter's threadbare office carpet. 'How could you not have seen what happened to this young woman?'

'Do you know the Albion?' asked Land angrily. 'It's a series of rooms, and we were out at the back having a game of arrows. How was I to know she'd been attacked?'

'Didn't you hear or see anything unusual at all?'

'No, I was playing for money and concentrating on my form. I don't think I saw another person in the pub apart from the barman, and he hardly speaks any English. This girl had apparently been stood up by her boyfriend – who is in the clear, by the way, because he was actually at a job interview in the Finchley Road Mercedes showroom and had forgotten he was meeting her. Besides, she had been sitting outside the whole time, so how was I supposed to see her?'

'Has Giles had a chance to conduct a full examination of the body yet?'

'No, he had to wait for the family to come in and ID her last night, but he says there's a piercing on the side of her neck consistent with the MO on the first two – or rather four, if we count the uninvestigated cases.'

'Our perpetrator is becoming angrier.' Giles Kershaw was unfurled in Land's doorway. 'Very nearly snapped the needle off in her neck, left a circular bruise where he pushed the syringe base right up against the skin, and it looks like such a high dosage that I should imagine she died in seconds. I'm heading back to Bayham Street. Jasmina Sherwin's father is probably going berserk.'

Kershaw flicked back his blond hair in the habitual gesture he had acquired from bending his tall frame over tissue samples. 'Something's out of whack. This one is different, the age, the ethnicity, the social background. I'd have said it was an entirely separate incident except that she was found in a pub and killed in the same fashion. Premeditation, obviously. But a fundamental paradox: the killer wants them to die so quietly that no one notices, and yet he chooses to kill them in public, often crowded places. It goes against all of our received wisdom.'

'Why has he switched to a young black girl after singling out middle-aged white women?' asked Land.

'His lacunae, the calm gaps between his acts of violence, are closing. It's only a few hours since he last took a life. Perhaps the need has now become so urgent that in this case it drove him into the nearest pub, and Sherwin was unlucky enough to be the only female there. The rest of the locations are grouped in roughly the same area. Does anyone mind if I take Renfield with me?'

'What for?' asked May.

Kershaw looked embarrassed. 'I think Mr Sherwin might come back and try to thump someone, probably me as I'm the weediest. We've never had anyone at the unit who could handle trouble, and I've heard Renfield is pretty good in difficult situations.'

'He gets very stroppy and shouty, if that's what you mean,' said May.

'It may be what's needed in this case,' said Kershaw. 'I'll return him, don't worry.'

'So what happens now?' asked Land, for whom events were clearly moving too fast.

'The press is making sure that this story will be all over London like a cheap suit. It's the fault of that woman from *Hard News* whose life we saved, Janet Ramsey.' The journalist had nearly come a cropper in her pursuit of a story, luring a killer to her apartment, only to be bailed out by the PCU. 'She agreed to get off our backs for a while but clearly has no gratitude, because she's already rung me about reports of a young girl's death in a London pub, says she's going to run something tonight.'

'It's the scorpion and the frog,' said Land despondently. 'She can't resist stinging because it's in her nature. The last thing we need right now is more negative publicity. What are you going to do about it?'

'What happened to *we*?' asked May in surprise. 'I thought you were on our side.'

'I've had enough crap fall on me in the last few months to drown a cow,' answered Land. 'I'm going to make sure I stay dry and sweet-smelling this time.'

'Oh, I see,' said May. 'When the going gets tough, the tough run for cover.'

'I never said I was tough,' answered Land. 'All I ever wanted was a quiet life.'

'Well, you'll get it if this goes wrong, won't you? Renfield will take great joy in filing a report to Faraday and Kasavian. In addition to pointing out that we were sitting on cold files connected to an ongoing investigation which he thinks we can't crack, he'll probably mention that Arthur's memory is so bad he managed to lose the ashes of his pathologist on the same night, while somehow hallucinating himself back into Victorian times, so you'll finally get your wish, to sit out your remaining working years in a police station the size of a cab-drivers' hut in a depopulated village on the Orkney Islands that's so quiet you'll be able to hear a duck break wind four miles away.'

'I don't know why you have to be so incredibly rude,' said Land indignantly.

'Because you might have saved a young woman's life if you'd been concentrating on your bloody job instead of drinking with your cronies. If you're so keen to have Renfield write out reports, tell him to put that detail in it.'

'We are going to get a lead in this case today, and we will stop anyone else from dying,' Bryant announced as he strolled into the office and tossed his walking stick into its stand, a sooty old chimney-pot he had rescued from the demolition of the York Way Jam Factory in 1982.

'Did I miss a meeting?' asked May. 'I love the way you just decide to announce these things. How are we going to accomplish this feat? We're still trying to sort out links between the victims.'

'We'll get the break. It may not seem to you like we're closing in, but we are. Perhaps it's someone who worked with them all.'

'Unlikely. Only Curtis and Wynley were at the Swedenborg Society. And we have no proof that they really knew each other – only that one woman was friendly enough with the next to put her number into her mobile.'

'Then perhaps you're approaching the investigation

from the wrong end. Ask yourself, what do we know about the killer?' Bryant dropped into his chair and swung it around. 'He feels at home in pubs, to the point where he can commit murder in them with total confidence. Unfortunately, due to high staff turnover, the barmaids and barmen rarely take note of regular customers. Also, his field of operation is in an area of the city which doesn't have local custom, and that allows him to slip unseen among strangers. Perhaps he's visited these pubs many times when he has not been moved to kill. Perhaps they mean something special to him, have some magic that can only be captured by taking a life.'

'You know I'm going to say I don't agree with you,' warned May.

'Yes, and therefore to prove a point, tonight the PCU is going on a pub crawl. I've worked the whole thing out. There have been five deaths in all, but there are only four public houses involved as the fifth appears to have vanished some decades ago. However, all five women have connections with other pubs, so we need to check those as well, which in my book makes a total of nine places to visit, and means we need to put every member of the PCU to work this evening. Here's the roster.'

Bryant flipped open a neat black leather Mont Blanc notepad, the one gift from Alma that he had managed not to lose. 'Janice is going to head for the Conspirators' Club at the Sutton Arms, where Jocelyn Roquesby was a regular, and Renfield will stake out the Old Bell Tavern, where she died.

'Meera will visit the Apple Tree in Clerkenwell, where Carol Wynley used to socialize after work. Colin has requested to join the speed-dating night at the Museum Tavern, Bloomsbury, where our most recent victim, Jasmina Sherwin, worked as a barmaid.

'John, you'll be going to the quiz night at the Betsey

Trotwood in Farringdon, which Joanne Kellerman had been known to frequent. Giles Kershaw has offered to spend the evening in the Old Dr Butler's Head, where she was found murdered.

'April will attend the Phobia Society upstairs at the Ship and Shovell off the Strand, which Naomi Curtis told her partner she visited because she suffered from claustrophobia, while our Dan Banbury will check out the Seven Stars, Carey Street, where she was killed.

'Raymond Land can go back to the Albion, Barnsbury, to see if he can find out anything more about Jasmina Sherwin's death. And I shall be joining a historical society, the Grand Order of London Immortals, which Dr Masters has recommended to me on previous occasions, because they know all there is to know about sociopathic behaviour in urban society. They've moved to the back bar of the Yorkshire Grey in Langham Place because their old haunt, the Plough in Museum Street, installed a plasma screen for the World Cup, an act for which they have never been forgiven.'

'And what good do you think all this is going to do?' asked May.

'As I believe I mentioned, I have an idea that the murderer is motivated as much by the locations as the victims. If that's the case, we need to spend more time in the kind of places he chooses as his haunts. I want everyone to be sensitive to their surroundings, and to make copious notes. Talk to people, be honest about what you're looking for. We'll meet back here after closing time and pool any information we consider relevant, or possibly irrelevant.'

'You think Renfield's going to go along with something like this?'

'We have Raymond's backing, so I don't see how he can stop us. Besides, we're covering all the official routes of enquiry. This is extra-curricular. It's going to be a long night, so no drinking alcohol. I don't want Renfield trying to disbar evidence because our intelligence sources were one over the eight.'

'That includes you,' said May.

'Bitter isn't alcohol, it's beer,' said Bryant. 'We will start to find a way of catching this man by the end of tonight, I promise you.' He checked his watch, more from habit than any useful purpose, as the little hand had fallen off in the blast that destroyed the PCU's old offices, and he had not got around to having it mended.

'You don't suppose you're still suffering the after-effects from losing your memory last time around, do you?' asked May. 'Remember when you blew up the unit and banged your head?'

'That was ages ago,' said Bryant. 'I've never suffered any recurrence since then. Besides, Mrs Mandeville says I'll start remembering all sorts of things any day now, if my internal organs can withstand the vigour of her root-vegetable diet. Right, I must be off. Call me later.'

'Do you have your mobile on you?'

'Actually I do. This is one of the first things Mrs Mandeville taught me to remember.'

'Good. Is it on?'

'We haven't got that far yet. I shall put it on now.' Bryant made an unnecessary pantomime of operating the device before setting off.

From his window, May watched his partner negotiating the shuffling drunks of Camden High Street. It was difficult not to worry about Arthur's safety these days, but Bryant seemed quite unconcerned. He waved his walking stick at a passing taxi, and glanced up briefly at the unit's windows as he climbed in.

Two minutes later, May received a text that read:

Stop Fretting Im Fine Have Fully Mastered Predictive Tghx
Will Call If I Need Ghzb

If he didn't keep finding ways of saving lives, he'd be the death of me, thought May.

19

CONSPIRATORS

Bryant's idea seemed sound enough, until you considered that nobody knew who this man was or what he looked like. Sergeant Janice Longbright studied the scrap of paper she had been handed and searched the street. The great shuttered block of Smithfield meat market dominated an area now replenished with upscale eateries and thumping nightclubs, but here was a pub like an ancient lithograph, with a grand lead-glass bay window, polished oak doors and sienna paintwork, the sign of the Sutton Arms picked out in gold glass on an umber background.

The interior had been given a peculiar timeless ambience of plaster busts, aspidistra pots and sepia photos that fitted in well enough with Belgian beers and the steak menu. A narrow staircase led to an overlit upper room, but Longbright could not gain access to it because a table covered in books and pamphlets had been placed across the entrance.

'Can I help you?' asked a sallow-faced man with deep-set eyes and tentacles of oily hair plastered across his bald head.

'I'm here for the Conspirators' Club,' said Longbright.

'Well of course, you would say that, wouldn't you? You could have read that on our website. Anyone could have read that, found out the address and just come in here off the street, and we'd have no way of knowing if they're friend or foe. Do you know the password?'

'Oh, give over, Stanley, how can she know the password when you keep changing it?' asked a pleasant-faced woman in her mid-forties. 'Last week it was Inkerman, this week it's Bisto, how are we supposed to keep track? Just let the lady come in, for heaven's sake.'

'Entrance fee is still two pounds – the money goes towards our fighting fund,' said Stanley, tapping a relabelled Kleenex box.

'It goes towards his beer money. He's a nuisance but he keeps out undesirables. I'm Lulu,' said Lulu. 'Come on in.'

'Do you get many nutters here?' Longbright could not resist asking.

'Mainly on anniversaries of assassinations, although our last meeting on St Valentine's night was tricky. A group of war-game strategists turned up and attempted to provide new theories about the fall of the Maginot Line using beer bottles and baguettes. Our members tend to be intense and easily persuaded, especially the single ones. Have you been before?'

'No, but a friend of mine has. Jocelyn Roquesby, perhaps you know her?'

'My goodness, you poor love, you're in the right place because we've been proposing theories about her. It's not the sort of thing we usually talk about. Mostly it's stuff like this.'

She indicated the books and brochures on the table. Several titles caught Longbright's eye: *Jim Morrison Lives On in Indian Spirit*; *The Bavarian Illuminati*;

Lockerbie and the CIA; *Christ's Blood and the Crown of Thorns*; *The UK Biochemical Cover-Up*; *The Search for Princess Diana*; *1968 Moon Landing Props Found in Vegas*; *Floridagate*; *Death in the Persian Gulf*; *Where Anna Nicole Smith Is Now.*

'They're not all as barking as they may at first look,' said Lulu. 'People think it's all about coming up with outlandish reasons for the Kennedy assassination – America invented all the juiciest conspiracy theories, after all – but these days most of our debates concern the limitations of world media and the way in which information is controlled. Many of these books expound surprisingly even-handed ideas, although I wouldn't believe the one about Kurt Cobain being reincarnated as the king of the lizard aliens. Would you like a drink?'

'Thanks,' said Longbright, immediately breaking Bryant's rule. 'I'll have a gin and French. You know, with Vermouth.'

'Good choice,' said Lulu. 'Perhaps we can introduce you to some interesting people tonight. I'll try to keep you away from the cryptozoologists. Get them on to Loch Ness and you'll be stuck here until closing time.'

'What usually happens at these meetings?' asked Longbright.

'Sometimes there's a book launch, or a talk or a debate. It's a lot more rational than you'd expect. We discuss theories about recent news stories and share ideas. It's an alternative to only getting your data from the mainstream media, which is partisan, conservative, and mainly concerned with scaring the living daylights out of Middle England.'

'I think I know that woman.' Longbright pointed to an elegant redhead in her early forties, dressed in a black sweater and jeans.

'She's a new recruit. Came here by mistake, thinking

it was an art appreciation class, but enjoyed herself so much that she ended up coming back. Let me introduce you.'

'Hi,' said the redhead, holding out her hand. 'I'm Monica Greenwood. You're a policewoman, aren't you?'

Longbright was taken aback. 'Is it my feet?' she asked. 'They've always been big. I shouldn't draw attention to them.' Admittedly, she was wearing Joe Tan crimson peep-toed pumps with ankle-bows.

'No.' Monica smiled. 'I've met you before with John May. I'm afraid I'm the one with whom he was having the affair. Paul Greenwood's wife.'

'Sorry, I knew I'd seen you before.' Longbright was taken aback by her forthrightness. She recalled the scandal of the academic's wife who had become involved with her superior during the investigation of a murder.

'I'm the one who should be sorry. I made things pretty tricky for your boss, didn't I?'

'Only for a while. I was sorry to hear about your husband.'

'I stayed by him while he was sick, but now that he's fully recovered and can take care of himself, we're finally getting a divorce. I should have done it years ago. What brings you here? Oh my God, you're not working, are you?'

Janice had never been a convincing liar. 'My attendance is connected to a case,' she admitted. 'A woman called Jocelyn Roquesby died near here in a pub called the Old Bell Tavern.'

'We were just talking about her. She was quite a regular. Naturally, there are some people here who take their conspiracies rather too seriously,' she indicated a group of barrel-stomached men in cable-knit jumpers gathered in the corner, 'and they think she was murdered.'

'I'm afraid in this instance they might be right,' said

Longbright. 'Is there any specific reason for them thinking that?'

'One of the main reasons she used to attend was because she had quite a few conspiracy theories of her own. Phillip, her ex-husband, was in some senior government post and she was supposedly well known on the Westminster dinner-party circuit. Reading between the lines, I'd say she became a bit of an embarrassment for him, a few too many indiscreet remarks made over the liqueurs, and he filed for divorce. Some of her stories sounded very plausible, though. There were plenty of people here who were prepared to listen to her ideas, and I daresay quite a few more will turn up now that she's dead.'

Longbright began to see how conspiracy theories developed. If Roquesby had just been a housewife and her husband had worked in the local post office, no one other than those directly involved would have questioned the circumstances of her death. You had to be in a position of some power before the seeds of suspicion could be sown and your demise could invite the status of conspiracy. How easy would it be to become tangled in the skein of half-truths and hearsay that encrusted themselves around the circumstances of a high-profile death?

'Did she make any good friends here? Or bring anyone else along?'

'She was ever so sweet, and rather lonely. Undergoing chemotherapy for cancer, I believe. She didn't say much during the general debates, but really enjoyed meeting new people.'

'What kind of stories did she used to tell?'

'You have to understand that she was very bitter about Phillip. She said he dumped her because she knew things about the government, but in fact I hear he left her for a younger woman with a firmer bust and a smaller mind, as they all do. Then one day she wouldn't talk about it any more. Said it was a private matter, but I think she was warned off by the gleam in the eyes of our conspirators. I imagine that coming here was a way of forgetting her personal troubles. The last thing she'd have wanted to do was to have them dragged out in public. These events can get very personal. Conspiracy theorists have little respect for privacy, everything is regarded as fair game. And conspiracies breed in the face of opposing truths. As a student, I created some crop circles with a friend down on Box Hill, taking step-by-step photographs of how we did it with a plank and some ropes. A couple of months later, I posted the pictures to the local paper. When the article appeared I received hate mail from people telling me I was deliberately trying to discredit the "Box Hill Circles". I became a victim in my own conspiracy.'

'Do you think if someone had gone up to Mrs Roquesby in a pub and started making polite conversation, she would have responded, encouraged him?'

'Not very likely. She seemed shy. I think it took a fair amount of courage just to come here. She told me she had no close personal friends at all, and hardly any family apart from her daughter.'

Which suggested that Jocelyn Roquesby had not known her attacker, and that he struck at random. It was the worst possible news she could have wished for, and the last thing she wanted to report back to Arthur and John.

Jack Renfield had been seated in the Old Bell Tavern for over an hour, and had switched from orange juice to lager because he was bored and angry. He eyed the rowdy office workers over the top of his glass, and longed to wipe the grins off their faces by nicking them for infringing by-laws, just because they were enjoying themselves. *That one*, he thought, *smug git trying to impress some bird from the office, he's probably got a wrap of coke in his pocket. I'd love to pull him up and see the look on his face*. Several of his mates were on the pavement, impeding the passage of passers-by. That was enough to get them arrested.

Renfield always felt like arresting someone when he was lonely.

How, he wondered, had he allowed himself to be manoeuvred into the PCU, where everyone hated him? He felt sure Bryant and May were laughing at him behind his back, ordering him to spend the evening sitting in a pub by himself, in the absurd hope that he might pick up some kind of information about the killer. Why weren't they hammering the fear of the law into relatives and colleagues, chasing down the recent contacts of the deceased and demanding answers? A nutcase wanders around the city's public houses armed with a syringe and nobody sees him – how the hell was that possible? And instead of trying to discover his identity, Bryant announces that they must first understand his motive. Crimes that produced no leads in forty-eight hours were virtually dead. No wonder the Home Office tried to shut the unit down every five minutes; the place was an anachronistic embarrassment, a division that fancied itself more at home in the pages of the *Strand* magazine than on the mean streets of Camden Town.

And yet . . .

He found himself staring at a man who was behaving most strangely. He had taken off his shoes and donned a pair of red tartan carpet slippers, and had sat back to read the top volume of a pile of magazines, just as if he were at home. But he was, in fact, assessing the young women who passed his table, surreptitiously studying their legs and buttocks until they moved out of sight.

The longer he watched the behaviour of strangers in the Old Bell, the more Jack Renfield began to think that there might be something to the PCU's methodology after all.

20

IRRATIONALITY

'Own up to being afraid,' said a thin ginger-headed man at the podium. 'It's the first step to acknowledging that you have a problem.' He pointed a plastic ruler at the top page on the board behind him, upon which a variety of phobias were spelled out. 'These are the fears of our current and past members. If yours is not listed here, I'd like you to step up now and add it to the list.'

April looked for *agoraphobia* among more obscure irrationalities: *aichmophobia*, fear of pointed objects; *ailurophobia*, fear of cats; *alektorophobia*, fear of chickens; *alliumphobia*, fear of garlic; *anthrophobia*, fear of flowers; *antlophobia*, fear of floods – and those were just the As. Presumably the young man's easel held twenty-six pages of terrors.

The group was seated upstairs at the Ship and Shovell pub behind the Strand, which Naomi Curtis, the second victim, had visited in an attempt to cure her claustrophobia. It was the only pub in London that existed in two separate halves, each piece a red-painted mirror image of the other, set on either side of a sloping passageway that led down to the Thames. 'Shovell' was spelled with a double 'L' because it had been the original owner's name.

For a bunch of people who lived in irrational fear of ordinary things – computers, snow, being touched – they seemed remarkably chatty and cheerful. The ginger man's talk lasted half an hour, after which there were questions, then everyone went to the bar except one woman, who was apparently perturbed by the sight of spilled beer.

'You're new, aren't you?' asked the speaker. 'I haven't seen you before. You didn't come up to the board.'

'I was agoraphobic, but it seems to be retreating now,' April explained. 'I've had various other phobias in the past – I was bothered by dirt and untidiness. I have a bit of a neatness fetish.'

'I suppose your doctor said you were spending too much time indoors, and developed other fears because you were looking to reduce your world still further. It's quite common. I'm Alex, by the way.'

'April.'

She held out her hand, but he shook his head. 'Can't do it, I'm afraid. Germs. Sadly, recognizing one's phobias doesn't necessarily lead to their cure.'

'And yet we're in an old pub where there are probably a couple of hundred years' worth of microbes festering in the carpets.'

'You know as well as I do that a phobia has no respect for reason.' They took their drinks to a corner of the room.

'I'm here on a mission,' April finally admitted. 'Did you ever meet a woman called Naomi Curtis?'

'Don't know. Hang on.' Alex fetched a diary from the table by the door and checked it. 'Some only come to the society once or twice. We try to keep a record of names, but it's rather hit and miss. Claustrophobic, wasn't she?

She attended a few times. We usually met outside. It was a little too cramped for her at the bar.'

'I can understand that. Did she have many friends here?'

'I think she came with another woman, someone from work. People don't like to visit by themselves. They think they're going to get some kind of sales pitch, but we're just a self-funding help group. Once they understand that, they relax more.'

'Do you ever cure anyone?'

'Sometimes. But fears have a habit of mutating. They'll vanish, only to reappear in a different form. We've managed to keep the group going for six years now, even though we have to keep changing pubs.'

'Why's that?'

'The landlords don't like primal-scream therapy. And once I accidentally released ants all over the saloon floor, and we had a tarantula go missing behind the bar. Never did find it. We had a disastrous meeting in the Queen's Head and Artichoke last year, when three old ladies got locked in the lavatory. They went in as autophobics – afraid of being alone – and came out as claustrophobics. Why did you ask about Miss Curtis – do you know her?'

'No. I'm helping to investigate her murder.'

'My God, I had no idea.'

'She was in a pub.'

'Not this one?'

'The Seven Stars in Carey Street, just down the road from here. She probably went there to meet a friend.'

'And you think it might have been someone she met here?'

'It's a long shot.' April had already told him more than she'd intended to.

'Maybe not so long,' said Alex. 'She did meet someone the last time she came – a bloke in his early thirties, funny haircut, black leather overcoat. I remember thinking there was something really creepy about him. It sticks in my mind because they sat in the corner talking intensely for quite a long time, then she left very suddenly, as if they'd had a row. Mind you, she was incredibly drunk.'

'Would you recognize him again?'

'Possibly. I think he had something wrong with his face, some kind of purple birthmark.'

'Was that what made him appear creepy?'

'No, God, I hope I'm not that shallow. You know the way some people don't behave how they should in company? He was hunched over his beer, openly staring at other women. We're used to autistic behaviour but this was different. I'm sorry, it's not much to go on, is it?'

'You'd be surprised,' said April. It looked as if Curtis's attacker had hit on her before. Perhaps he had even tried to hurt her, only to have his plans thwarted. All nine members of the PCU were out searching public houses tonight. If any of them turned up a similar description, they would finally have a suspect.

Dan Banbury found himself wedged against a wall in the claustrophobic Seven Stars pub, which was located behind Lincoln's Inn Fields and packed to the gills with boisterous, merry legal workers. Normally he would have enjoyed himself in such an environment, but his conversation with the bar staff had been turned into a shouting match by the deafening combination of courtroom rhetoric and cheap beer.

The barmaid who had served Naomi Curtis on the night of her death could think of no other details, and was too busy to concentrate on the subject for long. Banbury jammed himself further into the corner with his pint and wondered. What kind of man would she have allowed close? In his experience women preferred cocktail bars to pubs, especially ones this intimate and rowdy. He felt sure that she could only have come in here to meet a man. This kind of pub was the choice of a male.

With difficulty, he unfolded the spreadsheet April had supplied and checked the notes she had printed. The same injected overdose of sedative, giving symptoms that had been mistaken for heat stroke. A quick, virtually painless method of killing, putting someone to sleep so easily and quietly that their death could pass unnoticed in a crowded bar. Naomi Curtis wasn't rich, had no unusual beneficiaries, no one who might profit excessively from her demise. It seemed unlikely to have been anyone she knew, which meant that she had simply been in the wrong place at the wrong time.

This place was a crime-scene manager's worst nightmare, trampled flat day in, day out, vacuumed and disinfected, scoured by the scrum of bodies, sloshed with centuries of beer. In a way, the man they were looking for had hit upon the perfect location to commit murder. Every night in every pub there would be petty feuds, heated arguments, friendships forged, sexual liaisons proposed and relationships ended, the threats of tears and laughter. Alcohol heightened the emotions. Providing he did not draw attention to himself, a killer could easily hide inside such a world. Bryant was right: coming here had started to give him a different perspective on the problem. He studied the room again, screening out unlikely candidates. The loudmouths and drunks, the shrieking office girls and their stentorian workmates vanished one by one.

Banbury found himself left with a handful of introspective loners, any one of whom might be nursing an uncapped syringe in his jacket pocket.

21

DATING AND DANCING

Raymond Land indignantly refused to follow his own detective's orders to return to the Albion in Barnsbury, so Colin Bimsley and Meera Mangeshkar took on a double shift, first travelling to where Jasmina Sherwin had been found dead. After spending half the evening here, they planned to split up and tackle two further public houses.

For months, Bimsley had fantasized about being in a pub with Meera, a combination of pleasures that made him heartsick with delight. In previous investigations he had been happy enough to spend the night rummaging through suspects' dustbins with her, searching for pieces of food-stained evidence, but just when his wish had been fulfilled, he found that his changing attitude to the diminutive DC had robbed him of happiness.

In short, he had gone off her.

After putting up with her sulks, her tantrums, her cynicism, her sarcasm, her ability to start small bin fires with her pre-menstrual temper, the scales had finally fallen from his eyes, and he fancied he could see her as the woman she had become: bitter, bad-tempered, happy to keep him dangling on the promise of a date which would never be arranged.

As a consequence, the mood between them was polite but arctic. Seated side by side in the snug of the Albion, they stared into their soft drinks and allowed the silence to stretch between them.

Finally, Meera spoke. 'This girl, Sherwin, she was supposed to be young and streetwise. She wouldn't have let some creep just come up and touch her. We're not going to find anything here.'

'Well, that's a positive attitude. You're just saying that because you don't believe in Bryant's methods.'

'Colin, look around you. The place is virtually empty. What are we looking for? The barman who found her isn't even here any more, so he can't point out anyone he saw.'

'How do you know that?'

'I talked to the girl who served me these drinks.'

'Did she say anything else about him?'

'He was sent by the brewery to fill in for someone who hadn't turned up for work.'

Bimsley jumped up so quickly that he knocked his orange juice across the table. While obtaining a cloth at the counter he had a word with the barmaid, who wrote him a number on a slip of paper. He waited for an answer on his mobile, turning his back on Meera.

'The brewery never sent anyone,' he told her, returning. 'They didn't get the message in time. If he wasn't a barman, he could just have ducked behind the bar to serve her. That's how he got close enough to be sure of his latest choice. There was only one staff member on duty last night instead of two, and if she was in the kitchen or the other bar there would have been no one at all at the front.'

'We need to find someone else other than Raymond who was in the pub, someone observant.'

'This is the sort of place that has regulars. You can spot them a mile off. Those two in the corner, for a start, and that old guy by the fireplace. I'll do one end of the bar, you do the other. Look for unsteady hands and broken nose veins.'

Hard drinkers make unreliable witnesses. Several people professed to have seen someone behind the counter, but none of them could agree on a description. He was tall, thin, broad, blond, black, Asian, blotched with a crimson birthmark. Mangeshkar tallied her notes with Bimsley's, and they headed to their next destinations.

Speed-dating night was held at the Museum Tavern on the corner of Museum Street, where Jasmina Sherwin had worked and met her boyfriend. The pub retained the seedy bookishness of Bloomsbury, its crimson leather seats filled with half-cut proofreaders poring over drink-dampened manuscripts. Like the Cross Keys in Endell Street or the Bloomsbury Tavern in Shaftesbury Avenue, it remained constant in a sliding world: the distinctive odour of hops, the ebb of background chatter, muted light through stained glass, china tap handles, metal drip trays, mirrored walls, bars of oak and brass. The Victoriana was fake, of course, modelled on obsolete pub ornaments and anachronistically updated with each refurbishment to create an increasingly off-kilter view of the past, but the blurry ambience remained undisturbed.

The tiny round tables in the rear of the room had been arranged to accommodate the couples who were about to tackle their abridged liaisons. Bimsley was assigned a number by the evening's hostess, a pleasant-faced, overweight girl who reminded him of a character from a Pieter Bruegel painting. Her name-tag proclaimed her to be Andrea from the Two of Hearts Club. She spoke with the sing-song condescension of a suburban Kentish housewife, and probably had a heart of gold until it came to gays and immigrants. 'First time? Lovely! You're a nice big fellow, we shouldn't have too much trouble pairing you up. Pop your badge on and we'll get you settled in. What's your name, lovey?'

'Bimsley,' said Bimsley.

'I think it would be nicer to be on first-name terms with the ladies, don't you?'

'Colin.'

'Oh, we haven't had one of those for a while. There.' She patted a sticky yellow square on to his lapel. Bimsley looked around the saloon. There were several presentable, even sexy women, but the quality of the males was abysmal: a couple of boney-faced accountant-types with VDU pallor, a leaker with lank hair stuck to his forehead and sweat rolling down his cheeks, a middle-aged man dressed as a giant toddler in a sleeveless T-shirt and three-quarter-length trousers, an ageing media-type in club gear who was probably not as interesting as his haircut, a very old gentleman cruising for an heir or possibly an enjoyable way of having a heart attack. In Russia there were ten million more women than men, so at least there the males had an excuse for not bothering to look their best.

His speed dates were allocated just three minutes each, at the end of which he was required to give his women a rating of between one and three points. Bimsley's decision to ask questions about a murder victim instead of enquiring about hobbies, favourite films or dining out brought him looks of incomprehension, confusion and outright hostility until Andrea took him to one side and gave him some advice.

'I think you need to lighten up, darling,' she told him.

'Whatever you're asking these lovely ladies seems to be having a negative effect on their opinion of you.'

After achieving a rating score two points lower than the leaker, Bimsley decided to sit out the next batch of rounds and talk to the barmaid instead. This time he found himself on to a winner.

'I worked the same shift as Jasmina most nights,' said the pixie-faced Polish girl with earnest blue eyes whose name was Izabella, and whose jet hair framed her face like Louise Brooks in *Pandora's Box*. 'She was very nice, but I did not like her boyfriend.'

'Why not?' asked Bimsley, succumbing to a pint of lager.

'He was not interested in her. He had other girlfriends.'

'Did she ever come in here and drink on her nights off? Maybe with someone other than her boyfriend?'

'Oh, no. She hated this place.'

'Why?'

'Because she had a – what you call it? – a stalker. You get men in every pub who try and talk to you on quiet nights, but this one came in all the time.'

'Did you ever see him? What was he like?'

'Too old for her – probably in his early thirties. Brown hair, tall, with a red mark on his face. I was here one night when he started on her.'

'Can you remember anything he said?'

Izabella thought carefully. 'I think he'd been fired from his job. He was a bar manager. North London somewhere. We laughed about him after he left.'

'This is really important,' said Bimsley. 'I need you to make a note of everything you remember about this man.'

'Wait until I finish work tonight,' said Izabella with an impish smile. 'I will tell you anything you want.'

* * *

Meera Mangeshkar was at the Apple Tree in Mount Pleasant, which Carol Wynley had sometimes visited with her work colleagues, but asking questions of the staff and customers proved difficult because there was a country and western line-dancing night in progress.

This had been a postmen's pub for many years due to its proximity to the sorting office, but had now been refurbished for the benefit of tourists visiting from nearby hotels. As Dolly Parton warbled through 'Heartbreaker' on the speakers and couples in checked shirts and fringed cowboy jackets stamped their stitched boots on the ancient Axminster carpet, Mangeshkar was forced into stupefied silence on a nearby counter barstool. The combination of beery British boozer and traditional Texas toetap made her uncomfortable, partly because she was the only Indian girl in the room, and felt as if she might get shot. The well-drilled lines of dancers did not whoop and yell like their more liberated US cousins, but concentrated on their footwork, determined to master exercises more culturally alien to the London mindset than Morris dancing.

She became annoyed that, once again, she had been given an assignment that would yield nothing useful or practical, and was thinking about calling it a night when one of the men grabbed her hands and pulled her on to the dance floor for 'My Heroes Have Always Been Cowboys'.

For the next twenty minutes, Meera forgot her frustration and regret about moving to the Peculiar Crimes Unit as, much to her surprise, she discovered the joys of formation dancing to Willie Nelson.

22

QUESTIONS AND ANSWERS

'In the film *The Ladykillers*, what was the screen name of the old lady Alec Guinness and his cronies were trying to murder? We're talking about the original British version here, not the remake.'

May looked around at the hunched shoulders and lowered heads. The room in the Old Dr Butler's Head, London Wall, where Joanne Kellerman had been found dead, was silent but for the scratching of HB pencils. As he wrote 'Mrs Wilberforce' on the sheet before him, he accidentally caught the eye of the woman at the next table. She promptly glanced away, suspecting him of trying to cheat. *They want to be back at school*, he thought, *each vying to be top of the class once more.*

'Last question in our film round: give me the name of the ancient kingdom discovered in *Passport to Pimlico*.'

May wrote 'Burgundy' and turned over his paper, ready for collection. He looked around the room at the assembled players, trying to see if any were alone. *We always assume killers operate singly*, he caught himself thinking. *What if there are two of them, perhaps even a man and a woman?* Suddenly the conspiring, whispering pairs in the room appeared more sinister. The women had not told their partners, relatives or friends where they were going. Was that in itself significant? If the attacks were completely random and the killer moved to a fresh venue every time, catching him would be a matter of luck. *There are nearly six thousand pubs in London*, he thought. *What are we expected to do, close them all down? Suppose he switches to another hectic public place – inside the Tube, on rush-hour buses, or simply on crowded city pavements?*

The case had resonance with a number of other, more extraordinary killings that had occurred in London over recent years. A Bulgarian dissident, Georgi Markov, had been poisoned on Waterloo Bridge with the sharpened tip of an umbrella. Roberto Calvi, the Vatican banker, had been found hanged in a convincingly staged suicide underneath Blackfriars Bridge. And the former KGB agent Alexander Litvinenko was fatally dosed with radioactive thallium in a busy sushi bar. In all three cases there had been no guns, no knives, just the careful and quiet determination to remove a life.

It was difficult to shake off a sense of impending failure.

May was inclined to disagree with his partner, who felt that the attacks were based on opportunity and location as much as on the women themselves, but the fact remained that they had uncovered no common denominators other than the link between their mobile phones. None of the calls had been under surveillance, so there was no way of tracing what had been said.

And there was another problem: Jasmina Sherwin's mobile had been found on her body, so the killer wasn't using a consistent MO. *If it can be proved that they all knew each other*, he thought, *it might be possible to discover the identities of other women in danger.* He handed in his quiz form and sipped at his pint, watching the quizmaster at work. *That's who I need to talk to*, he decided. *He'll remember everyone who's ever come here to play. The kind of men who compile quizzes always do . . .*

The Grand Order of London Immortals were, in their own words, primarily interested in London's most infamous characters: political brigands, celebrity criminals, unapprehended murderers, and anyone else who had been stencilled into the city's collective memory by doing something notorious and getting away with it.

Dr Harold Masters knew that the order shared some members with his own Insomnia Squad, and had recommended it to Bryant as a group who might unwittingly shine a light on the path to uncovering a murderer. This month they were meeting in the Yorkshire Grey, Langham Place, a small green-painted Victorian establishment with hanging baskets, exterior tables and memorabilia from the nearby BBC on their walls. Workers from the garment district frequented the bar, but tonight the Immortals – a grandiose term for what was essentially a band of disgruntled scholars – were loudly holding forth in the rear of the saloon.

Bryant recognized a number of old friends who had helped him in the past, including Stanhope Beaufort, a bombastic architectural expert who volunteered advice on London's ancient monuments, and Raymond Kirkpatrick, a verbose English language professor who had been banned from lecturing at Oxford because of his habit of playing deafening heavy-metal music while he researched. The Immortals attracted their own groupies, not as glamorous perhaps as those who lurked backstage at rock concerts, but every bit as tenacious. Among these was Jackie Quinten, the maternal widow who had tried to tempt Bryant back to her kitchen with the offer of a steaming kidney casserole when they had met in the course of the PCU's investigation into the so-called 'Water Room'. He had turned her down, not because he disliked her cuisine but because she seemed to view him as potential husband material, which could only lead to tears.

He had spotted her sitting in a corner reading, and was careful to skirt the edge of the room in order to avoid her. Unfortunately, as he was creeping past with his head drawn down into the folds of his scarf, he caught his foot in her handbag strap and lurched forward, precipitating half a pint of Samuel Smith's Imperial Stout straight into her lap.

There was a detonation of yelping chaos followed by a commotion of mopping and sponging, during which time Bryant stood helplessly by, caught between the conflicting desires to apologize profusely and to sprint for the exit.

'Really, Arthur,' Jackie Quinten cried in exasperation as she wrung out her skirt, which was woollen and perfectly designed for absorption, 'there must be better ways of announcing yourself.'

'I'm most dreadfully sorry, Jackie, I didn't see you sitting there. You're rather invisible in that corner.'

'Thanks, you always know how to make a woman feel special.' When she saw the look of mortification on his face, she relented. 'Come and sit down for a minute, at least.'

Bryant squeezed in beside her, breathing in the yeasty scent of fermented hops.

'I suppose you're here on business.'

'After a fashion. I'm trying to stop a most unusual murderer.'

'You always are, Arthur. That's what you do, isn't it?'

'Yes, but this one is particularly slippery. He corners middle-aged women in public houses and puts them to sleep.'

'I know an awful lot of men like that.' Mrs Quinten did not appear in the least surprised. If anything, she looked as if her worst fears had been confirmed. Perhaps, thought Bryant, she had considered herself to be in London's last safe place, only to find its status suddenly removed. 'I presume they die in the process, otherwise you wouldn't be involved. Why would he want to do that?' she asked.

'He probably hears voices, or is appeasing a desire, or attempting to restore an equilibrium only he understands. Who knows? Ask why men kill and you open the door to one of life's most paradoxical mysteries.'

'So what are you doing here?'

'Trying to learn how you can make a pub disappear. What about you?'

'Oh, the usual, listening to a bunch of rambling old lecturers and writers talk utter rot. I have to get out occasionally, Arthur, otherwise I'd go insane. Besides, I've always had a soft spot for academics.'

'Their endless curiosity about the world does seem to keep them young,' Bryant admitted.

'And I can't stay indoors making chutney every day, you know. I refuse to watch the toxic drivel that passes for television these days. I thought that by coming to these sorts of events I might get a clearer understanding of the world. I wonder what it is that drives the old to such questioning.'

'I find I'm getting more rebellious as I age,' agreed Bryant. 'The young accept the status quo to an alarming degree. I do wish they wouldn't.'

'Have we merely been disappointed with our lives, do you suppose?'

'When I was young I fantasized about the future.' Bryant flicked a droplet of splashed beer from Jackie's sleeve. 'Now that I'm living in it, I find it all a bit tatty. I was expecting us to be on other planets by now. I wanted genetic transformations and orbiting cities instead of internet porn and small improvements in personal stereos.'

'I know what you mean,' Jackie agreed. 'Take this lot. They have plenty of ideas but no application. At least you might find them useful. Stanhope Beaufort sounds like your best bet, over there. He's an architect.'

'Yes, I know,' said Bryant. 'Do you mind if I go and talk with him?'

'No, but before you go, perhaps I can hold you to the promise of dinner. I'm not trying to lure you, Arthur. I'd make a rather unprepossessing siren. I just enjoy your company.' She seemed hesitant about continuing. 'And we'd appreciate your opinion about a private matter. On a professional basis, you understand.'

'On that basis, I'll do my best to oblige.' Bryant relented, rising. 'I'm free on Saturday.'

Mrs Quinten looked disappointed. 'That's the one day I can't do. I'm meeting one of my gentlemen academics.'

'Oh, what an enormous pity. Another time then.'

'Perhaps after I finished . . .'

'Oh, I wouldn't want to intrude and spoil your evening.'

He was aware of Mrs Quinten's eyes on his back as he moved across the room. *I'll admit she's a not unattractive woman*, he caught himself thinking. *I rather admire a firm maternal bust, but I'm damned if I'll eat her kidney casserole.*

23

VANDALISM

Stanhope Beaufort drained his pint and wiped his white beard. He had put on an enormous amount of weight since Bryant last saw him. Squeezed into a shirt clearly purchased before this gain, he looked like a sheep in a corset. 'What the hell are you doing here, Arthur?' he asked with characteristic brusqueness. 'You only track me down when you want something, so what is it?'

'Actually I happen to be a semi-regular among this crowd,' Bryant pointed out. 'But seeing as you're here too, tell me, how long would it take a man to build a Victorian pub from scratch and then dismantle it again? Could he do it in a single night?'

Bryant explained his predicament.

Beaufort's initial look of surprise transmuted into concentration as he applied himself to the puzzle. 'It would be easier to go the other way around,' he said. 'Hide the pub behind a shop, because the Victorians built things to last. They used stronger mortar, thicker tiles, denser metals. But you could get a shop front up in an hour just by whacking a few sheets of coloured perspex over the brickwork and holding them in place with a handful of screws. Cover the windows with posters, strip the interior furniture, hide the bar behind racks of magazines, hire some old guy to sit at a counter and fob you off with some story about how he'd been there for years. Pubs usually have the capacity to be brightly lit, because the lights are traditionally turned up after time has been called, so they wouldn't have to replace the lighting. I can see how that might just work.'

'I don't know,' Bryant admitted. 'It sounds loopy even to me.'

'I didn't say it was a sane idea, just that it's possible. There's one way to find out,' said Beaufort. 'I've got a crowbar in my car.'

'Are you suggesting we try to take the front of the store off?' said Bryant.

'You're a police officer, aren't you? You can do whatever you like.'

'Sadly we can't,' said Bryant. 'I have a tendency to get caught.' But he was already buttoning his coat.

They found a parking space for Victor, Bryant's decrepit Mini Cooper, in the next street over, and Beaufort slid the crowbar inside his coat as they walked to the corner of Whidbourne Street. The Pricecutter supermarket was in darkness. After checking that the coast was clear, Beaufort slid the implement from his coat and applied it to the oblong of orange plastic that covered the base of the store. He levered the crowbar back until there was a loud crack, and a two-foot-long triangle shattered, clattering to the pavement. Beaufort dropped to his knees and examined the brickwork underneath.

'The fascia is screwed directly into the stonework,' he pointed out. 'With the right tools it could be removed in a few minutes, all of it, but the bad news is that the stonework underneath dates from the 1970s. Nothing is left of the pub that used to be on this site.'

'Are you sure?' said Bryant. 'Couldn't we get one of the upper panels off?'

'This amounts to vandalism, Arthur.'

'It's a murder investigation.'

'All right.' Beaufort hoisted his bulk up on to the low window ledge and wedged his crowbar under the shop's nameplate. It came away in an explosion of brick dust and plastic. 'The same cement finish,' he tutted. 'Hopeless rendering, very disappointing. Still, the original structure of the building is intact. If you could get all this off, I suppose you'd be able to build a false front over the top of it, but you'd need several strong lads and plenty of specialist equipment. Help me down before I fall.'

'That's no good,' said Bryant, holding out a hand. 'I'm looking for a lone murderer, thin, slight build, late twenties or early thirties, not someone travelling around with a team of builders. Besides, even assuming that the killer arranged to meet his victim here, with all the real pubs in London to choose from, why would he feel the need to re-create one from the past? Damn, there's someone coming. We'd better get out of here.'

'I thought you'd be officially sanctioned to commit wanton acts of destruction,' said Beaufort.

'Er, no, not exactly,' Bryant admitted, looking around. 'Time to scram.'

Feeling like a pair of teenaged vandals, they shoved the broken plastic back in place and scooted across the pavement with Bryant using the crowbar as an impromptu walking stick. Dropping into the Mini Cooper, they struggled to regain their breath.

'Well, I'm stumped,' said Bryant, thumping his wheezing chest. 'I most definitely saw the victim in that street. The St Pancras clock-tower was directly behind her like a full moon. Can I give you a lift anywhere? I'm driving back to the PCU.'

'You're not going to carry on working tonight, surely?'

'Just a few notes. I've asked everyone to come back. We need to create a more accurate profile of this gentleman.'

'And how are you intending to catch him?'

'That's the tricky part. He appears to have come up with one of the simplest killing methods ever devised, which makes him either very smart or incredibly stupid.'

'And which do you think he is?' asked Beaufort.

'Both,' said Bryant.

24

HANGOVERS

'You've all been drinking,' said May, shocked. 'Look at the state of you, you're half cut.'

He glanced around the briefing room. Raymond Land was half asleep, Renfield looked sloshed, Banbury was poking about in a packet of cheese 'n' onion crisps and Meera was wearing a suede fringed jacket with THE KING LIVES written across it in red, white and blue sequins.

'Only in the cause of research, sir,' said Banbury, crunching crisps.

'Has anyone seen Bimsley?' asked May.

'Outside, sir. On the street.'

'What's he doing out there, for heaven's sake?'

'Snogging a girl, sir. Tongues and everything. Pretty hot stuff.' Banbury wiggled his eyebrows suggestively and looked about the room. Meera attempted to quell him with a well-aimed stare.

'He gave me his notes,' said April, unfurling a ball of paper and smoothing it out.

'Well, at least you've all been able to turn some in. I

think the evening has given us a chance to reflect on the events of the past few days. I know how these women came to meet their deaths. I want to know why.'

'With all due respect, old chap, we're not going to be able to crack that nut overnight,' said Kershaw. 'We don't have any clear suspects.'

'We now have witness descriptions,' said April, looking up from the collated notes she had laid neatly across the desk. 'Naomi Curtis and Jasmina Sherwin were both approached by a man in his early thirties, attractive despite the fact that he has a large wine-coloured birthmark covering the left side of his face. We think he might be a former north London barman who was fired from his job. It shouldn't be so hard to get a name.'

'That depends on whether he was using his own,' said Bryant. 'Bar staff sometimes pay substitutes cash in hand to take their shifts.'

'Then we have to hope this one was legally employed,' said May, glaring at his partner.

'There's something else,' said April. 'Three of the victims knew each other.' She held up a landscape photograph that clearly showed Naomi Curtis, Jocelyn Roquesby and Joanne Kellerman standing together in a bar holding glasses of red wine.

'Where on earth did you get that?' asked Bryant, amazed.

April pointed across the room to Renfield. 'Jack found it among the photographs of drinkers pinned behind the bar in the Old Bell, although it doesn't look like it was taken there. The décor is different,' she told the group. 'Dan, perhaps you could examine the shot and get some clue to the location.'

'The barmaid thinks it's a recent addition, because she doesn't remember it being there when she started working behind the bar last month,' said Renfield.

'Then it's conceivable that the killer was drinking or working in a pub on the night they met, and singled them out.' Kershaw tapped the photograph with a manicured nail. 'When it came to meeting up with them separately, he could pose as one of the other two, using Kellerman's mobile to send text messages. Could they have all been members of the same pub club?'

'They met in a public house because it was secure,' said Bryant.

'What do you mean?'

'It's what Masters said, a pub is neutral territory. Why, the very word "public" suggests openness. They wanted somewhere safe and busy to meet, so that they could discuss something where they wouldn't be bugged, watched or monitored, something common to all of them.'

'Or someone,' said Longbright. 'Jasmina was stalked.'

'The fundamental problem remains,' said Bryant. 'He's changed his MO and didn't taken Sherwin's mobile this time, so how do we predict whether he will strike again?'

'Start narrowing the search,' said Renfield. 'We put out a description to every pub in north and central London. He's not going to leave his hunting ground. You said yourself that he feels comfortable there, Bryant. He's local to the area. We could have him locked away by this time tomorrow.'

'That would require extra manpower, which means involving the Met,' Bryant pointed out.

'What, you have a problem with that?' Renfield wanted to know.

'We don't, but they do. They won't help us, or you, despite the fact that your mates are still there.'

'Bryant's right.' Land seemed suddenly alert. 'We'll have to do it ourselves. Let's start making the calls and getting people out of bed. Nobody goes home tonight.'

A collective groan rose in the room. The staff clambered from their perches and started to disperse.

'It still doesn't feel right,' said Bryant, shaking his head as the office emptied. 'We're looking at the victims instead of the victimizer.'

'You're trying too hard, Arthur,' said May. 'You always do.'

'No, this time my gut instinct is valid. I think – ' He rolled his eyes to the ceiling, as if searching for ideas in the dusty cornicing. 'I think I need to be alone with my books for an hour.' He rose with a grimace and stumped off to his room.

May knew it was pointless trying to control his partner. He could only follow and wait for revelations, no matter how wrong-headed they might be.

Dan Banbury had scanned the photograph of Naomi Curtis, Jocelyn Roquesby and Joanne Kellerman drinking together, and, section by section, expanded the background illuminated in the flash of the digital camera, a 3.5 megapixel by the look of it. There were plenty of mobiles offering that level of quality. The top left hand of the photograph showed the edge of a window. From its placement, he could tell that the pub was on a corner. The light suggested early evening. Through the window he could make out a swathe of green plastic, a canopy made of metal rods, rows of what appeared to be oranges and bananas: market stalls. Two small gold letters had been painted in reverse on the glass, E and X.

After that, it was simply a matter of running a search on all street markets in the central London area, and finding a corner pub with the letters E and X in its title. Only one fitted the bill: the Exmouth Arms, in Clerkenwell's Exmouth Market.

Banbury checked his watch and punched the air. The entire process had taken him less than fifteen minutes. He had a feeling they were finally getting somewhere.

'All right, come on, you've had your hour. What is it you're looking for?' May shut the door behind him as he returned to the office.

'I'm no good at understanding psychology,' said Bryant. 'I've always left that to you. But it seems to me that the taking of human life involves shame and regret as well as arrogance and cruelty.'

'I wouldn't say that was always true. Serial killers usually fail to produce normal emotional responses. What are you thinking?'

'That part of him wants to be caught. My problem is Jasmina Sherwin, the odd girl out. She's younger, more overtly attractive, different in every way from the others. She doesn't fit the pattern, and yet she's linked to the others by a description of the man who followed her. It doesn't add up, John. Then there are the locations, all grouped together in a tight circle. He's anxious to be stopped, and is trying to expose himself.'

'Then why wouldn't he just turn himself in?'

'Something is driving him on to these acts of violence. No, violence is the wrong word, because I don't think he hates women. The attacks are almost gentle, as if he just wants them to fall asleep in his arms.'

'All right.' May seated himself on the corner of the desk, thinking. 'If he was very lonely – if he felt that the birthmark on his face kept him from being attractive to the opposite sex – this might be his way of preserving a moment for ever, of keeping women by his side in a place where he feels happy and comfortable.'

'Then why aren't all his victims like Jasmina? Look,

do you remember when we were much younger, you tracked down a man who was attacking girls on Number 75 buses – 1968, I think it was. The first thing he said when you took him into custody was "Why did you take so long to stop me?" I think this is similar, and it makes me wonder if he's leaving me any more explicit clues.'

'You say leaving *you* clues. You don't think it's someone who knows you?'

'It has crossed what's left of my mind,' sighed Bryant. 'If only my memory was sharper. I've another appointment with Mrs Mandeville first thing tomorrow morning. She hypnotized me the other day, you know.'

'Did it help to improve your memory?'

'I think so. When I woke up, I suddenly remembered who I'd lent my electric drill to in the summer of '86. It seems I accused the wrong person of stealing it. I should never have filled his garage with bees. You know there's one thing about all these pubs, don't you? We've been to them before, every single one of them.'

'Yes, but so have thousands of other Londoners. If you like public houses, you're bound to have tried a few on the list at some time in your life.'

'I daresay. But I've told you, I don't think this is just about the victims. It's about the locations. Give me a hand, would you?' Bryant wobbled on to the seat of his chair and reached for a collection of tatty albums on the uppermost shelf. He passed them down to May, who caught some of the titles: *Signs of the Times: A Guide to London Names*; *English Symbols*; *The Secret Language of Codes*; *Urban Semiotics.*

'You don't honestly think these are going to help?' asked May.

'The others will be searching through employment records and contacting witnesses, tackling the prosaic tasks of criminal investigation,' Bryant reminded him, holding out a hand to descend. 'Leave me to potter in the past by myself, it's what I'm best at. I might surprise you yet.'

25

RITE OF PASSAGE

The atmosphere at the PCU had changed from a state of indecision to one of purpose. Like it or not, Longbright knew that this was partly down to Jack Renfield. There was a general feeling that his pragmatic approach to policing was just what the PCU might need to survive.

The detective sergeant was forced to consider the idea that her bosses' old-school methods were reaching the end of their natural lifespan. Renfield came from a world that dealt in quantifiable results. Under Bryant and May, the PCU was like an old-time company that nurtured talent and won out on aggregate, but its new accountability required it to operate on case-by-case wins. Longbright wondered if she was the only one to feel that something unique and precious was about to be lost.

She needed to be useful. There was no point in thinking about her passing life, her unpaid bills, her empty fridge and even emptier bed. Whipping out a mother-of-pearl compact made for Alma Cogan in 1958, she applied a fresh layer of make-up, then repainted her eyes. Within seconds she began to feel calmer. *Right*, she thought, cracking her knuckles. *Witness statements – let's close the net on this son of a bitch.*

'You missed the debrief.' Meera Mangeshkar was not good at hiding her feelings. Right now she had a face like a half-sucked lemon. 'Everybody else managed to get here.'

'I got a lift,' Bimsley explained. 'Someone kindly dropped me off.'

'From what I heard, you had trouble getting out of the car.'

'What do you care? I thought I didn't exist in your world. The only time you stop ignoring me is when you've got something horrible to say. Stop the press, a woman found me appealing.' He glared at her.

'Are you going to see her again?'

'What am I, stupid? No, don't answer that, I think I know where you stand on that question.'

'You were supposed to be working, not picking up girls.'

The room temperature dropped another eleven degrees.

If Bimsley was even dimly aware of the reason for Meera's annoyance, he might have displayed a glimmer of understanding, but he was not, and so could not. Instead he blinked and stared and frowned and fidgeted, before his confusion was replaced with the warm memory of Izabella's perfumed embrace, at which point he smiled with a scrunch of his freckled nose, only to recoil in surprise when Meera stormed past him and slammed out of the room, making the same kind of noise that Concorde managed when it passed through the sound barrier.

On Friday morning it was decided to split-shift the unit so that a team would be working around the clock, and Renfield seemed happy to be put in charge of the organization.

After grabbing a nap on his couch, Bryant headed off for the second of his hypnosis sessions with Mrs Mandeville. Everyone was searching for a lead on their common suspect. In the meantime, April and Janice Longbright ducked out for a working breakfast on the terrace of Camden Town's Roundhouse, the site of the giant railway turntable that had been renovated as a concert venue.

Longbright patted the pockets of her blazer. 'You haven't any gaspers on you, I suppose?'

'Why would anyone smoke these days?' asked April, studying the menu.

'Actually I don't. It's affectation. Gesturing has more of a point with a snout in your hand. You're right, though, I shouldn't. I've been a little wound up lately.'

'You certainly have your own style,' said April approvingly. 'Your shoes, your Ruth Ellis haircut, the weird colours of lipstick you find, the way you grind out a fag-end in an ashtray when you're angry. You always manage to be so noticeable. I feel quite invisible beside you.'

'Listen, darling, I grew up in a household where the rent money was always spent by mid-week. After the war, my Auntie Dot was employed as a theatrical costumier at the Duke of York's. When she died she left me her entire wardrobe, so I adopted it. I found her old ration book inside one jacket pocket. The smell of mothballs never bothered me. I tried the look and it stuck. I can't be doing with modern clothes. I'm too fleshy for most of them.' She looked out across the stables, early-morning sunshine striping the roofs. 'You wouldn't have been able to sit out up here a few weeks ago. Too much open space.'

'My agoraphobia seems to have subsided,' April agreed, 'but I can't help feeling it will resurface in some other form the next time I get stressed. It always does. I have a compulsive personality. My mother had me checked for autism.'

'Everyone has some damage. You learn to work around it. And at least yours is put to practical use at the unit.'

April barely heard her. She pushed her newspaper across the table. 'My God, check this out. They're running a front-page article about the dangers of women drinking alone in pubs.'

'This is going to be a godsend for the tabloids,' said Longbright. 'They'll be able to attack any number of targets, from promiscuity to the collapse of the family unit, before pleading for higher security and more police on the streets.'

April scanned the subheads. 'THE BREACH OF THE LAST MALE STRONGHOLD: WHY NO WOMAN CAN NOW FEEL SAFE. How they love to explain the dangers of independence to us. I hope we can expect plenty of rebuttals from women journalists.'

Sensing a juicy public debate, the talk shows had already begun to line up their guests. It was all as Bryant had predicted: the tense issue of safety in public areas was set to return to a level last seen in London during the IRA pub bombings of the 1970s, but this time around, no one knew what they were looking for. Everyone was suddenly a suspect. In the rush to apportion blame, it seemed that only the victims were ignored.

'These were the kind of crimes our unit was created to prevent,' said Longbright. 'How difficult can it be to put a name to this guy?'

'The problem is the nature of pubs themselves. They're intimate places full of total strangers. You can have an argument about politics, fashion or football with someone for an entire evening, and leave without any clue to their identity. People seem to drop into an amnesiac state in pubs. They emerge without any knowledge of what's occurred in the course of the evening.'

'Which reminds me, have you had any luck locating Oswald's urn?'

'Not really,' April admitted. 'It seems certain that somebody removed it from the bar during the wake, but the barmaid didn't see who it was. I'm afraid I wouldn't make a very good detective.'

'Rubbish, you've got exactly the right attitude. You quietly watch and see how everything fits together, and keep us supplied with all the information we need. We never had someone who could do that before John brought you in.'

'I know the others think I got the job because I'm his granddaughter.'

'That might have been true at first, but you've earned your place with us.' Longbright smiled over the coffee nestled between cherry-glossed fingernails. 'Your grandfather and Mr Bryant still have what it takes, you know. They're a wonderful team. The place wouldn't survive if anything happened to either one of them. Did you know they sent me flowers the other day, for my birthday?'

'That was Uncle Arthur's doing,' said April. 'I know because he asked me to remind him of your address on Friday night.'

'But even I had forgotten the date. I never celebrate it. How did he remember something like that when he's supposed to be suffering from memory loss?'

'Well, if there's nothing wrong with his mind, that would mean he really did walk into the past after Oswald's wake.'

'Or someone wanted him to think he had,' said Longbright. A thoughtful silence fell between them. Longbright's coffee cup was marked with a fluorescent arc of lipstick. 'Listen, we'd better get back before they miss us.' She rose and pushed in her chair.

'I think Meera's going to leave the unit. She seems really unhappy about something.'

'She's very angry with herself.'

'Why?'

'Because she had a chance to be much happier than she is right now, and she blew it.'

'She has a lot to prove to herself.'

The DS shook out a melancholy smile. On her left hand there was still a pale line where her engagement ring had once been. 'Look, we've all made tough choices. It's a rite of passage for just about everyone who's ever worked at the PCU. Lost friends, missed loves, wasted opportunities. Maybe it's something we have in common with the women who've been preyed upon in pubs.'

'What do you mean?' asked April.

'We're the ones who chose different paths, and to someone out there, maybe it's as noticeable as a birthmark.'

26

NOMENCLATURE

If the notorious gangster-twin Kray brothers had taken to bare-knuckle sparring with each other in East End boxing clubs until they were melded into a single flat-nosed, cauliflower-eared entity, they would have looked like Oliver Golifer, the ridiculously monickered owner of the Newman Street Picture Library.

Golifer's terrifying demeanour was greatly at odds with his delicate, somewhat theatrical personality. He was a contradictory hulk, heavy of tread but light on his feet, with an erudite intelligence that hid behind the appearance of a particularly gruesome monkey. He knew an awful lot about London, largely gleaned from the immense collection of rare prints and monochrome photographs he had amassed in his three-floor shop.

'I thought I might be getting a visit from you,' said Golifer, opening the door to usher in London's oldest detective. 'The case is all over the papers, and I couldn't imagine anyone at the Met being able to get a fix on it. What are you looking for?'

'Public houses, Oliver,' said Bryant, digging into his

raincoat to produce a bulky bag containing, among other things, his pub list. 'I want photographs of all these boozers. Old ones, new ones, I don't care, as many as you've got.'

'What you said on the dog and bone about the locations attracting him, I didn't follow that.'

'My worry is that even if we caught him right now, we might never find out how or why he's been attacking women. Perhaps you can help me shed some light.'

'I can try.' Golifer wrinkled the meaty stump that passed for his nose. 'What else have you got in that bag?'

'Sweets. They won't let me smoke at the unit. Today I've got Menthol and Eucalyptus, Liquorice Pontefract Cakes, Old English Cloves, Winter Warmers or Army and Navy Tablets.'

'I don't want any, I just wondered what the smell was. Come with me, let's go down to the basement.'

Golifer led the way to the wrought-iron spiral staircase at the rear of the store, past dusty corkboards filled with pinned pictures of peculiarly English memories that made Bryant smile as he passed them.

The Reverend Marcus Morris appearing before a crowd of excited lads in 1950 for the launch of his British boys' paper *The Eagle*, intended as a healthy alternative to the 'lurid' American comics that GIs had introduced to the nation's youth.

A thoughtful mother watching while the police combed bleak ridges of Saddleworth Moor for the young victim of deranged lovers Ian Brady and Myra Hindley in 1965.

A bandaged Jack Mills, beaten, traumatized and due for an early death because he had been victimized in the Great Train Robbery in 1963.

The shattered wreckage of the BEA Elizabethan plane on the frozen runway of Munich Airport, where the

Busby Babes, England's greatest football team, had died in 1958.

A faded copy of the *Daily Express* hailing Neville Chamberlain's 1939 peace agreement with Hitler, with the headline: THIS PAPER DECLARES THAT BRITAIN WILL NOT BE INVOLVED IN A EUROPEAN WAR THIS YEAR, OR NEXT YEAR EITHER.

The walls became more crowded: a montage of barricades and protesters, police and politicians, moments of loss, elation and cruelty, the shocked faces of men and women caught by the vicissitudes of fate. Golifer's library reflected its owner's fascination with his country and the way it reacted to world events.

'Show me those names.' The archivist held out a meaty fist. 'It would help if I knew what you expected to find.'

'If I knew that I wouldn't need your help, would I? Something to do with pub histories and how they got their names. I can't help thinking the murderer might somehow have left us some pointers.'

'Why the hell would he do that?'

'Because he wants to be caught.'

'That makes no bleeding sense at all, but I suppose you know what you're doing,' said Golifer. 'All right, here, first one up, the Seven Stars, back of the law courts. A nice little boozer, I've been there a few times myself.'

'It's where the second victim, Naomi Curtis, died. Does it say how the pub got its name?'

Golifer turned the photograph over and read the typed caption that ran across the back. '"Penderel's Oak is the name of the oak tree which Charles II hid inside after the Battle of Worcester, is why so many public houses are named the Royal Oak."'

'No, Oliver, that's the wrong caption.'

'Bugger, they've been transposed. I had an assistant here for a while, but had to fire him. Hang on.' They searched for the photograph of the Penderel's Oak pub, and checked its description. 'Right, here's the Seven Stars. "Built 1602, this public house was originally named the League of Seven Stars, the sign representing the seven provinces of Holland." Is that any help?'

'I don't know.' Bryant screwed up one eye in thought. 'The number seven . . . a Dutch connection . . . could be anything. Go back to the first pub, the Old Dr Butler's Head in Mason's Avenue.'

Golifer riffled through the folds of photographs, but came up empty-handed. 'No pictures, but I know about that one. It's named after some nutter, Dr Butler, who reckoned he was a neurologist, but his treatment consisted of chucking his patients down a trapdoor into the Thames from London Bridge to scare the *merde* out of them. Apparently James I thought it was a worthwhile pastime, because he appointed him court physician, but then James was obsessed with the idea that witchcraft would destroy the fabric of England. He wrote a barking-mad treatise on demonology that resulted in hundreds of Scottish people being put to death and buried under the streets of Edinburgh. Old Butler developed a brand of ale with so-called medicinal properties, and set up a string of taverns to sell it in, and that – the Old Dr Butler's Head – is the last surviving pub. Try me on another.'

'You're a mine of fantastically useless information, Ollie. How about this, the Old Bell Tavern, Fleet Street, scene of the fourth victim's death. Anything on that?'

After a few minutes of diligent searching, the archivist pulled out a dog-eared Victorian photograph and flipped it before Bryant.

'The frontage is right, but that's the wrong name.' He tapped the picture. A sign hanging above the entrance depicted seven golden bells.

'Maybe it used to be called the Seven Bells. Doesn't

mean anything.' Bryant consulted his list. 'All right, how about the Victoria Cross, Bloomsbury, which Carol Wynley died outside?'

They dragged out several mouldy cardboard boxes from beneath the counters and emptied their contents across the floorboards. 'You're a pain in the arse, Arthur,' Golifer complained. 'Do I get anything out of this disruption and chaos?'

'The sense of inner calm that arises from knowing you've helped London's finest in the course of their duty,' said Bryant. 'This place is a fire risk. Have you got insurance?'

'Don't you threaten me, mate. Here we go, look at that.' He slipped a creased sepia photograph from its protective sleeve and held it up for Bryant to examine. Two straw-hatted publicans stood proudly in front of a pub window. Above them part of the signage could be read: *Ales – Stouts – Porter – Established 1845 – The Vict—.*

'That's the sign I saw. What exactly is Porter?' Bryant wondered.

'The name of the drink changed. It used to be called Three Threads, because it was made up of stale old ale mixed with good young beer to freshen it, plus a third stronger beer called Twopenny. The threads refer to the taps on the casks. The resulting mixture was dirt cheap, so it became the chosen tipple of the Covent Garden porters, and the name Porter stuck.'

'How could I have seen a pub called the Victoria Cross eighty years after it was demolished?'

'You couldn't, old chum.' Oliver chucked down the picture. 'There wasn't such a place.'

'What are you talking about?'

'The Victoria Cross wasn't awarded until 1857. When this pub was built, the medal didn't yet exist. The name must have been changed after that date. Old pubs sometimes dumped their original names if they got bad reputations.' Golifer pulled out a photographers' magnifier and examined the lettering above the window. 'Judging by the width of this frontage I reckon the first name was shorter, probably the Victoria.'

'But I specifically remember the date – 1845 – and I remember the painted sign depicting the medal.'

'There's a simple explanation,' said Golifer. 'They changed the sign but not the etched detailing on the glass.'

'No. All of the other building details match the pub I saw,' Bryant insisted. 'It's some kind of deliberate anachronism, put there to trick me.'

'Do you realize how bloody paranoid that sounds?' Golifer handed him the photograph. 'Go on, take it, at least I'll be able to bill you.'

'I agree, it's utter madness,' Bryant said miserably, 'but how am I supposed to rationalize what I saw? Try one more for me, the Exmouth Arms, Exmouth Street. It's where three of the victims were photographed together.'

Golifer sighed and began searching the alphabetized racks again. This time he found a more recent photograph, colour, taken in the 1970s, featuring hipsters with shaggy haircuts striking a pose outside the pub, surrounded by black plastic rubbish sacks left in one of the many refuse collectors' disputes of the time.

'OK, a case in point – the sign carved into the wall of the saloon says 1915, see?' Golifer held the picture so close that Bryant had to back away to examine it clearly. 'But the back of the photo has 1816 as the pub's foundation date. Says here it was originally named after the first Viscount Exmouth, 1757 to 1833, a Vice-Admiral who turned up in the Horatio Hornblower stories. He was the hero of the bombardment of Algiers in 1816 that ended Christian slavery. And according to this, he was also the father of one Pownoll Bastard Exmouth. Bloody extraordinary choice of name for his son, I must say. So, as the pub was there before the rest of the street, it must have lent its name to Exmouth Market. Anything of use so far?'

'Not that I can think of.'

'Exmouth's family motto is *Deo Non Fortuna* – Through God Not By Chance. Nice family crest, silver argent, red chevron, three silver mascles. Natty painting of the admiral on the pub's sign.'

'What was the viscount's actual name?'

'Edward Pellew.'

Bryant's eyes widened. 'Holy Jumping Moses, I think my memory suddenly improved.'

'Why do you say that?'

'I remember that name. Let me think. I need a cuppa, strong, Indian, lots of it.'

Golifer had been hoping to get some work done, but now resigned himself to acting as a butler to his old friend.

'It was back in 1994,' Bryant told him once they were seated in Golifer's cramped kitchen behind the store. 'We had a case of suspected kidnap come in. A teenaged girl had been missing for over forty-eight hours, and it seemed clear to us that her boyfriend was somehow involved in the disappearance. At first he refused to speak to anyone, but John and I tricked him into admitting that he had been with her on the night of her disappearance. During the subsequent interview, we discovered that he had rendered her unconscious and imprisoned her in the basement of his mother's pub. Luckily, we found her and were able to effect her release. The odd thing was that he really seemed to care for her, and simply couldn't help himself. It was a very unusual case.'

'What happened to him?'

'He was judged to be in possession of his faculties at the time of the kidnap, but a subsequent court of appeal found him mentally incompetent to stand trial. He was committed to the secure wing of an NHS mental hospital called Twelve Elms Cross, somewhere in East Kent. I distinctly remember the case because John went down to see him soon after his admission, when he was undergoing therapy. He was very interested in the boy. I think we both thought there was a benefit in understanding what drove him to act the way he did.'

'I don't see what this has to do with Viscount Exmouth,' said Golifer, mystified.

Bryant raised a knowing eyebrow. 'Maybe nothing. But the lad's name. It was Anthony Pellew.'

27

LAST ORDERS

'Don't you see?' said Bryant. 'He was leaving clues in the histories of the pubs, knowing we'd track him down. The Seven Stars – seven victims, perhaps some kind of Dutch connection. The Victoria Cross – an anachronism, an impossibility I was meant to pick up on. It's true that there are some pubs I haven't worked out how to fit into the picture yet, but then there's the Exmouth Arms, chosen because it bears his own surname. How desperately he wants to be caught! We must oblige him immediately.'

'Really, Arthur, this insatiable desire of yours to tie everything into neat parcels is infuriating.'

'Then prove me wrong. Contact Twelve Elms Cross and find out if Tony Pellew was released before the first murder occurred.'

May made the call while Bryant impatiently slammed about among his books, but it took the best part of an hour for staff to collate the information they needed. With the receiver crooked under his ear, he gave his partner an update.

'Looks like you're right. Pellew was transferred to the

Broadhampton Clinic two years ago, then released back into the community three weeks before the death of Joanne Kellerman, the first victim.'

Bryant's face crumpled in puzzlement. 'The Broadhampton's not a secure hospital, at least not in the same way as Twelve Elms Cross. Pellew was dangerous – you of all people know that. Why would they have transferred him at all?'

'The head nurse sounds uncomfortable. She says it's a matter of some delicacy. I don't think she'll give us anything else over the phone.'

'Then we must go and see her at once. Tell her we'll come today.'

The train from Victoria was almost empty. 'I wasn't planning to leave London again for a while,' said Bryant, removing sandwich wrappers and beer cans from his seat before heaving himself into it. 'Not after our trek into the snowdrifts of Dartmoor. That little escapade played havoc with my chilblains.'

'Nobody has chilblains any more,' said May. 'This is the twenty-first century. Global warming has knocked them on the head.'

'A glance at my plates of meat would reveal a different story.'

May sighed. 'Come on then, get it all out – bunions, chilblains, Pakamacs, cap bombs, Jamboree Bags, MacFisheries, bombsites, Shirley Abicair and her zither, real coal fires, smog, gabardines, milk stout, rag-and-bone men – let's hear about all the weird old English stuff you miss from the past,' he cried in exasperation. 'It's amazing how you never remember the dreadful things like TB and whooping cough and only two channels on the telly. I wish you could hear yourself sometimes.'

Bryant gave a disdainful sniff. 'You can still get milk

stout, actually. Trains have lost the odd smell they had when the carriages were separate, have you noticed? There was an odour of iron filings, mica and dust. Now we all have to be communal and watch each other eating while staring through windows savaged by graffiti. Did you see the youths on the platform back there? When I was a kid we had to go to the circus if we wanted to see the fat lady and the tattooed man. Now they're all over the place.'

May fell wearily back into the seat and snapped open his newspaper. The annoying thing was that he knew Bryant was playing with him. He caught the twinkle of his partner's eye over the top of his page and decided to let the old man blow off steam. During the journey, he was treated to a detailed description of the usefulness of the Adlestrop Railway Atlas, a diatribe on the unoriginality of the modern criminal mind, a complaint about the discontinuation of Fry's Five Fruit Chocolate, and sundry reminiscences concerning London's burglars, thieves and confidence tricksters of the late 1950s. Bryant's monologues were rarely less than entertaining, but today he wasn't in the mood. He was quite relieved when the train finally pulled into Otford railway station.

'You're very quiet today,' Bryant observed as they alighted. 'I hope you're not having a mid-life crisis.' He hastily threw up his hands. 'I jest, I jest.'

Twelve Elms Cross was a melancholy yellow-brick mansion built on the gentle slopes of royal parkland three miles beyond the station. Since 1902 it had provided a secure home for some of the country's most disturbed mental patients, but now the listed interiors were proving unsuitable for modern health care, and the building was in the process of being decommissioned.

The chief warden, Abigail Cochrane, was also its curator. She led the detectives from her office to the patients' quarters via a corridor reserved for visitors. It spared them the discomfort of seeing the inmates, and vice versa.

'Why do they always have to line these places with horrible daubs?' whispered Bryant, referring to the patients' paintings that hung on the passage walls. 'Being bonkers doesn't make them more artistic, it just shows how bored they are.'

'Once in a while,' May whispered back, exasperated, 'it wouldn't hurt you to be a little more politically correct, would it?'

'I'm criticizing the system, not the patients.'

'The hospital was designed to incarcerate rather than rehabilitate,' Nurse Cochrane explained. 'The grounds are pleasant enough, but the day-rooms are pitifully inadequate, and the personal quarters are too small. The Edwardians had rather fixed ideas about the amount of private space that should be allocated to offenders. I tend to think they treated the institution as if it were some kind of human zoo.'

She pushed back a door leading to a wide corridor with a floor of polished linoleum and institutional green-and-cream walls. The faint scents of cabbage and disinfectant hung in the undisturbed air. 'As I'm sure you'll remember, Mr May, Tony was of above average intelligence. Under different circumstances he could really have made something of himself. He was rather a favourite of ours, even though I felt he was likely to be a repeat offender.'

'Why was he transferred to a low-security clinic?'

Nurse Cochrane withdrew a large, old-fashioned key and unlocked the iron door they had stopped before. 'Because of this,' she told them, gesturing about the room. 'We never got around to clearing it.'

The cell was ten feet by twelve, little more than a space for a bed and desk, without separate bathroom facilities.

A single barred window faced out on to the pasture where the twelve elms must once have existed. The cell walls were cream-painted brick, but had been obscured by dozens of taped photographs and reproductions of paintings. Most of the art was from the late nineteenth century, and showed groups of men sociably smoking, drinking, bantering. A few pictures featured pugilists posing in pleasure gardens.

The photographs were all of one person, a blowsy middle-aged woman in heavy make-up. Her features showed the signs of poor diet and too much drink. 'Tony was distraught when his mother died. He worshipped her, even though she never once bothered to visit him. Tragic, really. We contacted her so many times over the years, whenever he was ill or particularly hard to settle, but she only ever responded once. There.' Cochrane pointed to a taped postcard with the words '*Tony wishing you better love Kate*' scrawled across the back. 'I think she only wrote that to get him off her back for a while. When he found out she had died from cirrhosis of the liver, the fight went out of him.'

'Are you saying there was something more than a normal mother–son relationship going on?' asked May.

'I'm not able to comment on that.' He sensed that a shutter had closed between them, and knew she would cite patient confidentiality if he tried to press her.

'This is an ongoing murder investigation, Miss Cochrane. We'll sequester his hospital notes if we have to, and remove any files we feel might pertain to his case if it means we can prevent him from harming anyone else.'

Nurse Cochrane's cold manner thawed a little. She had simply not realized the gravity of her former charge's situation. 'I'm sorry, sometimes it is necessary to protect our patients from the eagerness of the public to condemn and demonize. I'm sure you understand.'

'Then perhaps you could help us to understand him more fully,' Bryant suggested. 'Did he ever talk about the girl he kidnapped?'

'There are extensive therapists' notes in his case history, but I can probably save you a lot of time with a précis. His story is sad, but hardly uncommon. Tony's family was originally from Zandvoort, in Holland. His father had been in and out of jail all his life. He was a violent alcoholic whose first two sons had been taken into care. He met Tony's mother in the pub where she worked, and their relationship was a familiar cycle of alcohol misuse and physical abuse. She left him, taking Tony with her, and gained employment in the City of London pubs, usually in bars that had live-in premises above them. Although we have only anecdotal evidence, it seems likely that she supplemented her income through bouts of prostitution. Oddly, I think Tony was at his happiest during that period. He would have been about eleven then.'

'Camus suggested that we spend our adult lives seeking to restore childhood's brief moments of happiness,' said Bryant.

'Tony told me he felt safest during those evenings he spent waiting for his mother to finish behind the bar, or waiting for her to return after seeing a punter. She always left him in the pub. He tried to strangle his first girlfriend, did you know? It didn't take long for a pattern to emerge. He would latch on to girls he met in his mother's pub, come on too strong and scare them off by trying too hard to keep them with him.'

'The serial killer Denis Nielsen murdered because he wanted companionship,' May reminded them. 'He was not only lonely but incredibly boring. The only way he could make his victims stay around was by rendering them unconscious.'

'Tony told us something similar,' said Cochrane. 'He reckoned he had all sorts of scenarios worked out to keep women by his side. He didn't need to kill them to re-create his happiest hours – merely make them immobile. It seems he experimented for a number of years without getting caught, although there were a few close calls. He felt at home in pubs, and dreaded the sound of the last bell, knowing that the place would empty out and he'd be left alone.'

'The girl he kidnapped was anxious to point out that she was never hurt by him in any way,' said May. 'And yet it seems he decided to start killing them.'

'You say he changed after his mother died,' said Bryant. 'How did that change manifest itself?'

'He'd always been boisterous, eager to join in and organize meetings. He enjoyed a good argument with the others, although he had a poor attention span and tended towards over-excitement. After the funeral he withdrew from everyone, wouldn't talk or think for himself, exhibited the classic signs of depression, became morbidly introspective, lost weight, spent too much time asleep.'

'If he was unwell, why was he transferred?'

'This building has been sold, Mr Bryant. It is about to become offices and luxury apartments. The pressure is on for us to place all of our patients elsewhere as soon as possible. Tony Pellew was apparently no longer considered to be a threat to himself or anyone else. It was decided that the Broadhampton was better equipped for his needs.'

'Are you aware that he's no longer at the Broadhampton, either?' asked May.

'I knew the board decided to release him recently, because they contacted me in order to obtain his personal files,' Cochrane explained.

'Don't you think their decision was rather odd?'

'Not so much these days. You'd be amazed if you knew about some of the people that get sent back out on to the streets.'

'You must have made your own judgement as to whether he was in any fit state to be released.'

Cochrane regarded Bryant with a cool detachment that suggested she had an opinion but wasn't keen on sharing it. 'I'm afraid you'll have to take that up with the staff at the Broadhampton,' she said.

As the echoing rooms of Twelve Elms Cross were emptied and barred, it seemed as if their past melancholies would fade and die with them, to be replaced by the bright, light cubicles of a luxurious new prison.

28

MATERNITY

Bryant was unusually quiet on the journey back. He stared out of the scarred windows with his chin resting on liver-spotted knuckles, lost in thought, impervious to conversation. May was confident that it would be only a matter of hours before they would find Pellew, and his partner's silence perplexed him.

'All right, out with it,' he said finally. 'What's wrong?'

Bryant turned to fix him with translucent blue eyes that were, for once, unreadable. 'You would say that we understand each other to an unusual degree, wouldn't you?' he asked. 'I mean, over so many years, due to the extraordinary way in which we've been involved in each other's lives?'

'Indeed. I never know exactly what you're thinking, but I usually have a pretty good idea. I can't imagine anyone knows you better.'

'And that's how I feel about you. I know you leave the TV on all the time, and love buying those hideously vulgar new suits. I know your sister in Brighton thinks I'm a bad influence on you. I know you lost the wallet I bought you for your birthday, and purchased an identical one so I wouldn't find out. I know you hate beetroot and suffer from hayfever. I know you still blame yourself for the death of your daughter, even though there was nothing more you could have done for her. I wonder, therefore, if you've been entirely honest with me.'

'What do you mean? What about?'

'The past, John. The past. There were, of course, a few periods when we weren't working together, and I know I didn't see enough of you during the time you were married. That's understandable: you were in love, and were having to deal with the onset of Jane's mental problems; I was wrapped up in troubles of my own. I suppose I always realized there were – omissions – in your life. I forgot about them for a while, but I started wondering again during Oswald Finch's wake.'

May furrowed his brow, but decided to say nothing. It was better to let Bryant clear his head without interruption. Perhaps it was time for the conversation he had so long avoided.

'I got to thinking. Instead of floral tributes, Oswald asked for contributions to a ward at the Broadhampton Hospital. When I asked you about it, you refused to catch my eye. In fact, considering the number of times we've had cause to check with the Broadhampton's patients in other investigations, you've always seemed uncomfortable with the subject. I think it's time you told me the truth.'

'What about?' May played for time. He had not lied so much as omitted details, but after all this time he knew that the inconsistency felt like deception.

'Jane, your wife. Surely you couldn't have lied to me about her?'

Any answer May could have made dried in his mouth. He stared helplessly back.

'On more than one occasion you told me she was dead,

or at least you suggested as much, but it was the way you said it. You meant *dead to me*, as if you had simply cut her out of your life after the divorce. That was how I phrased it when I was writing our memoirs. Of course, you'd been apart for quite a while by then, and I thought, *Well, if that's how he's dealing with it, it's his affair.* Then out of the blue, you told me you'd take me to meet her, and I could only assume you were making some kind of off-colour joke. You really had led me to believe she was gone, hadn't you?'

'I wasn't deliberately trying to mislead you, if that's what you're thinking.'

'I knew she'd had a breakdown. I assumed she'd died in the Broadhampton, and that Oswald knew about it, which is why he wanted contributions sent there.'

'No,' said May, shaking his head. 'No, she didn't die, Arthur. She's still there.'

'Then it's true. My God. I don't understand. Why would you keep such a thing from me?'

May felt the shame of a betrayer. 'It was less a lie than an omission. You don't know what I went through with Jane.'

'You could have told me, I might have been able to help.'

'Arthur, you have no patience with people. This was a private problem, something I couldn't find a way to share with you. I had to find a way of getting through to her on my own. Mental illness is so terribly misunderstood and I wanted to see if I could help her.'

'Even you can't undo the past, John,' said Bryant sadly. 'How is she now?'

'She has her black dog days. The death of Elizabeth will always stand between us, but the trouble began long before she died.' May had good reason to sometimes think that his family had been cursed. First, Jane's illness and their subsequent divorce, then the death of their daughter. Alex, their son, had left for Canada and would still not talk to his father. 'I kept thinking that if I had understood Jane better in the early days of her illness, I might have been able to keep us all together.'

'When was the last time you saw her?'

'About four months ago. Oswald used to come with me to visit her. That's why he wanted to leave money to the hospital.'

'Does she recognize you?'

'Certainly. But it's difficult to hold a conversation with her. Sometimes you think she's perfectly fine, but she's very good at pretending that nothing is wrong. She's in her seventies – hardly the age it once was, of course – but she hasn't been right for such a long time that I can hardly recall a time when she was ever truly well. I've lost track of the number of times she's tried to kill herself. Elizabeth's death removed her reason for living.'

'But what about April? Does she know about this?'

'No, and I agreed with Jane that we wouldn't tell her. She's been through enough without finding out that her grandmother is still alive. What is the point in opening up old wounds? Jane is in no fit state to see her granddaughter, and April has only just made her own recovery. I don't hold with all this stuff about *closure* and *moving on*. Sometimes I think it just causes more damage.'

'Perhaps she needs to decide that for herself,' said Bryant carefully.

'Don't you see? Once the subject is reopened it can't be closed up again. April is not strong enough. I have to protect her.'

'Nor is she a child, John. What happened to Jane?'

May sighed. 'It was a long time ago, and we had a very sixties marriage. You must remember what she was like, how wild she could be. It's a miracle we stayed together as long as we did. After the separation, I told you she went off with someone who was a bad influence on her, some kind of TV producer, so he said. I expected him to tell her lies, but not to give her drugs. Anyone with an ounce of sense could see she was not the sort of person – well, I was looking after the children, you were off in France sorting out troubles of your own with Nathalie's family, we weren't working together much, you and I – I meant to tell you what had happened, but the time never seemed to be right.'

'You told me a little about the accident, but not much.'

'Jane was driving the Volkswagen when it mounted the pavement right in the middle of Tottenham Court Road. Her boyfriend was killed instantly. She had no licence. They found LSD, cocaine and alcohol in her system. She was too fragile to deal with police and doctors. She suffered a mental collapse and was deemed unfit to stand trial. She wouldn't see me, or anyone else for that matter, and although her doctor thought she would eventually recover, she seemed to slip away from us to some private place inside her head. She became a danger to herself and was admitted as a patient to the Broadhampton. I had to sign her papers. It was the worst day of my life. She showed little improvement, and seemed desperate to take up long-term residency. She wanted no responsibility for her own life. When you returned, I told myself I would talk to you when the time was right, but I kept putting it off. I visit her every once in a while, but she doesn't always know who I am.' May looked from the window as if searching for answers. 'It seems I can help every family except my own. My son thinks I dumped his mother in a clinic and encouraged his sister to join the police. To think that I could have lost April as well . . .'

'But you didn't, John, you brought her back,' said Bryant gently. 'You should be proud of that. You know we have to go to the Broadhampton next, don't you? Would you let me visit Jane?'

'Wouldn't you rather remember her as she once was?' asked May, as the train passed across the glittering grey Thames on its approach to Victoria Station.

'Yes, but I'd still like to see her once more.'

'Then I should call ahead.' May took out his mobile.

'No, don't do that. We need to find out why Pellew was released early, so let's catch them on the hop. I don't want any prepared answers.'

May tried to read the look on his partner's face, but for once failed to do so.

The Broadhampton Clinic in Lavender Hill, south London, was an orange-brick Edwardian building with central columns of white stucco, pedimented wings and a small bell-tower. It possessed the aura of paternal authority common to civic buildings of the era, and made one feel vaguely diminished just by approaching it.

The detectives met with an apologetic young intern named Senwe who did his best to help, but was unfamiliar with the patient in question. After conferring with other nurses and registrars, Senwe returned to the office where he had left the detectives waiting.

'There is a lady who knows about the release of Anthony Pellew,' he explained, rounding his vowels with a crystal African accent, 'but she is away on holiday. Her department have given me this for you.' He handed over a single folded sheet of paper.

Bryant fiddled his reading glasses into place. 'Let's see, what have we got? "A. Pellew, thirty-seven years of age, adjudged by the medical assessment committee under conditions established by the Revised Mental Health Act of 1998 to be of such mental sufficiency that he may be released under his own cognizance conditional to regular examination and palliative care" – God, who writes these things?'

'It looks like the board decided he met enough of their criteria to be placed in a halfway house, so long as he continued to take medication for anxiety,' said May, reading over his shoulder.

'So he was kept on the happy pills and packed off to a flat on the De Beauvoir Estate, off the Balls Pond Road in Islington. There's an address here. We could nip back and get Victor.'

'I'm not driving around town in that lethal hippie rust-bucket, thank you,' May warned. 'We'll take my BMW. You shouldn't be driving.'

'You're a fine one to talk. Alma hasn't forgiven you for buggering up her Bedford van.'

'We were stuck in a snowdrift, Arthur, it's hardly surprising the radiator cracked. Any next of kin listed?'

'None, but there's a social-services officer. Actually, it's someone we've dealt with before, Lorraine Bonner, the leader of the Residents' Association at the Roland Plumbe Community Estate. At least we know where to find her.'

'Then that's our next stop.' He paused, uncertain. 'Do you still want to see Jane?'

'Yes, I'd like to.'

May led the way upstairs and along the cheerfully painted corridors, to a ward separated from the rest of the floor. Nodding to the duty nurse, he headed towards the corner room and gently pushed back the door.

'Jane, it's me.' There was no answer. 'I've brought somebody to see you. You remember Arthur Bryant, don't you?'

Jane Bryant appeared not to have heard. She pulled his grey cardigan a little more tightly over a long pleated skirt. Her white sneakers had no laces. She had kept her figure and removed any trace of grey from her auburn hair, but when she turned around, Bryant saw the tumult of the intervening years etched on her face, a topography of past torments that had removed the focus in her eyes, as though she was no longer interested in searching for answers. After a moment of composure, during which she absently touched a hair into place, she drew a breath and seemed to grow a little.

'Jane, do you remember Arthur?'

She raised a finger at him and tried to smile. 'Yes, we've met, but I'm afraid I don't know where – '

'I came to your wedding,' said Bryant gently.

'My wedding. How nice. Of course you did. You were always so kind.' The smile held, the eyes even twinkled, but her concentration was disturbed by the movement of branches beyond the window, the scrappy flight of a magpie, a murmur of conversation in the corridor. 'I wonder if – ' She stopped, a cloud of anxiety crossing her features. 'We could go to the coast. I'd like that, John. On a day when it's sunny, a day like today. I'd like to walk on the cliffs. But it must be warmer.'

'I know you don't like the cold, Jane, but spring will be here soon. I'll come for you then.'

'You've always been so good to him, Arthur.' She reached out for Bryant's arm, gently plucking a thread from his sleeve. He glimpsed the scribble of scars whitening the flesh of her arm as she did so. 'I felt sure you would have both retired by now.'

'Oh, no, we're in this together right until the bitter end.' There was indulgent gaiety in Bryant's chuckle, but he could see a lasting winter in her eyes.

'Well, I feel terribly special today. It's good to see you both. I'm very privileged. Perhaps you'll come back another time. Come and see me again.'

The audience was over. Her attention had started to

diminish, like a boat pulling away from the shore. She turned away. 'I'm quite happy here. I know everyone. You needn't rush back, not if you don't want to.'

'Jane, did you meet a patient here, a gentleman called Tony Pellew?' Bryant could not stop himself from asking.

Her waning interest was suddenly checked. Here was something she could grasp, someone she could recall from recent days. 'Of course I did. He spoke to me.'

The answer had come too quickly. He doubted she was telling the truth. 'Really? You knew him?'

'Long brown hair, slight, undernourished. They let him out.'

'That's right.'

'He seemed decent enough, very bright, but such a mother's boy. There was something too soft in his eyes. He talked about his mother all the time. He told me that when she died, all the clocks in the pub stopped at two minutes past eleven.'

'What pub?'

'Where she lived. They let him leave. He wasn't well enough, in my opinion. You can tell which ones are well enough to go.' She pulled her cardigan a little tighter. 'How is my little girl?'

May looked guilty. 'She's well, Jane. Much better than she's been in years.'

'You must take very good care of her. She's all I have now.' She looked away, touching a finger beneath her eye. 'Perhaps one day you can bring her here.'

'We discussed this, Jane. If the doctor feels you can cope – '

'I know, I know, it's a stupid idea.' Her features set in a smile of practised hospitality. 'Well I must go now, or I'll miss my lunch.'

Bryant looked back once as he walked away, and

wished he had not seen her. The tiny, hunchbacked figure framed against the window bore no resemblance to the woman he remembered laughing between their linked arms. The tragedy of losing those she loved had robbed her of the right to happiness.

29

WRAITH

Lorraine Bonner was a broad black woman with a laugh like someone unbunging a sink and enough courage to make the surliest delinquent think twice about disrespecting her. They found her surrounded by cardboard files in the chaotic first-floor office of the council estate's main block.

'I didn't think I'd see the two of you again,' she said, pouring thick brown tea from a steel pot the size of a bucket. 'I thought that thing with the Highwayman was all over.'

'It is, Lorraine, but Mr May and I have a new problem,' said Bryant, 'and we wondered if you might be able to help us.'

'Can you walk with me while I do my pensioners?' Mrs Bonner delivered meals to the mobility-challenged seniors on the estate every lunchtime. When their own relatives could not be bothered to look after them, she was there to dispense patient kindnesses that had sophisticates sneering, while offering such practical help that they felt ashamed.

May explained their mission as she manhandled her protesting trolley into the corridor.

'A lady from the Broadhampton phoned Islington Council to add Tony Pellew to my roster,' she told them. 'They'd got him a one-bedroom apartment on the De Beauvoir estate. He didn't want to live in south London. His family was originally from around here. Normally we try to return home, don't we? It's only natural. You'll want the address of his flat.'

'How can we get that?'

'My filing system's in my head, love.' She took a card from May and wrote on the back of it.

'When did you last see him?'

'Well, I got him settled in and popped over a couple of times during the first week, but then he went missing. He didn't have many belongings, just enough to fill a backpack, but the wardrobe was emptied out and the bed hadn't been slept in.'

'How do you know he wasn't staying at a friend's?' asked May.

'Both pairs of his shoes were gone. You don't take all your shoes unless you're not coming back, do you? I had to make a report to his probationer.'

'What was he like?' Bryant wondered, intrigued.

'Very quiet and sad, needed fattening up. The sort of man an older lady would like to take under her wing, you know? I heard he'd had a difficult upbringing. I'm not trying to excuse what he did, you just want to understand, don't you? Well it's only human nature, isn't it?'

'Do you have any idea at all where he went?'

Mrs Bonner gave a shrug. 'They come and go, these lost souls, can't settle, don't feel comfortable in themselves, do they? Just take off one day. London can be so lonely. He can't leave the country because he hasn't got a passport. And I don't think he wants to go far from where his old mum lived, even though she disowned him. He'll turn up in a shelter somewhere, if he hasn't already.'

Tony Pellew's apartment had an air of abandonment. Its resident had moved on, taking his clothes and the few personal belongings he possessed. Beneath the smell of dust and damp carpeting was the musk of stillness and solitude. The flat had been used by dozens of short-term residents who had passed their time here, seated forlornly on the candlewick corner of the single bed, or propped at the square Ikea kitchen table, staring from the window into an unforgiving future. Discoloured edges on the carpet mapped furniture phantoms. Pale squares on the wall left ghosts of old picture frames. Pellew had left no mark on the apartment.

The first thing to do was check that he had not tried to return to his former home. Bryant pushed back the door of a kitchen cupboard with the tip of his walking stick and peered inside. The few tins he found were the kind of staples stocked by someone with no interest in food. 'He must have left something behind. Everybody who moves house leaves some faint trace. I want to know this man's history. The bloody cheek of the Broadhampton, palming us off with a bit of paper.'

'It's not their fault,' said May defensively. 'They provide some of the best care in the country. Someone there has been stepped on by the assessment committee. Get April on the phone and have her call the clinic on the half-hour until someone gives her the full story.'

While May made the call, Bryant wandered from room to room, wrinkling his nose in the stale, dead air. They were about to lock the place up and head back to the unit when Bryant saw the newspaper cutting that lay pressed behind a sheet of glass on the kitchen table. Withdrawing his reading glasses, he read through it and called May in.

'It looks like he was going to frame this, John. It's his mother.'

The photograph was of a blonde crop-haired woman with a hard, almost perfectly square face. Her son's grainy photograph was inset, and showed a boy with a bowed head emerging from court, his features in shadow.

'She sold her story to our friends at *Hard News* just a few weeks before her death. WHY MY SON MUST NEVER BE FREED. Looks like she used the article to envisage what he would do if he was ever granted his freedom. Do you think she'd heard he was being assessed for release? My godfathers!' He sat down and peered closely at the page. 'It reads like a blueprint of his activities over the last week. In his state of mind, it's hard not to think that he'd have seen this as some kind of fateful prediction. "Mrs Anita Pellew, the manager of London's famous old Clock House pub in Leather Lane."'

Bryant slapped his hand on the glass-covered sheet. 'That's where he's gone.'

30

SOLIDARITY

Janice Longbright was ahead of them. April's search for Pellew's trial coverage had already picked up his mother's interview. As the information was distributed and digested around the unit, Longbright threw on her jacket and headed for Farringdon before Renfield could try to stop her.

The Clock House occupied a shaded corner of Leather Lane. As she passed beneath the heraldic red lion and white unicorn over the front door, she wondered how a building with so many windows could remain so gloomy inside. The tobacco fug that had obscured the mirrored interior for more than a century was now beyond dissipation by a mere smoking ban. Making her way through a saloon crowded with market traders and local office workers, she introduced herself to a barmaid, another pretty Polish girl, called Zosia.

'I understand that a woman called Anita Pellew lived here,' said Longbright.

'I don't know – I'm new here. You should talk to Patrick over there.' She pointed at the old boy collecting glasses.

'That's right,' said the Irish pot man, thinking. 'She went to the hospital and didn't come back.'

'Were her rooms above the pub?'

'First floor.' He put down his pint mugs to point at the ceiling.

'Can I get up there?'

'It's all locked up,' said Zosia. 'The new manageress has the keys, and she's gone out.'

'What about the basement? Does that stay locked?'

'No, because the bar staff have to get down there to change barrels.'

'Is there just the single staircase behind the bar?'

'No, there's an access door outside as well.'

'Thanks, I'll need to take a look.'

Zosia raised the bar for her and led the way to the cellar door. 'I can't leave the bar,' she warned Longbright. 'Call me if you need anything.'

The floor below occupied a far greater area than the bar overhead. At least six rooms opened from the central battleship-grey corridor, their doors pulled shut. The dusty overhead bulb provided barely adequate light. Down here, only the faintest murmurs and footfalls could be heard from the saloon.

The first two rooms were filled with metal beer barrels and crates. Beyond these, a small office had been set up for the manager to work on the accounts. Had Mrs Pellew once sat here adding up figures while her son played in the bar?

Longbright felt for the Bakelite light switches, as round and high as pudding bowls, clicking them on as she went. At the far end of the corridor, a door opened on to a narrow, stepped passage originally designed for the delivery of coal. Its latch was easy to slip up. She knew it meant he would be able to come and go without anyone in the pub seeing him.

It took a lot to frighten the detective sergeant; she had spent too many years searching London's derelict buildings, climbing through its rubbish-strewn yards and alleyways, chasing panicked men over scraps of waste ground and across windswept car parks. The evidence suggested that Pellew had no intention of causing women pain, even though he killed them. But to Longbright, this paradox made him all the more disturbing. It left a gap in his genetic make-up, a void that could not be explained away. It made him impossible to read.

When she opened the door of the darkened end-room and saw a green nylon sleeping bag on the floor, she knew she had found him. She stepped inside, drawn by the desire to rummage through the empty white packets beside his bed, and realized they were boxes that had contained clear plastic drug ampoules, diabetic needles so small and fine that nobody would notice them.

What she failed to notice was that the door had started closing silently behind her.

A rag of shadow flung itself forward, seizing her in a practised grip. She should have been able to throw him over her head, but he had caught her off-balance.

Stupid, stupid, she thought as she fell. *I didn't consider myself old enough to be a target, but of course I'm exactly the right age.*

The needle must have been tiny, similar to the one on an insulin pen, because instead of sliding in hotly it just plucked at the skin of her arm like an insect. A warm dental numbness flooded her body with astonishing speed.

His arms extended to catch her as she fell, to ease her to the floor, but she was heavier than he'd expected and slipped through his welcoming embrace. She jarred her hip and the side of her skull as she slammed on to the cement ground.

Anaesthetists always suggested counting to ten. She tried that now, but struggled beyond the number four. *Will I die?* she wondered distantly. *Have I joined the sisterhood of his victims? Will this be my last conscious thought?*

He wanted to stay with her, but the circumstances were not right. She should have been seated next to him in the warm ochre light of the saloon bar, her thigh lightly touching his, her glass almost full. She should have been watching him with his mother's eyes, listening intently, smiling and nodding as music and laughter surrounded them in soothing sussurance. The time – somewhere between nine p.m. and the bell for last orders – would have stretched to an eternity. But instead she was lying on the floor of the cellar, dying.

Knowing it was time to leave, he grabbed his backpack from the floor, ran out into the corridor and headed for the coal steps.

Longbright had been face-down on the cement for about twenty minutes when John May found her. Her breathing was shallow, her pulse faint but steady. When he saw the emptied ampoule beside her, he immediately searched for the mark on her exposed skin. Her hands and feet were still warm. He could only think that Pellew had underestimated her size, that the amount discharged had not been enough to kill her.

The ambulance had trouble reaching the pub because a bendy-bus had become wedged across the turn at Holborn Circus, and the traffic was backed up in every direction. When the medics finally arrived, they took her to University College Hospital.

'We should have gone with her,' said May, climbing back into the driving seat of the BMW.

'Right now we're more useful going after him,' said

Bryant. 'The ambulance boys say she's going to be all right, and we have to believe them. We'll need someone to meet us there.'

'Where? You know where he's heading?'

'He finds sanctuary in pubs, and probably salvation. Before Anthony and his mother lived at the Clock House, they came from south of the river – Greenwich. He grew up in a pub, remember? We think that was most likely the Angerstein Hotel, on Woolwich Road. It's the only other location he mentioned to nurses from the old days.'

'Do you think it's still there?'

'I hope so. I'm meant to be playing in their skittles tournament this summer.'

'There may have been other pubs in between. I thought he and his mother moved around a lot.'

'Pellew was at the Angerstein from the ages of eight to fourteen, his formative years. And I know the place, it's huge. That makes it the likeliest venue. He clearly feels most comfortable living and even killing in a crowd. Hardly the usual lone wolf.'

'You can be as alone in a city like London as you can in the secluded countryside, Arthur.'

'Poor Janice, she shouldn't have gone ahead without us. I'll never forgive myself if anything happens to her. We have to find him today, John. Judging by the number of empty ampoule boxes in his room, he's carrying enough lethal doses to take out a dozen people.'

Back at the unit in Mornington Crescent, Dan Banbury had looked in on May's granddaughter and found her frowning over her computer screen. He was starting to worry about how much time she was spending at the PCU. The others were used to it; April had only just managed to reconnect with the world, and he couldn't help feeling she had swapped one cage for another. 'You've got that look on your face again,' he warned, seating himself beside her. 'What's the matter?'

'I've been studying the photograph,' said April. 'Naomi Curtis, Jocelyn Roquesby and Joanne Kellerman. I don't think they just bumped into each other in a pub and had their picture taken together.'

'Why not?' Dan studied the digitized photograph on her screen.

'Look at the way they're standing. These women haven't just met. They're too close. I'd only relax like that if I was with a best mate. It doesn't look right.'

'Maybe they had to squeeze in for the photo.' Banbury squinted at the picture, tilting his head. 'It bothers you?'

'Enough to make me run some more checks. I finally managed to track down their CVs for date comparisons. It looks like they all changed jobs at the same time, September, three years ago.'

'You mean they were working together?'

'No, that's just it.' She pulled up the documents and opened their windows beside each other on the screen. 'Curtis was at a place called Sankani Exports, Roquesby was at Legal and General and Kellerman worked for a loss-adjustment company called Cooper Baldwin, but they all left in the same month.'

'Probably just a coincidence.'

'That's what I thought. So I called Legal and General's HR department, just to get a general idea about why she left. No one by the name of Jocelyn Roquesby ever worked there. And it gets better. Sankani Exports in High Holborn ceased trading in 1997, and according to Companies House, Cooper Baldwin doesn't even exist.'

'People exaggerate their CVs.'

'Come on, Dan. Three impossible jobs, three matching departure dates, three deaths?'

'What about start dates?'

'They're all different.'

'Have you checked the other two victims?'

'I've ruled out Jasmina Sherwin because she doesn't fit the pattern, and I'm waiting for Carol Wynley's partner to email me back. It should be in any minute.'

'Then hold off until you've got Wynley as well,' advised Banbury. 'If they did all know each other, it would mean Bryant was right; they weren't chosen at random.'

'I don't know where that takes us,' April admitted. 'I never go to a pub unless I'm meeting someone. What if Pellew worked with them somehow, perhaps even employed them? He arranges to meet each in turn, which is how they let him get close enough to jab them with a needle.'

'I don't see how that could happen. He'd been locked up for years.'

'Do you think he would have had internet privileges? Could it have been some kind of online deal?'

Banbury rubbed at his eye, thinking. 'I don't know. How can we tell if Pellew's even the right man? He's not in custody yet.'

'There's one other thing. Cochrane, the warder at Twelve Elms Cross, sent through Pellew's medical file. There's a photograph of him taken at the age of eight without the crimson blemish on his face, and another one taken when he was seventeen – still no mark.'

'So if it's not a birthmark, what is it?'

'A disguise,' said April.

31

THE ANGERSTEIN

It was said that the Angersteins were descended from Peter the Great himself, that John Julius Angerstein was the illegitimate son of either Catherine or Elizabeth, Empress of Russia, but the truth was somewhat less salubrious. John Julius, a Lloyd's underwriter, had grown rich from his West Indian slaves, and parlayed their miseries into an art collection that became the envy of kings, and the foundation of the National Gallery.

The Angersteins made their home in Greenwich, the birthplace of Henry VIII and the home of time itself. Woodlands, their house in Greenwich Park, was built to house John Julius's growing collection of Rembrandts and Titians, and a grand Victorian hotel commemorated his name.

But part of the maritime town had been allowed to die. Away from the splendours of the Royal Naval College, the Royal Observatory, the Queen's House and the *Cutty Sark*, east Greenwich grew dusty and rotted apart, its community shattered by the roaring motorway flyover that split the quiet streets in half. Here, the great

Angerstein hotel, now just another shabby pub, was situated. Like so many other public houses of its era, it had been repaired with thick layers of paint, blue-grey this time, and its windows were rainbowed with the lights of gambling machines and posters for karaoke nights.

John May edged his BMW through the isthmus of the one-way system and parked by the entrance just as Meera Mangeshkar arrived on her Norton, with Bimsley riding pillion. He opened his window and called over to the two young officers.

'We've spoken to the pub's manager. He was a bit shocked when I explained he might be harbouring a murderer in the building, but he's going to cooperate. He says Pellew's hiding place can only be upstairs, as the basement is passcode protected.'

Shielding their eyes from the breaking rain, they looked up at the hotel, as arrogant and imposing as a battleship.

'Looks like more than twenty rooms, plus a fire escape and a basement exit,' said Bimsley.

'The first and second floors are accessible by a small side entrance round the corner, but the manager keeps the gate locked. If he's in there, Pellew's only escape route is down through the bar and out of the front, or down the rear fire escape.'

'How do you want to do this?'

'You two, cover the floors above. Arthur, you're staying on the ground floor. The bar staff are ready to close the main doors once we're inside. I'll get the fire escape.'

'No one except the manager sees what we're doing, understood?' said Bryant. 'If Pellew is panicked into running again, he may hurt someone or try to take a hostage. There's no way of getting all the drinkers outside without tipping him off. Don't forget that he's armed with the kind of weapon we may not even notice him discharging.' He struggled to unlock his recalcitrant seatbelt. 'For heaven's sake get me out of this bloody thing, John.'

They went in. 'Bloody hell, it's heaving!' said Meera. 'What's going on?'

'Charity match,' a punter shouted back. 'Charlton Athletic.'

Just as she asked, a mighty cheer went up. The crowd was watching their local team charge across a luminous emerald screen.

'You know what he looks like. Shut everyone else out of your vision and concentrate on his face,' said May. 'The birthmark makes him stand out.'

In the narrow sepia-wallpapered first-floor corridor, Bimsley ran lightly forward with the manager, a slender Asian man armed with a fat bunch of master keys for the rooms. 'We've hardly anyone staying here at the moment,' he explained. 'Certainly no one fitting your description. There's a service room at the end, a storeroom and another guest bedroom, but we've stopped letting it out because it's got some damp problems.'

'Open it up.'

The room smelled of wet wood, old newspapers, standing water. Black stalactites crawled down the discoloured plaster cornicing of vines and grapes. A reproduction of a painting, a black boy dressed in a golden turban, leaned against the mantelpiece. It was an attractive piece until one considered it in the light of John Julius Angerstein's background. There was no sleeping bag this time, though, no cigarette butts, no ampoule boxes – no sign of habitation at all.

'What else have you got?'

'Laundry room on the floor below. There's another small room beside it where the linen is kept.'

They moved lightly down the fire stairs and checked each room. Bimsley made a supreme effort not to crash into anything. There was no sign of human occupancy except a few muddy trainer-prints, an empty pack of gum, and a crumpled piece of notepaper which Bimsley pocketed.

And yet there was something, a disturbance in the stillness of the atmosphere, a faint trail of warmth that was enough to tip off an experienced officer that the room had been recently entered.

'He's around here somewhere.' Bimsley sniffed the stale air as if picking up spore. 'I'd put money on it.'

In the raucous bar the game had reached half-time, and the punters were heading back to order more beers.

Bryant leaned against a table and studied the crowd. His fingers were closed around the mobile in his right pocket. After years of dropping them down toilets and reversing over them in his Mini Cooper, he had finally managed to keep this one in working order. He watched and waited.

There was a high shriek at the corner of the bar, but the cry dropped and curled into hysterical laughter. A collective roar went up from a pride of males. Someone else shouted to mates across the room. Bryant peered through the scrum, watching the behaviour of the pack, the passing of pints over heads, the bellowed orders, the arms rested on shoulders, the hands pressed against backs, the fingers raised to catch the barman's attention.

The barman.

The cocky little sod, Bryant thought. *I don't believe he's actually working here!* But was it Pellew, though? As he turned, no crimson birthmark was revealed. His complexion was quite clear. There was no mistaking his profile, however, or the feral wariness of his eyes, like the dim and dying light within a man suffering from a serious physical illness.

He's watching the crowd as well, Bryant thought. *Why is he doing that? Surely he's not thinking of taking a victim here, in front of all these people? Yes*, he told himself, *because he wants to be seen and stopped so badly that there's no other course of action left open to him.*

Their eyes locked, and in the brief exchange of recognition, Pellew bolted.

The counter flap banged up in a crash of glasses and suddenly he was shouldering his way forward into the human forest.

Bryant flipped open his mobile and hit Redial, knowing that the call sign would trigger his partner's return. He made his way towards Pellew, pushing drinkers aside with his stick.

One of the other barmen was standing in front of the door, blocking it, suddenly aware of fast movement. A stool rose above heads, wavered and was pitched, smashing the largest window in the saloon.

He saw Pellew's back and shoulders rising above the assembly as he climbed up on to a table, heard the crunch of glass as he vaulted out into the street. The others were arriving now, and all hell was kicking up, the crowd startled into action, the barman getting shoved aside, the main door slamming back, and then they were out on the road running after him.

Bryant could not keep up, and leaned against the wall trying to catch his breath as Bimsley shouted for their suspect to stop.

Meera had been on her way down the stairs when Pellew made his move. Now she too was outside, sprinting after him as he hammered around the corner into Westerdale Road, not realizing that he had blundered into a cul-de-sac created by the motorway ahead.

As she closed in fast behind him, she thought, *Where*

can he go? Into one of the houses? She was drawing neck and neck with Bimsley when Pellew threw himself at the pebbledashed concrete slabs of the motorway wall. She knew that if he managed to cross the six lanes to its far side, he would be home free.

'Colin, no,' she called as the DC showed no signs of slowing down. 'You'll get killed.'

She knew he could hear her but would not stop, and watched in horror as he too jumped at the wall, curling his broad hands over the edge, swinging his legs to one side and hauling himself to the top before vanishing over the other side.

Colin found himself facing the Friday-night rush-hour traffic – three lanes of sunset headlamps and three beyond that of tail-lights, racing into the city dusk. Ahead, one lane in, Pellew had lurched to a stop amid honking horns, teetering on the broken line, waiting to run again. If he managed to vault the wall on the far side he'd hit the railway embankment, which branched and ran for miles in a multitude of directions.

Having been diagnosed with the hereditary syndrome that caused diminished spatial awareness, Bimsley was the wrong man to be dodging speeding cars. The ground always seemed further away from him than it was, and when he walked down a passage he had to concentrate on not blundering into the walls. Now he needed to judge the relative speeds of six lanes of vehicles, and allow enough time to run across the tarmac between them.

Pellew, on the other hand, was a natural. He avoided launching himself into the paths of trucks, knowing that they would try to brake slowly to avoid shifting their loads. Instead he concentrated on the mid-sized family roadsters that sold themselves on safety features, anti-skid devices and superior braking power. He reached the central reservation with ease and hopped the steel barrier to do the same on the other side.

As Meera watched with her heart in her mouth, Bimsley windmilled his arms and threw himself across two lanes at once, causing vehicles to swerve around him. He had decided that his only way of making it through alive would be to reduce his peripheral vision, so, with his eyes now partially shut, he lumbered towards the central divide and tried not to listen to the sound of squealing brakes.

Pellew was on the move again, pausing, darting, timing his bursts of energy, nimbly bypassing a Sainsbury's truck as Bimsley reached the central barrier.

Only one more lane. Pellew drew breath and lurched forward once more. This time, he failed to spot the car that the truck had just overtaken. As he glanced back at Bimsley, who was making a dash directly at him, he was hit full-on by a new silver Mercedes saloon.

Pellew's body rose and smashed against the windscreen before bouncing away into the path of cars in the slow lane, where he was hit a second and third time.

One of the swerving vehicles winged Bimsley, flipping him around and hurling him back on to the central reservation.

He landed hard against the corrugated steel barrier, but this time he had the good sense to stay until the other officers arrived.

32

PIGMENTATION

These days, Arthur Bryant seemed to be spending more and more time in hospital, less for himself than to visit others. So many of his friends had reached the age where their ailments required overnight stays rather than a mere course of tablets. This evening, he had Bimsley in one ward getting his ribs bandaged and his left tarsals strapped into a sprain-anklet, Longbright sleeping off the effects of her poisoning in a nearby bed and Anthony Pellew downstairs in the morgue. Their suspect's legs had been shattered by the first impact, but his skull had been crushed by the second, and he had died in seconds. Although the traffic had been moving at a fairly swift pace, none of the drivers had ended up joining them in the wards.

Bryant shambled through the ward looking for Bimsley, pulling back curtains and frightening patients. 'Ah, there you are,' he said. 'The shop was out of grapes so I brought you a hat.' He tossed a baseball cap that read WORLD'S BEST MUM on Bimsley's bed and plonked himself down beside it. 'Oh, and something for you to read.' He fished out his dog-eared paperback of *An Informal History of the Black Death.* 'You'll be up on your feet – or at least, foot – in a day or two. You were bloody lucky.'

'If you call getting hit by the wing mirror of a Ford Mondeo lucky,' Bimsley complained. 'It couldn't have been a Ferrari, could it?'

'If it had been, you might not be here. What's the damage?'

'My hip's pretty bashed up, some torn ligaments, one broken rib, left ankle sprained, some surface cuts.'

'I don't know what you're making such a fuss about, then,' said Bryant. 'Pellew's legs are facing the wrong way and his head looks like a dropped meringue.'

'Yeah, but I'm on the correct side of the law, sir.'

'Righteousness does not protect you from injury. I know you meant well, going after him like that, but you might have panicked him into the traffic. Pellew was a former mental patient, after all. Renfield's furious with you, but I've persuaded him not to make a fuss about what happened.'

'Pellew had been released, sir, even though he was still dangerous.'

'Well, we've still to get to the bottom of that. It's looking like he deliberately targeted his victims after all. April discovered that three of the five victims falsified their CVs. It would seem they didn't even tell their partners or families the truth about their jobs, just trotted off to work every day and came home in the evening as if everything was normal.'

'I don't understand,' said Bimsley. 'What does that mean? Where were they going?'

'Where indeed?' Bryant narrowed his eyes. 'To a place where they might have come into contact with Anthony Pellew, perhaps.'

'The Broadhampton.'

'No – we've already checked the clinic's employment records. Somewhere else. Have a think while you're lying there, old sausage, it'll give you something to do.'

'Do me a favour and open that, sir.' Bimsley pointed to his locker. 'There should be a piece of paper inside.'

Bryant pulled out the single mud-stained sheet and gingerly flattened it.

'I found it on the floor of one of the rooms in the Angerstein. It's not much, but it might have come from him.'

Bryant found himself looking at a scribbled doodle. It appeared to be of a bird sitting atop a tree stump. 'Thanks. No idea what this might be but I'll check it out.' He rose to leave, then stopped. 'By the way, young Meera wanted to come and see you, but I had to send her to interview Carol Wynley's partner.'

'I don't suppose she could be bothered to leave me a message.'

'Would it raise your spirits and aid your recovery if I told you she did?'

Bimsley attempted to affect an air of disinterest. 'It might do.'

Bryant thought for a moment. 'Fine, she said to get well soon and hurry back . . . No, I'm joking, she didn't say anything at all. Sorry.'

'What the bloody hell were you doing there by yourself?' asked Renfield, who was attempting to keep his voice down on the women's ward. 'You're not supposed to conduct a search like that unaccompanied.'

'How long have you been here?' asked Longbright, trying to focus on the sclerotic sergeant perched on the edge of her visitor's chair.

'Just for a while. I've been watching you sleep,' Renfield admitted.

'I didn't need you to come with me.' Longbright pushed at her pillows, trying not to disturb the saline drip attached to her wrist. 'Arthur said that Pellew wanted to be stopped. I've done this sort of thing plenty of times before.'

'And that's exactly why you had your guard down,' said Renfield. 'You'd be in a body-bag downstairs if he hadn't misjudged your size. Pellew didn't turn himself in, so part of him must have wanted to remain at large, and that made him dangerous. Your boss had it wrong.'

'Have they said how long I have to stay in here?'

'They've got to finish flushing out your system. You'll be allowed home tomorrow.' He fought down a smile.

'What's so funny?'

'I've never seen you without make-up.'

My God, thought Longbright, *I don't think anyone has ever seen me without make-up.* 'I'll stay until the doctor has been. Give me something to do until then, Jack. Get me the case notes.'

'You're supposed to rest.' Renfield looked about the ward. Two constables were walking a shouting, handcuffed drunk woman past the beds.

'All right, Steve? Joey?' Renfield called. They nodded curtly to him, but carried on without stopping to speak.

She watched the officers pass. 'You must be missing your mates in the Met.'

'Well, they don't bloody miss me,' said Renfield, looking back. 'They won't even say hello to me now.'

'So you finally know how the rest of us feel. Look at the state of your fingernails. It's stress.' Longbright lowered her head back to the pillow. 'Being on the unit takes over your life until there's nothing else left. From the day I joined the PCU even the duty officers at Bayham Street stopped talking to me. They thought I was waving two fingers at them, getting out to move on to a cushy number. They didn't know I took a drop in pay and position just to work where my mother once worked. I slogged away in the Met in order to build up respect and credibility, and lost it all on the day I moved across to join John and Arthur. My partner left me, my civilian friends went away, I have nothing left but the unit. The same thing will happen to you.'

'It already did.' Renfield looked down at his toecaps. 'Four years ago last month. My girlfriend died in Manchester, on duty.'

'I never heard about that.'

'I didn't tell many people. She'd been working up on Moss Side, liaising with immigration officers for a couple of years. One Saturday night in the middle of winter some bloke had a go at her outside a rough-as-guts nightclub – just a punch in the neck, but she'd had a couple of rums before she went on duty. She went down heavily, bruised herself, suffered a bit of shock. Went home not feeling well and died in bed that night. Those two drinks meant the difference between burial with full honours and dismissal with nothing at all. You wonder why I prefer to stick to the rulebook. So when you say you have nothing left, you know how I feel.'

'I think I preferred you when you were being unpleasant to everyone,' she sighed.

'You know I don't approve of the way the PCU goes about things, but I'm trying to learn, understood?'

Longbright gave a small smile and held out her unfettered hand. 'Understood.'

Giles Kershaw was below the pavement of the Euston Road, in the UCH morgue, talking to Alex Reynolds, the admitting surgeon. The remains of Anthony Pellew lay in the tray before them, being cleaned, opened and weighed.

'No birthmark on his face,' noted Kershaw, holding back his hair as he leaned over the body.

'You were expecting one?' asked Reynolds. 'You should be wearing a cap, or don't they bother with them at the PCU morgue?'

'Actually, we're skilled enough to sort out our own fibres from those of our suspects at the PCU, thanks,' said Kershaw coolly. 'We've got this man down with *nevus flammeus*.'

Reynolds could not recall the term. 'Remind me.'

'Port-wine facial markings. They're formed at birth.'

'Then you've got the wrong man, haven't you?'

'No, I don't think we have. I need to get a tissue sample.' Kershaw took a closer look. Pellew had not been taking care of himself. His nails were split, the cuticles bitten and torn. A cracked front tooth, bad skin due to a poor diet, worn-out underclothes, worn-over trainers. And deep in his hairline, minuscule red specks.

Kershaw withdrew tweezers and lifted the dots into a small plastic pouch, but he could already identify the substance by its odour: lipstick. Pellew had applied the so-called birthmark with artificial colouring. Why? Was it due to some mental aberration, a form of tribal disguise, part of the ritual of killing? Or could there be a stranger reason that added method to his madness?

This case isn't over, he thought. *It looks like the real work is only just beginning.*

33

CONSPIRACY

They met on the bridge, always on Waterloo Bridge, because the light was sharper here, because the sky was high and wide, because for them it gave the greatest view of London.

In all the years they had been meeting above the river, the northern horizon had never changed as quickly as it was changing now. Instead of the barges and blackened warehouses, the working cranes and silhouetted derricks, glass balconies protruded from blank pastel walls like boxes at the theatre. The Thames itself had been transformed from a pulsing aquatic artery to an empty scenic backdrop provided for the amusement of shore-dwellers, a cosmetic alteration that in Arthur Bryant's opinion mainly benefited the rich in their penthouse flats. What else would be provided for them, he wondered, the kind of gaudy floating pageants that had been staged in the presence of *le roi soleil*? Fireworks and hot-air balloons? But of course the mayor, following in the great tradition of London mayors, was already providing them with such distractions. To be the Lord Mayor of London was to accept the city's poisoned chalice, and always be hated by at least half the capital's residents.

In his younger days, Bryant had passionately supported marches, rallies and protests through the capital, even though as a public servant he was required to be non-partisan. His partner had managed to avoid taking sides, simply because he felt that the science of investigation should be considered away from distracting influences, and he regarded himself as an impartial technician. However, this stance had lately been eroded by the continued efforts of the Home Office, whose attempts to close the unit had become tiresome and predictable, just another obstacle to factor into any protracted investigation.

Bryant leaned against the balustrade of Waterloo Bridge and looked across at the graceful glass span connecting St Paul's to the Tate Modern. The new bridge had drawn attention away from mere stone river-crossings like Waterloo.

'I hate small-mindedness,' he suddenly announced after several minutes of contemplative silence. 'The notices everywhere warning us not to trip over or turn left or take our dogs off leads. That annoying recorded voice in the post office telling you which counter is free. I bought some peas in the supermarket last week and do you know what it said on the packet? "Does not contain nuts." I hate the endless admonishments of a nanny state that lives in fear of its lawyers. While colonies of dim-witted traffic wardens swarm about looking for minor parking infringements, nobody seems to notice that our very social fabric is falling apart.'

'What's brought this on?' asked May, puzzled. 'Have you got another court summons over your car?'

'Several, in fact, but that's not the point.' Bryant poked his pipe between his lips and lit up. 'Once our children played on bombsites and collected unexploded shells.

Now they're driven to school by paranoid parents in armoured cars. The determination of dullards can always be counted upon to challenge the merits of innovators.' He noisily sucked on his pipe until the bowl's embers sparkled against the cloud-grey waters. 'To be popular in this city you have to be average. Our unorthodox approach to the attainment of excellence won't allow us to survive.'

'No one else can handle something like this,' said May. 'We'll be here so long as there are such crimes.'

'I don't think so. Have a chocolate banana.' Bryant pulled the pocket fluff from a sweet and passed it over. He felt guilty having a smoke without giving May a sweet. 'I bet Raymond can't wait to slam the lid on the Pellew investigation. He'll be able to let Faraday know that there's no more danger lurking in the capital's public places.'

'Kershaw reckons he's got a couple of skin flakes from two of the women, but I suppose it'll take a while to see if there's a DNA match with Pellew's tissue samples. We don't rank very highly in the queue for equipment use these days. You're not in any doubt about him, are you?'

'Me?' asked Bryant. 'Didn't you hear? Kershaw's also got a complete thumb-print from one of the emptied plastic ampoules Pellew left in his room at the Clock House. A straight match. We just need to complete the link by making sure that the residue inside it has the same chemical composition as the drug we found in his victims' bloodstreams.' He tightened his collar against the early evening mist. 'No, it's not his identity that bothers me now, there's no question of that, it's his motive I find troubling. I went over April's background notes again. There's a very peculiar disparity I find myself unable to account for.'

'Perhaps I can help.'

Bryant raised his head to look May in the eye. 'What do we now know about Anthony Pellew? That he was a disturbed and lonely child, brought up in pubs by an alcoholic, unfaithful father and a mother who turned tricks when they were short of cash. As a kid I imagine he was probably left hanging about in the beery haze of the bar room while the girls flirted around his old man. Upon his father's death, he and his mother settled into the Angerstein, and later, after she'd been kicked out for soliciting, they moved to the Clock House. Anthony hit adolescence only to find himself ignored and unable to talk to the opposite sex in any place other than the pub.'

'He also started drinking heavily.'

'So, after his mother was taken ill for the first time, he kidnapped a girl and kept her locked up in the basement of a boozer, staying with her, talking to her. Agreed so far?'

'I think so.'

'After his trial and incarceration Pellew supposedly underwent rehabilitation, and had frequent assessments. Somehow, we still don't know how, he managed to secure an early release. But unbeknown to the doctors, his desire to re-create the small comforts of the past had twisted into something darker. He knew that if he kidnapped another girl, the authorities would come for him and take her away, so it seems he decided on a new method of fulfilling his dreams. He could keep these women with him for ever by fatally drugging them. They would simply fall asleep by his side in a place that made him happy. No sexual assault, no violence, just the everlasting companionship he craved, and found he could create by taking lives.'

'You think the women he picked reminded him of his mother?'

'I wondered about that. But it would make everything so psychologically neat, wouldn't it? Even the phoney birthmark makes sense because the argument would be that he was using it as a mask, a way of proving that even though he had deliberately made himself unattractive, he could draw a woman to his side. What he was really doing, though, was marking himself out to us. Pellew could be regarded either as a tragic figure doomed to recreate the only moments of happiness he had ever had, or as an arrogant grotesque preying on the lonely and vulnerable. With the exception of Jasmina Sherwin, he only selected women with maternal instincts.'

'Either way, Raymond is right to close the case,' said May.

'Except for one fact that unravels this neatly bow-tied little package. Three of these gentle, harmless ladies knew each other. So the notion of a lonely, embittered, mentally ill man wandering from pub to pub looking for random victims is suddenly thrown out, because his acts are carefully premeditated.'

'Unless it's sheer coincidence. Look at the make-up of city pubs and you'll find workers from the same professions, many of whom know each other.'

'A fair point. You can talk to someone in a pub and yet hardly acknowledge them in another environment. So many overlapping circles.'

'I should produce a set of Venn diagrams.'

'Please don't.' Bryant exhaled a wreath of blue smoke around his head.

'And what if one victim led to the next? He makes friends with Kellerman, and she leads him to Curtis, who leads him to Wynley and then Roquesby. Was any one of them aware of what had happened to the others? Presumably not, or they'd have steered clear of doing the same thing, standing around alone in a pub. Although no one's ever really alone in a pub, are they? That's the attraction.'

'Perhaps, but I'm not at all happy,' said Bryant firmly. 'And I won't let Raymond shut the case until I am. I want to see the psychiatric evaluations that got Pellew released from the Broadhampton. I want to know how those women came to be in that photograph, and why their employment records were falsified over the same periods. We have to go back and take another look at the pubs. Why did I see a Victorian public house that never even existed under that name? Most of all, we need to find out how on earth an outpatient under observation was able to lay his hands on such highly toxic drugs.'

'That's going to take time,' said May, 'and Land wants this wrapped up fast.'

'Then he'll have to wait.'

'But if no one else is attacked—'

'I don't care,' said Bryant stubbornly. 'We've missed something essential.'

'Not to the outcome of the case, Arthur, only to your personal satisfaction. You know we don't always get every last detail correct. It would be like suggesting we've solved the mysteries of human nature. It's not simply a matter of genomes, there are social variables and—'

'I know it's not an exact science, John, but there's something here that simply. Does. Not. Make. Sense.' He thumped his walking stick on the pavement for emphasis.

'Then tell me, what do you think that is?'

Bryant punched him in the chest with a mittened hand. 'What have I always told you? The kind of crimes that reach our little unit can best be appreciated and resolved through a consideration of the laws of paradox. Pellew himself led us to him, then fled when we arrived. Why? Although he wanted – needed – us to catch him, why did he run to his death on a busy motorway?'

'He was trying to get away and made a mistake.'

'No. You saw him hesitate and look back. He knew that we couldn't be allowed to take him alive. If we did, he would find himself charged and interrogated, and he couldn't afford to let that happen.'

'Why in God's name not?' asked May, mystified.

'Because under interrogation he would incriminate someone else,' said Bryant, looking out into the incoming mist.

'But Arthur, there *isn't* anyone else. He operated alone, acting for the private gratification that he alone could receive.'

'So it would seem. And we are presented with the textbook apparatus to understand his motivation. In fact, there's little left for us to do beyond conducting a few scientific matches and placing the case in archive. The Broadhampton's medical faculty will be at great pains to justify their decision to release Pellew into the community. Everyone walks away with their hands clean.'

A police launch passed beneath them, a white arrow cleaving sepia waters.

'And there's something else,' added Bryant. 'I thought about the drawing Bimsley found on the floor of Pellew's makeshift hiding place at the Angerstein Hotel, a scrappy rendering of a bird with a long tail, sitting on a tree stump. Bimsley gave it to me when I visited him at the hospital.'

'What of it?'

'It only took me a few moments to come up with the pub name – the Magpie and Stump, opposite the Old Bailey. But I was a little slower in making the connection. Pellew left us a more deliberate clue than any of his clumsy earlier attempts. What does the name Thomas Spence mean to you?'

'The Cato Street Conspiracy,' said May. 'Spence was a former schoolteacher who believed that if all the land of

Britain was shared out equally, every man, woman and child would get seven acres each.'

'Very good, you know your history. Did you also know that he founded the Society of Spencean Philanthropists? They believed that instead of a centralized governing body, Britain should be run by small groups based in public houses. I made a list . . . hang on.' He rooted out another of his scraps of paper and squinted at the huge lettering on it. 'The Spenceans met at the Nag's Head in Carnaby Market, the Carlisle in Shoreditch, the Mulberry Tree in Moorfields, the Cock in Soho, the White Lion in Camden and a host of other pubs. In rented rooms in Cato Street, they hatched plans to assassinate a group of government ministers attending a dinner party in Grosvenor Square. They were caught by police and tried at the Old Bailey, while their supporters watched from the windows of the Magpie and Stump public house. Some of the accused were executed, some transported. So, we get a second "seven" after the Seven Stars pub, a third with the Seven Bells – the former name of the Old Bell pub – and on top of the other keywords Pellew has given us, we must now add "conspiracy".'

Bryant balled the paper and tossed it down into the fast-flowing river. 'Look at the view we take so much for granted. Politicians are fond of telling us how much cleaner the Thames is now, how you can catch dace and sole in its reaches once again. Everyone wants to believe in appearances. What was the Thames ever but a gigantic sewer, somewhere to empty the waste of a wealthy nation? The steamships churned up so much shit that the fine people crossing this bridge died of cholera. You can burnish a city's image, but you never really change its nature. There's something hidden and corrupt running beneath it, there always is, and this time it's not just the acted-out fantasies of a lost soul.'

'Oh really,' May complained. 'You're saying you see some kind of city-wide conspiracy at work?'

'Most definitely.' Bryant nodded with vigour. 'And I intend to discover exactly what it is.'

'If you're wrong, our reputations will be ruined once and for all.'

'Given the nature of my suspicions, I pray I'm wrong,' said Bryant gloomily.

34

GAZUMPED

Raymond Land was perched uncomfortably on the cracked red-leather seat of a nineteenth-century tapestry-backed chair in Leslie Faraday's office, nervously waiting for the minister to return.

As he toyed with a loose thread, he wondered whether he would be able to curry favour from the case's fast conclusion. His superiors would see that the PCU could compete with the Met in terms of efficiency, and as he was acting head of the division he would surely be commended for resolving a situation that might well have caused a national panic. The monotonous regularity with which the HO attempted to shut down the unit would be ended, and its officers would finally be allowed to continue in an atmosphere of mutual respect.

He looked down and realized that the tapestry thread was wrapped around his fingers. Peering over at the back of the chair, he saw to his horror that he had unravelled a substantial portion of the ancient design. The shepherdess now had no head, and two of her sheep had partially evaporated.

Faraday waddled into the room rubbing his hands. 'Ah, there you are, Land,' he boomed cheerfully. 'I'm having Deirdre rustle us up some tea. You're white with two sugars, if memory serves.' Faraday's memory always served. Indeed, it was his singular talent, and all that kept him from being booted from his fine Whitehall office into the gutter. Faraday was as slow as treacle, but remembered where all the financial corpses were buried, and therefore it was expedient to keep him where ministers with more competence and cunning could keep an eye on him. 'I must say you've done jolly well to put this frightful business to bed. I thought it would be a good idea to tell – '

A chill breeze trembled through Land's heart. He suddenly knew who Faraday had told.

' – Mr Kasavian,' said Faraday, holding open the door. 'He wanted a word with you himself.'

This could not be good. Whenever the cadaverous Home Office security supervisor became involved in their affairs, babies cried, women cowered, innocence was punished and blame was wrongly apportioned. As he entered the room, Land fancied he heard the distant sound of noosed bodies falling through trap doors. Certainly the sun went in, draining all warmth from the room.

Oskar Kasavian did not smile so much as bare his lower teeth. As Land rose and held out his hand, he realized that his palm was still filled with material from the damaged chair. Like a shamed schoolboy, he let it drop on to the floor behind him.

'I understand our public houses are once more safe enough for the populace to become drunk in,' said Kasavian, waving Land back into his seat. 'Although it would have been preferable to bring the malefactor to justice rather than spreading him all over the A102.'

'My officers risked a great deal trying to prevent the flight of a mentally unstable man,' Land explained.

'Quite understood.' Kasavian examined his nails as though checking for evidence that could link him with murder. 'Trying circumstances for everyone involved, and I look forward to reading your full report. But I am here about another matter entirely. The Peculiar Crimes Unit currently occupies the site at 1B Hampstead Road, does it not?' Kasavian opened a folder and produced a photocopied map of the area, with the footprint of Mornington Crescent station marked in shaded lines.

Land was thrown. He leaned forward, peering at the proffered document. 'That is correct.'

Kasavian tapped a long hard fingernail on his front tooth. It made a sound like water dripping from a corpse on to an upturned tin bucket. 'You see, the thing is, there has been a rather unfortunate oversight. Probably no more than a clerical error, but an error all the same. Your lease – '

' – extended to 2017. I signed the documents myself,' said Land hastily.

'Indeed you did, but for some reason I can hardly begin to fathom, the document was never notarized by the Land Registrar. Which means that the lease was never officially extended.' Kasavian had employed his legal team for over a month, searching for some loophole by which to remove the PCU from his sight. The unratified lease had fallen into his etiolated hands like disinterred treasure.

'Then surely it is simply a matter of presenting the lease once more,' said Land hopefully.

'Would that things were so simple.' Kasavian wrung his hands together so tightly that Land expected to see drops of blood fall from them. 'With the lapse of the lease, all existing documentation between the former leaseholder and the Crown Estate, which owns the site, is voided.'

'Can't we draw up new documents based on the previous arrangement?' asked Land, already knowing the answer.

Kasavian gave him a dry, hooded look that suggested he could not be bothered to come up with any more excuses. 'The unit is required to vacate the premises at noon on Monday.'

'But tomorrow's Saturday,' squeaked Land. 'Where are we to be rehoused?'

'Alas, we do not have the facility for rehousing such a government unit at present.'

'Then what are you suggesting we do?'

Faraday pretended to spot something of great interest outside the window, which was unlikely as he was facing a brick wall in Horseferry Road. 'Mr Kasavian has kindly agreed to place all members of staff on partially paid leave until the situation can be sorted out,' he said.

'We hope to find new premises for you within three to four months. Meanwhile, we will be offering a generous "opt-out" scheme to your staff, for those members who feel unable to continue with the unit.'

'Do you know how many times the Home Office has tried to disband the PCU and failed?' said Land hotly. 'Without us, this type of crime would go undetected and unsolved.'

'That remains to be seen,' said Kasavian. 'The unit has clearly had its fans in the Home Office, but many members of the old guard are reaching retirement age and handing over the reins. There are reasons why you never made superintendent, Land, just as there are now reasons to assume that the Metropolitan Police Force could handle this kind of work with greater cost-efficiency.'

'So that's what it comes down to?' asked Land. 'Money?'

'It's a matter of security. It may have escaped your

notice, but the capital is on a permanent severe terrorism alert. There is no room for your little cottage industry detection unit. You're an anachronism, an unacceptable security risk, you've admitted so yourself.'

'That was in the past, before—'

'Before your detectives won you over? Ask yourself, Land, what has changed? The answer is *nothing*, and that's the problem.'

'Is there anything I can say to make you change your mind?' Land pleaded. He glanced back at Faraday, who had just noticed that his tapestry chair was ruined.

'It's too late for that,' said Kasavian. 'I'm afraid the building has already been sold. Tomorrow is your very last day at Mornington Crescent. You'd better go and tell your staff to pack up their belongings.' His smile was as mirthless as any carnival huckster's. 'Don't worry, we won't do anything as drastic as changing the locks. I remember only too well what happened the last time we tried that. We're all civilized adults, Mr Land, I'm sure we can reach an amicable agreement.'

'You mean you'd like us to reach a compromise on the terms of moving out?' said Land hopefully.

'Good God, no,' said Kasavian. 'It's merely an expression. There's nothing you can do now except go.'

35

INTERPRETATION

A pair of disembodied legs sealed in black fishnet tights and crimson satin garters was balanced gracefully on a mound of red plastic poppies. Nearby, a torso clad in a basque with lavender rhinestones set in its staves glittered menacingly.

DS Janice Longbright peered into the window of a shop called 'Yield to the Night' and sighed at the clothes she could not afford. She was tired of being broke and unloved. Checking her watch, she realized that she was running late. Carol Wynley's partner was awaiting her arrival in the flat beside the shop.

Shad Thomson had suffered a stroke in his late fifties, three years earlier, and the apartment he shared with Carol Wynley had been adapted to allow his motorized wheelchair to pass easily from room to room. Although she was unsure how much help she should offer her host, Longbright suggested making tea for them both, and he comfortably acquiesced.

'I suppose I got lazy living with Carol,' he told her. 'It's surprisingly easy to let someone do everything for you.'

'You must miss her a great deal,' Longbright said.

'I'll never know anyone else like her,' he replied. 'She knew me before the stroke, so she remembered a different person, the one who was still on his feet, racing around town taking meetings, hitting deadlines, thinking that work was so damned important. No one will ever see me like that again. Carol was the last person to really know me. I'm someone else now. I can never go back.'

'How long were you together?'

'Seven years. I met her in a pub, the Seven Stars in Carey Street. I remember it had some kind of connection with Holland. She had worked for a law firm in Amsterdam, and we got talking about the history of the place. I'm a journalist. At least it's a job I can still do like this.'

'Carol was still working in a law firm, wasn't she?'

'That's right, as a legal PA for the Swedenborg Society.'

'Where was she before that, do you remember?'

'Of course. She was at the Holborn Security Group, a firm of specialist solicitors on Theobald's Road.'

'When did she leave that job?'

'I printed out her CV for you. Here.' He handed over the pages.

Around the same time that the other three left their non-existent jobs, thought Longbright. *Where had they all been? What were they really doing?*

'Did you ever meet anyone she worked with at the Holborn Security Group?'

'I met one of her bosses, some kind of consultant,' said Shad. 'And once a woman of about her age dropped her off here.'

'One of these three, perhaps?' Longbright showed him the photograph of Roquesby, Kellerman and Curtis taken in the pub.

'That one,' said Shad, pointing at Roquesby without hesitation. 'I think she and Jocelyn briefly shared an office. I remember because Mrs Roquesby was an old colleague of Dr Peter Jukes. You must have read about him in the papers.'

'I don't think I have,' said Longbright, but she could vaguely recall someone at the PCU mentioning his name.

'I did some work on his case, purely out of interest. Have a look on that shelf for me, would you?' He pointed to a rack of plastic folders above his workstation. 'Dr Jukes.'

Longbright found a slender yellow file with the doctor's name written across the top.

'He originally came from Salisbury, Wiltshire,' Shad explained, tipping the sheets out into his lap and examining them. 'Last year his body was found floating off Black Head on the Lizard peninsula, Cornwall. The coroner thought it was a simple matter of death by drowning, but a local newspaper decided to take up the case, and their reporter reckoned that Jukes had sustained some unexplained injuries, the inference being that the coroner didn't do his job properly. Jukes' boat was washed into a local harbour more than fifteen miles further down the coast. The coastguard thought it unlikely that he had fallen into the sea, because local tides and currents would have taken both the body and the boat into the nearest shore. Jukes told some drinking pals he was going fishing with a mate, but no friend was ever found. I got bugged by the story for a while, even asked Mrs Roquesby about it when she came by. I thought she might have heard something that didn't get into the papers.'

'Why were you so interested?' asked Longbright.

'I did my training on the regional court circuit,' said Shad. 'When you hear the names of certain litigious organizations come up time and again, alarm bells go off in your head. In this case I was intrigued because Jukes was a consultant at Porton Down.'

* * *

'Roquesby's colleague was a doctor who worked for the Ministry of Defence,' Longbright told the detectives when she met them an hour later. They were seated in the Hope and Anchor, sipping a dark malty liqueur poured from a mysterious and rather dusty brown bottle Arthur had ordered down from behind the bar. It was nearly eleven p.m. and they had sent the rest of the crew home.

'Jukes was chief scientist for chemical and biological security at the MoD's main laboratory. There was some kind of scandal over part of the lab being outsourced into the hands of privatized companies.'

'I thought that happened all the time,' said May.

'One of them had been under investigation for allegedly offering bribes. It made a couple of the papers, but the story was dropped pretty sharpish. You once talked to me about the case, Arthur. You said something about turning up darker connections.'

'Did I?' asked Bryant, surprised. 'I don't remember at all. Not that that's saying much.'

Longbright thought for a minute. 'This would have been back in the summer. You told me something about witches or warlocks – no, Druids.'

'Wait a minute . . . that's right, I do remember.' Bryant was genuinely amazed. 'I told you that Jukes had formerly belonged to a Druid sect – his family had insisted it was only a hobby, but according to the Sunday rags he had drifted into Satanist circles.'

'You didn't tell me about this,' said May, grimacing over his bitter drink.

'Well no, Janice and I look into all sorts of interesting stories behind your back, don't we, Janice? But there's not much point in bringing them to your attention if we don't think they'll fly.'

'So what happened?'

'Oh, the Met detectives refused to believe there was a connection between his injuries and his interest in black magic. They vindicated the coroner and agreed with the verdict of accidental death. But you know how my mind works.'

'Not really, no.'

'I couldn't help wondering if Jukes had become an embarrassment to his employers because he was operating under the Official Secrets Act. I'm not suggesting they assassinated him, of course, merely that they encouraged people to believe that he was mentally unstable. I actually petitioned the Home Office for a look at his notes, but the Defence Secretary refused to acknowledge that there was a case at all. He pointed out that Jukes had been suffering from clinical depression for a number of years, and had long been recognized as a security risk, so I let it drop. And now it turns out he knew Jocelyn Roquesby. Well, well.'

'So what do we have?' asked May. 'Carol Wynley worked for another company that doesn't exist – April couldn't find any specialist law firm under the name of the Holborn Security Group.'

'And Shad Thomson has another set of employment dates that match those of his girlfriend's murdered companions,' Longbright added.

Bryant stirred the thick sediment in his glass thoughtfully. 'Four women lie about where they work. One of their colleagues commits suicide or accidentally drowns. Then, in the space of two weeks, the women, plus a fifth, are put to sleep in public places by a former mental patient.'

'It may be that none of these facts are connected. You know how often we're criticized for jumping to conclusions; I think we have to be very careful this time, and only build the case with documented facts. We could be looking at the result of information gaps, misinterpreted events, simple clerical errors.'

'No. I spoke to one of the doctors who signed Pellew's release form. Hopelessly evasive about the procedure, pleaded patient confidentiality. And I keep coming back to the pubs in which they died. The Old Dr Butler was named after a deranged doctor, the Seven Stars and the Magpie and Stump give us "seven" and "conspiracy", the Victoria Cross is the name of a pub that could not even exist, the Exmouth Arms provides the name of Pellew himself. My God, he couldn't have left us much plainer clues.'

'You're forgetting the Old Bell,' said May.

'Well, I don't have anything interesting on that one, other than the fact that it used to be called the Seven Bells.'

'Seven belles.' Longbright raised her eyes from the dark liquid in her brandy glass. 'Seven women.'

'The mad see things differently,' said Bryant. 'It's just a question of interpretation.'

'You think he intended to take the lives of two more victims?'

The little group sensed the room growing colder as they considered the possibility that more lives were in danger.

36

GREATER DARKNESS

The icy night dragged past in a knot of sweat-soaked sheets and twisted blankets. At three thirty a.m., Bryant disentangled himself and stood at the window in his dressing gown, staring out at the glittering garden. A strange aura of disturbance had settled over him. He sensed that things were coming to a head. Pellew's case bothered him more than he cared to admit; it was a sure sign that something was wrong when Raymond Land felt confident enough about the investigation to go running off to the Home Office.

You didn't work this long without knowing when something bad had happened. The ground was shifting, the tide was turning against them. Perhaps it was already too late for them to save themselves.

The street outside was quiet. Frost sparkled in the lamplight, as if the air itself was gelid and starting to crystallize. He felt slow-witted and incomplete, unable to grasp the significance of the week's events. Mrs Mandeville's memory lessons were working wonders but something continued to elude him, some passing remark that had pricked his interest, only to return to the indistinct background of bar chatter that had filled the last few days.

Five years ago, this is not something I'd have missed, he thought angrily. *I'm becoming slow and lazy.* He dug out his tobacco pouch, stuffed and lit a pipe, watching as the aromatic smoke curled against the condensation on the window. Two more women – possibly three if you did not count the death of Jasmina Sherwin – were still at risk, but how and from what? A dead man?

A larger fear assailed Bryant, that the neat confluence of reasons driving Pellew to commit murder was deliberately misleading. Their murderer might have re-created the comforts of his childhood, killed for the companionship that brought relief from his nightly fevers, but his psychosis wasn't the whole story. Something else had driven him, and perhaps was working still.

The nurse at the Broadhampton had insisted that her patient was of above-average intelligence. Pellew had sent his would-be captors messages, but he was no historian. He just liked pubs because he felt safe inside them. The clues he'd left behind had been simple enough to decipher. But where they led . . .

The embers in the pipe glowed and crackled. Bryant had always felt possessed of, well, 'psychic ability' was perhaps the wrong term, but a sensitivity, faint and tremulous, to the fluctuations of his waking world. That mental gauge had been shaken badly during his investigation of the Highwayman, the murderer who had courted fame in the tabloids by killing failed celebrities on London's streets. Now it was vibrating again, more violently than ever before. Some greater darkness had empowered Pellew, making him as much a victim as a murderer.

You needed to see the complete picture, not just a corner . . .

'Are you going to be smoking that disgusting thing for long?' asked Alma Sorrowbridge, making him jump.

'Good lord, woman, can you not go creeping about the house in the middle of the night? Especially not looking like that.' She was standing in the doorway in a vast red-and-yellow-striped nightdress, with crimson silk ribbons knotted through her hair.

Alma placed her formidable fists on her hips. 'Like what?' she demanded to know.

'Like a marquee for a particularly disreputable travelling circus. What are you doing up, anyway? I suppose you've been at the fridge again.'

'I hear you moving about because the floorboards creak. You're thinking about work.'

'How do you know that?'

'It's all you ever think about.'

'Nonsense, I frequently have other thoughts about – things,' he finished lamely. 'It so happens that I'm stuck on a problem.'

'Maybe you should do what you usually do, go and see that crazy devil-woman. I can't help you with your case, but I can help you sleep. I'll make us some hot chocolate with vanilla pods and cinnamon.'

'I'm sorry, Alma.' Bryant's appreciative smile would have been more attractive with his teeth in. 'I haven't been very nice to you lately, have I?'

'I haven't noticed, you're always horrible.' Alma sniffed. 'But I know you don't mean any harm, so I never pay much mind.'

'You're very good to me, you know.'

'I know.' Unimpressed with this late display of sentiment, she went off to make the chocolate.

It was early morning, and the streets were still milky with mist. Bryant rang the doorbell again, and this time the sound of the vacuum cleaner stopped. He looked around at the front garden, where a motor scooter had been carelessly parked on top of some diseased-looking begonias. There were slates that had fallen off the roof, and a pair of front-door keys was sticking out of a flowerpot of dead snowdrops, where every thief in the neighbourhood could see them.

He waited while somebody thumped and crashed towards the front door. He usually went to the deconsecrated chapel in Prince of Wales Road, Kentish Town to see his old friend, but this morning he had decided to catch her at home in her little terraced house on Avenell Road, Finsbury Park. Maggie Armitage, the white witch from the coven of St James the Elder, opened the door in yellow rubber gloves and a purple pinafore. Bryant wondered if she had been taking fashion tips from his landlady.

'I'm afraid you caught me hoovering,' said Maggie, snapping off her gloves to give him a hug. She had dyed her hair bus-red and painted on the kind of lipstick that could only be removed from a collar with a nail-brush.

'I thought you preferred things dusty.' Bryant gave her a squeeze. 'You shouldn't leave your keys in the flowerpot.'

'It's all right, I put a curse on them. And I don't mind a bit of dust, but I draw the line at involuntary emissions of ectoplasm. Maureen had a visit from Captain Smollet last night and got it all over the place. It might be good for the purging of tortured souls but it's a bugger to get out of the carpet. Her familiars are all military men. I'm not sure if it's because she held her first séance near the Chelsea Barracks, or if she just likes a man in a uniform. Come in and have some breakfast.'

Maggie remained the unit's affiliated information source for all crimes involving elements of witchcraft or psychic analysis, but she was prepared to offer advice on any number of subjects, from numerology and necromancy to pet horoscopes and the care of orchids. Her information was spiritually sound, but lacking in logic and probability.

Bryant entered the hall, climbing past a bicycle and all kinds of junk, including what appeared to be an old Mr Whippy ice-cream machine. Her little house was always overflowing with dead people's belongings, which made it simultaneously cosy and creepy. 'What do you know about conspiracy theory?' he asked.

'Not really my subject, lovey. You need Dame Maud Hackshaw for that.'

'Can I contact her?'

'I imagine so, she's in the kitchen straightening out my spoons. She's been practising her parapsychology on my cutlery. Come through.'

Maggie ushered her visitor through to a kitchen cluttered with Wiccan icons, headless Barbie dolls and mouldering seaside souvenirs. Dame Maud Hackshaw, a mauve-haired, pearl-festooned Grade III witch from the coven of St James the Elder, stared at Bryant through the thickest spectacles he had ever seen.

'Hello ducks, how are you?' she asked. 'We met in an army truck outside Dartmoor, remember? And this week I was introduced to your lovely lady sergeant at the Sutton Arms. She's got the gift of second sight, which is nice for her. Doesn't realize it at the moment, of course, still a bit too young. They never do until they're in their second blossom.'

'Maggie says you know a thing or two about conspiracy theories,' said Bryant, gingerly examining several teaspoons that had been twisted into silver spirals.

'They're usually supposed to involve covert alliances of the rich and powerful, brought together to deceive the general populace,' said Dame Maud, rubbing hard at a set of fish knives. 'The most common ones involve a 9/11 cover-up, Zionist global domination, Kennedy, Monroe, the Bavarian Illuminati, the moon landings and the New World Order. For some reason, they seem to be mostly American these days. They've been described as "the exhaust fumes of democracy", a kind of release valve for the pressures of living in an intense consumer society, but of course such theories go back to Roman times.'

'I see.' Bryant was unfazed by women like Dame Maud. He had been around them all his life.

'Europe is traditionally associated with old-world conspiracies to do with the Vatican, the Knights Templars, the hidden meanings of the Codex Argenteus, basically anything with Latin derivatives. It's human nature to try and make sense out of chaos, to join the dots and come up with a picture. And of course it's a guilty pleasure, as long as you don't take it all at face value.'

'What do you know about the Cato Street Conspiracy?' asked Bryant, accepting Maggie's offer of a slice of strangely heavy bread pudding.

'That was real, of course, a plan to bring down the government, like the Gunpowder Plot. Conspiracies are not necessarily the product of overheated imaginations.'

'Would you say there are ones we could consider true today?'

'Almost certainly,' said Dame Maud, shining the cutlery and carefully replacing it piece by piece. 'There are corporate conspiracies to keep company prices artificially inflated, and government schemes to slip through parliamentary bills under the cover of controversial world events.' She indicated the fish knives. 'I didn't bend these with the power of my mind, unfortunately, but with my fingers. It's the oldest parlour trick in the world. I was just showing Margaret how it is done.'

'You think your murderer was playing a similar trick

on you,' said Maggie, smiling as she set down tea. There seemed to be holly in her hair, although Christmas had long gone.

'What makes you say that?'

'You wouldn't be here otherwise.'

'Do you think he was? Playing some kind of a trick on us? I told you my doubts on the phone. I feel I've been hoodwinked somehow.'

'You have no reason to disbelieve this person's history, have you?'

'That's the problem, I don't,' said Bryant, a little perplexed. 'It's all true. And his culpability has been proven beyond doubt.'

'Then he must be cleverer than you imagined.'

Bryant munched his pudding thoughtfully and somewhat carefully. 'But to what end?'

'In conspiracy theory there's the issue of *cui bono*, "who stands to gain?" You must ask yourself the same question. If your chap Pellew is found guilty of murder, who is the beneficiary? Certainly not the doctor who discharged him, for he can only appear in a bad light after the confirmation that his patient has been released to commit murder. Who else? Five women are dead. Who gains an advantage from their deaths?'

'Someone who featured in all of their lives. Someone who was important to each one of them.'

'Someone you haven't found.'

'We've made detailed examinations of their recent movements,' sighed Bryant. 'There's a dark patch on the X-ray, so to speak, a period when they all just – went missing.'

'There you are,' said Dame Maud, who had been so sensible up until this point. 'Alien abduction.'

'No, dear, he thinks they worked together,' Maggie explained, 'doing something they couldn't tell their relatives about.'

'Oh, ladies of the night? Jezebels, is it? Painted harlots?'

'No, in an office,' said Bryant, giving Dame Maud a wary look. 'Legal secretaries.'

'I'm confused. Why would they lie about working in an office?'

'That's rather the question,' Bryant admitted.

'ATM machines,' said Dame Maud, perking up suddenly. 'They'll have needed lunches, won't they? Find out where they drew their money from. Women have to eat in the morning, it's a metabolism thing. Read their journey details from their Oyster cards, then check the coffee bars nearest to the stations from which they all alighted.'

'Are you sure you haven't worked with the police before?' asked Bryant. 'You have a criminal turn of mind.'

'No, dear, I haven't worked with the police.' Her mooneyes swam innocently behind aquarium glass.

'You've been in trouble with them a few times,' Maggie pointed out.

'It wasn't my fault that last time, it was your Maureen and her familiar, pulling my skirt off like that.'

'You were in the Trafalgar Square fountains swearing like a navvy.'

'I was in a state of advanced transcendentalism.'

'You were in a state of advanced inebriation, dear.'

As Bryant left the witches arguing in the little terraced house, he found himself wondering what a handful of kindly, maternal legal secretaries could have done to place themselves on the death-list of a deranged killer.

37

OPEN AND SHUT

'What do you mean, the case isn't shut?'

Raymond Land looked like someone had just thrown a bucket of iced water over him. Bryant had never seen him looking so tired. There were bags like holdalls under his eyes, and for once he hadn't tried to plaster his remaining strands of hair across his head.

'I've just told you, we think there may be at least two more victims, people we haven't considered. They could have been kidnapped by Pellew before he made a run for it. There's something else. Pellew was being monitored by a community warden called Lorraine Bonner. When he skipped his apartment, she notified his probation officer. The authorities knew he'd broken the terms of his release, but it looks like they did nothing about it. Why?'

'I can't go back to Faraday and tell him the case is still open, he'll have kittens.'

'I don't care about upsetting Faraday's little world when there may be human lives at stake.'

'And anyway – I suppose I'd better tell you – there's

another problem.' Land's sigh was like air leaking from an old accordion. 'Kasavian's closed the unit.'

'*Again?* My dear Raymond, every time we take on a case he closes the unit. It's getting so that people come here half-expecting to find us shut at odd hours. We're a crime division, not a French patisserie.'

'Listen to me, Arthur, this time it's for good. They've removed our lease on the building with immediate effect. We're required to vacate the premises.'

'Don't be ridiculous,' Bryant scoffed, before suddenly losing confidence. 'You're not serious?'

'As a heart attack. They've sold the property. There's another department moving in on Monday at noon.'

'How long are we supposed to vacate for? Where are we to go?'

'Kasavian says we'll be re-housed eventually, but I don't believe it for a second. It really is the end of the line.'

'Oh, you've said that before. We'll continue on, we always do. I haven't finished my biography yet.'

'For God's sake, Bryant, be realistic for once in your life,' Land shouted, startling them both. 'We have no funding, no offices, nowhere to work, no support, nothing, you understand? It's all gone. Everything you worked for all these years, it's finished, over.' He dropped his head into his hands, surreptitiously eyeing the aspirin bottle on his desk. 'Go home, I can't talk to you any more.'

'Well, I'm very disappointed that you won't go to bat for us,' said Bryant. 'It can't end here, you know. So long as we can prevent a single death, there's cause to go on.'

'Really? Are you sure you're not doing this for yourself, because you know that without the unit you have absolutely nothing left?'

'That was cruel, Raymond.' Bryant did his best to look

hurt. 'You've been hanging around with people from the Home Office for too long. It's made you hard. There was a time when you cared about doing the right thing.'

'I have to be practical about this. I looked inside the envelope you put in my jacket at Oswald's wake, Arthur. I know I wasn't supposed to, but curiosity got the better of me. You'd reached the decision to resign, and I know how you feel. Out of step with the present day. Heaven knows I've felt that often enough. I have no idea what people are thinking any more, all I know is that I don't like anyone very much. Some evenings I walk to the station and it seems as though every Londoner under forty is completely drunk. I'm getting to the point where I hate everyone. No wonder people shut themselves away. So you see, I understand your position. That's why I have to accept your resignation.'

'But I don't want to resign now. I have a reason for not doing so.'

'The case is closed.'

'No, it's not.'

'You identified the murderer.'

'Yes, I did.'

'You caught him red-handed.'

'Yes, that's true.'

'And now you're saying he didn't do it after all.'

'No, I'm saying he did.'

'Then how in God's name can someone else have done it?'

'I. Don't. Know.' Bryant realized they were shouting at each other, and turned his hearing aid down a fraction. 'But. I. Am. Going. To. Find. Out.'

He saw Land turning red and shouting something back, but had no idea what he was saying. 'Good,' he said. 'I'm glad that's settled. I'll get back to work.'

Land's next sentence was more creatively constructed

than anything he had said in the last five years, mainly because it was spectacularly obscene, but Bryant heard nothing at all as he left the room.

'I've got something for you,' April told her grandfather, commandeering his laptop and flipping open a file before him. 'You'll love this, it's technology gone mad. In November 2005, Jocelyn Roquesby caught a flight to Ancona in Italy, returning from Rome five days later. Giles found a torn piece of the ticket stub in the bottom of her handbag. He gave it to Dan Banbury, who used the information to locate her British Airways frequent-flyer number. By buying an online ticket in her name, he was able to access the rest of her personal data.'

'You can do that?' asked John May in surprise.

'We're simply stealing the tricks of the identity thieves,' said April. 'From that tiny row of digits Dan was able to get her passport number, her nationality and her date of birth. But better still, they led us to Roquesby's home address, her academic qualifications, profession and current-account details. We can tell you what car she drives, how much she bought her house for – and where she was working. Dan reckons most machine-readable ID documents carry flaws that make them pretty easy to crack. Although the new RFID-chipped passports demanded by the US have military-standard data-encryption technology, they're unlocked by supposedly "secret" keys that use readily available information. There are identity thieves who just work the airports, reading documents over travellers' shoulders and entering data into mobile phones.'

'So who was Jocelyn Roquesby working for?'

'A company called Theseus Research, based in King's Cross but registered out of Brussels. Dan cross-checked their employment records and came up with a total of seven names in the same London department, employed over roughly the same dates. Guess who they were?'

'Roquesby, Joanne Kellerman, Naomi Curtis, Carol Wynley and Jasmina Sherwin.'

'Close. You're right about the first four. But it looks like Uncle Arthur was correct about Sherwin not being part of the canonical selection of victims, though, because we have new names in fifth, sixth and seventh places.'

'The ones we haven't found.' May leaned forward and read down the screen. 'My God, I recognize one of them.'

'You do?'

May found himself looking at three further female names: Mary Sinclair, Jennifer Winslow and Jackie Quinten.

'Mrs Quinten has helped the unit out in the past. She's the lady who keeps trying to get Arthur to come over for dinner. Have you tried calling them all?'

'I've spoken to Jennifer Winslow – she's currently working at Ohio State University, and we can therefore assume her to be out of danger, at least until she returns next week. Mary Sinclair is at home in London, and we're providing her with immediate police protection, although from what or whom I have absolutely no idea. Right now, Jackie Quinten is the problem. There's no answer from her land-line or her mobile. Meera is on her way to Mrs Quinten's house in Kentish Town to see what's happened.'

'Poor Arthur,' said May. 'I think he has a bit of a soft spot for her. He knocked a drink over her at the Yorkshire Grey and had a moan about her harassing him for a dinner date, but I know he secretly loves being pampered. He'll never forgive himself if something has happened to her.'

38

DISAPPEARANCE

Meera Mangeshkar peered in through the kitchen window and saw rows of polished copper pots, steel utensils, framed maps, memorabilia collected from canal barges, Victorian vases and jugs filled with dried flowers. But of Mrs Quinten, there was no sign.

'You're wasting your time,' said a gap-toothed pensioner who was unnecessarily clipping the front hedge next door. 'She's gone out.'

'Do you know where?' asked Mangeshkar.

'She's got a sister in Hemel Hempsted, but I don't know if that's where she is. The lights have been off since this morning.'

'She could still be inside. She might have had an accident. Is there a side door?'

'You're a copper, aren't you?'

Meera bristled. 'Is it that obvious?'

'We don't get many coppers round here any more. You can come over my garden wall, it's an easy climb. She always leaves the back window ajar. She knows it's safe because I never go out, so I don't miss anything. But you're wasting your time, because I saw her go out over an hour ago.'

'Did she seem all right to you?'

'Fine, dressed for the shops, coat and boots, not like she was having a funny turn, if that's what you're implying.'

'Anything unusual about her?'

'I remember thinking she looked a bit worried.'

'You didn't ask her what about?'

'Oh no, I mind my own business.'

'And you're sure she didn't come back?'

'Positive, because I was watching at the front window.'

'In that case,' said Meera, 'I think I will hop over your fence and take a look around.'

Her arms were slender enough to fit through the gap in the window and unclip the latch. Climbing through, her boots touched down in the darkened lounge. Once inside, she opened the curtains. Hundreds of neatly rolled maps were stacked against the walls almost to the ceiling, but apart from that, everything appeared as it should be: magazines folded, cups washed, an ashtray emptied. A single wooden hanger lay on the bed, left when Mrs Quinten had donned her overcoat.

It appeared that she, like the others, had set off to meet someone.

Meera checked the cluttered noticeboard in the kitchen and searched the rooms for an appointment diary, but found nothing. A call to her mobile from someone masquerading as a friend, a work colleague, a dead woman?

As a child, Meera had blocked out the sounds of the estate by reading detective stories from the library. *It has the ingredients of an Agatha Christie without the logic*, she thought. *If this was Christie, the killer would be a dead woman who'd turn out not to have died. According to Mr Bryant, Mrs Quinten knew about his case. She understood that middle-aged women were at risk, so why would she be so trusting? Because she knows the killer.* She looked around the cosy room, praying that its occupant would live to see it again.

When Meera returned to the unit, she sought out Bryant and asked him about the conversation he'd had with Mrs Quinten in the upstairs bar of the Yorkshire Grey.

'I don't think she had any inkling of what had happened to her colleagues,' he said, concentrating on the recollection of events, 'because she expressed no concern to me. If anything, she complained of being bored recently. I didn't give her any names, so how could she have realized that she knew them? Although there was a moment at the end of our conversation . . .' He beetled his brow, trying to recall what was said. 'She was always inviting me over, but I got the feeling she wanted to consult me about something on a professional basis.'

'She didn't say what?'

'I don't think she felt comfortable about talking to me in public, said it was a private matter. She said *we*. So if she knew the other victims, perhaps they wanted to consult me as a group.'

'For all you know, she could have wanted to talk to you about her historical maps,' said May, overhearing.

'I'd forgotten about those. She collects them, doesn't she? Meera, did you see any at her house?'

'You couldn't miss them. They were everywhere, stacked against all the walls.'

'Where do we start looking for her?' asked May.

'Get April to track down the sister in Hemel Hempsted and find the addresses of any other relatives she might have wanted to visit, starting with the nearest.'

'She was meeting someone she felt comfortable with,' said Meera suddenly.

'How can you be sure of that?' asked Bryant.

'I questioned the next-door neighbour, who said she was "dressed for the shops". Warmly clothed, not dressed up.'

'She thought she was meeting the others, or at least one of them. That's what they all thought when they went out to their deaths, that they were going to meet each other.'

'If she'd known that any of them had been killed, she wouldn't have gone, would she?'

'Not unless it was very important.'

'A meeting so urgent that you have to risk your life?'

'It's someone she trusts,' said Meera. 'A former boss, someone in authority. Someone we haven't reached yet.' She looked around the room and realized that a pair of workmen were packing computers and files into boxes. 'What's going on?'

'We're being shut down again,' Bryant explained. 'Take no notice. I never do.' He tossed the end of his scarf around his neck.

'Wait, with all this going on, where do you think you're going?' May asked.

'If one of them lied about working for Theseus Research, they probably all did,' replied Bryant. 'I'm heading for King's Cross.'

39

SECURITY

Arthur Bryant had once shepherded bemused tourists on guided tours around King's Cross, and had perversely grown to love the area.

It had always been in a state of turbulence, of sickness and health, pleasure and vice, cruelty and grace. In its way, it was the most quintessential and paradoxical part of the entire city. The railway station was constructed on the site of the London Smallpox Hospital, and yet there had once been in its vicinity a pair of iron-rich spa springs and public pump rooms, near to which Eleanor Gwynne, the favourite of Charles II, had passed her summers in an idle procession of concerts and breakfasts.

In 1779, the Bagnigge Wells, as it was then called, had been described as a place where 'unfledged Templars first as fops parade, and new-made ensigns sport their first cockade'. Its banqueting hall boasted a distorting mirror and an organ, tea arbours draped with honeysuckle, swan fountains and fish ponds, bowling greens and skittle alleys, gardens and grottoes. But this most fashionable of resorts could not remain so for long. In 1827 it was written, 'The cits to Bagnigge Wells repair, to swallow dust and call it air.' Highwaymen and whores moved in for the rich pickings, the upper classes sneered at their new lowly companions and quickly moved on.

Just along the rain-polished road from where Bryant now found himself, the Fleet river broadened into a ford at Battle Bridge, a spot still filled with barges. The brickwork ashes that had accumulated on the grounds had been sold to Russia, to help rebuild Moscow after Napoleon's invasion, but who now could separate fact from fiction? Certainly, the immense octagonal monument to George IV that once sprawled across the road junctions had provided King's Cross with its name. Here sprang up some of London's roughest pubs, the Fox at Bay and the Pindar of Wakefield, the smoky homes of gamblers, drunkards and resurrectionists. Here, too, was the hellish Coldbath Fields prison, infamous for the severity of its punishments.

After the Second World War, the elegant terraced houses were carved into bed-and-breakfast lodgings for the dispossessed. And just as the railway terminus had once brought about the desecration of King's Cross, the wheel had turned and it was now the area's saviour, for the rail link to Europe arrived, a new town growing in its wake. The whores and dealers, modern versions of the nightflyers and pleasuremongers who had always flitted around the crossroads, had been scooped from their pitches and dumped elsewhere as chain stores moved in to attract new money.

At the moment, though, the area was still a battlefield of water-filled ditches and workmen's barriers, tourists clambering past one another with suitcases. Bryant loved towns in transition, and King's Cross was a core-sample of London at its most tumultuous. The Victorian buildings that had housed laundries, pawnbrokers and watchmakers had been rehabilitated into stripped-back modern offices.

It was here that he found the headquarters of Theseus Research.

Black-painted iron gates sealed a courtyard, beyond which a glass wall separated a security guard from the cold. The desk behind which he sat was so large that Bryant could only see the top of his head. He pressed the entry buzzer and awaited admittance. Instead of the gate swinging open, the guard emerged from the building into the rain and approached him.

'This building is not open to the public, mate,' he told Bryant through the bars, keeping his distance.

'Hello there, I run the King's Cross Rambling Club.' Bryant pressed his official London Tour Guide licence against the railings. 'There's a public right of way that runs through the middle of your building, and we want to include it on our tour.'

The guard's cold eyes reminded Bryant of a mackerel he had seen on a Sainsbury's slab. 'There's no access here. You can't come through here.'

'Then I'd like to speak with your public-relations officer.'

'We don't have one.'

'Well, whoever deals with your general enquiries, then,' he said, smiling and waiting with more patience than he could usually manage.

'We don't have general enquiries at the weekend.'

'I thought you did. My grandson works here, you see.'

'Then maybe you should call your grandson and get him to let you in.'

Bryant knew of a few certainties in life. One was that you should never rub your eyes after chopping chilli peppers, another was that you should be wary of using red telephone boxes after drunks had been in them, and now to this list he could add the fact that the guard on the door was never, ever going to admit him to this building.

'I'm an old-age pensioner,' he said forlornly, looking up at the guard with pathetic, watery blue eyes. 'I've come from miles away to organize this walk. I thought my grandson would be here, but he's not. Please, is there at least someone I can call?'

'You could try the general switchboard.' The guard sounded more sympathetic, but none too hopeful. Bryant dug out his mobile, flicked several Licorice Allsorts from its casing and began to punch out a number.

'Hey, you can't do that from here,' warned the guard.

'Why not?'

'You've got a camera on that. This is a secure area. Official Ministry of Defence property.'

'Really?'

'Yeah. Everyone who works here has to sign the Official Secrets Act. Even the cleaners.'

'But it's not as if they're making bombs or chemical weapons inside, is it? This is a built-up area. There are railway stations.'

'No, but they make plans here. For terrorist attacks and stuff like that.'

'Well, in that case, I shall tell our ramblers that they can't have access. We musn't interfere with the government's plans to protect us. Thank you – ' Bryant squinted at the guard's nametag, ' – Mandume. You've been very helpful.'

It was obvious, now that he thought about it. There could never have been any other explanation. *They were provided with cover stories because they were working for the Ministry of Defence*, thought Bryant as he raised his umbrella and walked back into the rain.

40

RECOLLECTION

'I say, how do we get access to Ministry of Defence files?'

Bryant asked the question casually as he caught up with a distraught Dan Banbury in the corridor of the PCU. The unit's computers had been removed and packed up in boxes that all but blocked the main passage. Most of the rooms had already been emptied of files and personal belongings.

Banbury released a snort of incredulous laughter. 'We don't,' he said. 'When it comes to the MoD, the same restrictions apply to us as to everyone else. By the way, there's a strange man in the evidence room putting everything in black plastic bin-bags. There's another one in the kitchen measuring things. He's taken our kettle. I can't find anything.'

'Yes, but what if it involves possible breaches in the law of the land? Surely we have the power to act in the public interest if ordinary citizens are at risk? I'm afraid I'm a bit of a neophyte when it comes to the workings of the government. How do we stand on that sort of thing legally?'

Banbury turned to look at him. 'Who do you think has a bigger say in the running of this country, Mr Bryant? The police or the National Defence Department?'

'Ah, I take your point. Then I'm not sure what to do. We've never had a situation like this before. Where we started at the beginning of the week isn't where we seem to be heading now.'

'With all due respect, where we're heading now is outside on to the pavement,' said Banbury. 'In case you haven't noticed, they're kicking us out of the building. How are we supposed to work?'

'I don't know. I haven't had time to think about it. Have a word with the others about accessing secure information, would you? I suppose we'll have to get everyone to regroup at my place for a while. Alma won't be pleased, but John's poky little flat isn't large enough to hold us all. Nobody's told us to actually stop work, it's just a matter of relocation as far as I'm concerned.'

'Are we going to be going right through the weekend then? Only it wasn't on the roster.'

Bryant gave a theatrical sigh. 'Yes, Dan, we are going to carry on until we get to the truth. Is there a problem?'

'Only that I'm looking after my nipper for a couple of days. He's at the age where he's a right handful, but I'll have to bring him with me.'

'Where's your wife?'

'With her new fella, a boiler-fitter from Stevenage she met at one of her sister's wine-tasting nights. She's leaving me. I suppose she didn't want me to feel left out.'

'About what?'

'Being the only person at the PCU in a satisfying relationship, sir. Thought I'd fit in better as an embittered workaholic loner.'

'Sarcasm will be the ruin of you, lad. Go and fetch the others.'

'Mr Bryant wants everyone to meet him at his house in Chalk Farm,' said Longbright, leaning her formidable chest against the door-jamb. 'Are you coming, Raymond?'

'How would it look if I did that?' said Land. Whenever he was faced with conflicting emotions, he became static with indecision. 'I can't be seen to take sides, Janice.'

'If we can get a conclusion on this over the weekend – '

'The case has already been closed, and I cannot reopen it without official approval. How are you going to continue investigating something that doesn't officially exist?'

'You're technically in charge of the unit. Surely you can do it.'

He didn't like the way she said *technically*, or how she used his first name while according Bryant the dignity of a surname. 'I can't without producing quantifiable evidence for doing so.'

'So you're just going to walk away from us?'

'Haven't you seen? They're impounding our files, sealing everything for later examination. I can't go along with you, Janice. Take whatever you need and leave, get out of here before they try to stop you. If anyone asks me, I didn't see anything.'

'Well thanks a lot, Raymond, you really know how to put yourself on the line for us.' Longbright slammed the door behind her, only to reopen it. 'And don't forget to collect Crippen's bowl and litter tray before you go. It's your turn to take him home with you.'

Alma Sorrowbridge was not thrilled with the idea of nine members of the PCU putting their boots all over her freshly vacuumed rugs. She made them tea and left warm yellow cornbread on the sideboard where they could help themselves, then beat a hasty retreat to the Evangelical church on Haverstock Hill.

As everyone arrived and settled in, John May laid down the files that the group deemed relevant to the proceedings by mutual consensus. Soon they had covered the floor of the lounge. May rocked back on his thighs and glanced across the labelled autopsy photographs, the CVs, the personal data files, the murder-location photographs and toxicology reports.

'Well, we know that Pellew never worked with his victims,' he announced, 'because he was in the secure wing of the Twelve Elms Cross hospital during the period that our ladies worked at Theseus.'

'The company has a website of sorts,' said April, turning her laptop around to show them, 'but as you'd expect it's not very forthcoming about their activities.' The screen revealed the anodyne silver logo of Theseus Research, together with a mission statement padded out with words like 'safety', 'protection' and 'excellence', but not much else. 'They're clearly an outside resource for the MoD, with no familiar names on their masthead. There are several authors of articles mentioned by name, though.'

'I don't recognize any of those.' Kershaw read down the screen.

'Wait, I know that one,' said Banbury. 'Katherine Cairns-Underhill, she was formerly attached to Porton Down as a virologist. She was one of the leading UK consultants during the Sarin gas attacks in Japan. Keep going.'

April continued to scroll through the site. 'I know that one,' said Kershaw. 'Iain Worthington, he's a senior epidemiologist at the Royal Free Hospital.'

'Skin diseases?' asked Bimsley.

'Epidemics, pathogenic spread. It sounds to me

like Theseus Research is involved in the prevention of chemical warfare.'

'Arthur, where did they get their name? You must know all about the myths surrounding Theseus.'

'I can remember bits and pieces,' said Bryant. 'He was a founding hero of Greece, a great reformer. There was something about him recovering his father's sword and sandals from beneath a gigantic rock. He slew the Minotaur with the help of Ariadne's thread. He even survived a trip to Hades. I think the key part here is his trip through the labyrinth to locate the Minotaur. It's analogous to the process of scientific discovery. But I don't think we can piece much more together from a few incomplete scraps of information.'

'We need to figure out where to look for Jackie Quinten,' said Meera. 'Do you think she could be inside their building?'

'Is there still nothing on the police reports about her?'

'Her description has been issued,' said May, 'but I don't know how we'll find out what's going on from – forgive me, Arthur – a converted toothbrush factory in Chalk Farm. I do wish you'd kept your old Battersea flat with Alma.'

'There are still a few people who owe me favours in the Met,' said Renfield. 'I can call around.'

At a little before seven p.m. the clouds above the house split open and rain lashed down the banks of the garden, running beneath the back door. The hall quickly became flooded, and rivulets trickled as far as the lounge. By this time, the unit's staff were sprawled out on armchairs and sofas throughout the building, like fractious members of a house party trapped indoors by the weather.

'All those times Jackie spoke to you,' said May in some

exasperation. 'You've even been to her house. Don't you remember her telling you anything about herself?'

'I wasn't really listening,' Bryant admitted. 'You know what I'm like.'

'I suppose you were multi-tasking.'

'No, I was just thinking of something else.'

'Now's the time to use the memory-training techniques Mrs Mandeville's been teaching you.'

Bryant thought long and hard. 'It's no good,' he said finally. 'I need to smoke a pipe.'

'All the windows are closed,' said Meera. 'Do you have to?'

'It always helped Sherlock Holmes.'

'He was a fictional character.'

Bryant decided to light up anyway, and produced some matches. He squinted at the yellow label on the box, then donned his reading glasses. 'I say, has anyone noticed this?' He held up the matchbox, studying the logo in amazement. 'That's us. "Bryant and May – England's Glory". I don't know why I never thought of that before.'

After three pipes the room was filled with fragrant smoke. 'Can we open a window now?' asked Meera. 'It smells like burning tulips.' She didn't explain to anyone how she knew.

'Can you really remember nothing you discussed with her?' asked May.

'All I'm sure of is that Jackie didn't know about the deaths when I bumped into her at the Yorkshire Grey,' said Bryant, thinking the matter through. 'And the time I saw her before that, we talked mainly about the first law of behavioural genetics, I have no idea why. We discussed map-making, too. She runs the local-history society. Told me a lot about London's geography.'

'She might not have been meeting anyone,' said Longbright. 'She might simply have become frightened and gone away until everything has blown over.'

'No, she was definitely seeing a friend, she told me so herself.'

Everyone looked dumbfounded. 'What do you mean?' asked May.

'When I saw her in the pub she said something about going out on Saturday to meet one of her gentlemen academics.' It was typical of Bryant to leave out a piece of information anyone else would have felt compelled to pass on, but in this case he had only just remembered.

'You might have told us earlier,' said Longbright. 'You don't suppose she killed them, do you? And somehow blamed Pellew?'

'That makes no sense at all,' May told her.

'The DNA matches were perfect on both blood and sweat,' Kershaw reminded them, 'and the thumb-print matched Pellew's. We know it was him. *Quod erat demonstrandum.*'

'But he was the symptom, not the cause,' Bryant insisted. 'The most dangerous element in this case was not Pellew at all, but the person who impelled his actions. I don't think we have a way of dealing with the matter now. We're simply not equipped.'

He needed to give the others some air. Clambering up and heading for the back door, he stepped outside, breathing deeply, standing beneath the eaves as rain fell in sheets before him.

Pellew and Quinten, he thought. *There's really no connection between them. How could there be? Did Pellew really go to the Exmouth Arms, just to leave behind the clue in the photograph?* He had never come across a case remotely like this. Nothing hung together, none of it was linked. *Anthony Pellew. A research laboratory. A clinic for mental disorders. Five – no, seven*

– lonely, maternal women. The Ministry of Defence. If only my memory—

And then he remembered, something small, no more than a single sentence. *Thank God for Mrs Mandeville,* he thought. *I take it all back, your system works!*

He shot back to the lounge much lighter in his step.

'Arthur, we've been talking this round in circles,' said Longbright, 'and we're convinced that you must be able to remember something more about Jackie Quinten. Do you have any idea who it was she went to see?'

'Oh, I think I know now. I just don't understand why, or what her connection is with him.'

'Oh, for God's sake, Arthur, spit it out!' cried May finally.

Bryant widened his eyes. 'She went to find Dr Harold Masters.'

'Wait a minute – your old friend Masters, the lecturer, the one I met in that odd little tavern?'

'I'm afraid so. Anyone will tell you that academics have a tendency towards sociopathic behaviour, and I think my old friend has finally overstepped the line.'

'I don't understand,' May admitted. 'What has he got to do with Jackie Quinten?'

'That I'm not sure of yet. But I think he's got a lot to do with this,' he told the others, dragging on his overcoat. 'And I can guess where to find Mrs Quinten. There's no time to waste. I've known Harold for years, if only in a sort of distant way, but I'm familiar with his habits. He's likely to be in one of three places. Colin and Meera, I need you to go to his house in Spitalfields. John and I will try the pub he told us he frequents. Janice, I'd like you and Sergeant Renfield to head for his office at the British Museum. And be careful. By now he may well be ready to kill in order to protect his secret.'

41

THE PATH OF HOPE

'He told me himself where he spends his evenings.' Bryant hurried his partner through the fine soaking rain towards the car. 'He's a creature of habit, and he doesn't know we're looking for him.'

May's immaculate BMW wound its way down through the fading light towards Smithfields, and the welcoming lights of the Hope Tavern in Cowcross Street. The roads around them were deserted. They would not come to life until the clubs started up later in the evening.

'The pub usually opens early for the market's meat porters, and apparently derived its name from the Path of Hope,' Bryant told him, 'a section of the route taken by condemned prisoners from Newgate on their way to execution. The market didn't appear until around 1855, but the pub's curved-glass bay windows date it from an earlier time. Look at the etched windows, mythical birds surrounding twined Ts and Hs.'

'This is no time for one of your guided tours, Arthur.'

'Many years ago I took it upon myself to educate you, and I have not yet given up hope. Don't feel bad, it's been a reciprocal process. You showed me how to use my mobile phone correctly. Those calls I was accidentally making to Kuala Lumpur were costing me a fortune. Why have you got a tennis ball in your glove compartment?'

'Leave that alone,' warned May. 'It's there in case I lose my keys again.'

'I don't understand.'

'Something Renfield taught me. You make a small hole in the ball, stick it over the lock and punch it. The air pressure pops the lock open.'

'That man has a touch of the tealeaf about him,' said Bryant with a look of disapproval.

'What do you expect? He was dealing with thieves on the street all day before he came to us. Anyway, you could learn a bit from him.' Like other members in the unit, May had begun grudgingly to reassess the sergeant.

As they alighted and locked the vehicle, Bryant started examining the pub's woodwork until May pulled him inside.

'I think Jackie Quinten did discover that some of her colleagues were dead, and at that point she must have realized what connected them all,' Bryant declared, heading straight for the bar. 'She needed to confide in someone, to visit a person in a position of trust. The Official Secrets Act remains in place after you leave a government establishment. She couldn't unburden herself to an outsider. It had to be someone she had known through the company she had worked for.'

'And you think she came here?'

'I'm convinced of it. I tried a couple of Kiskaya Mandeville's memory techniques and remembered something Masters said to me when I went to see him, about Christ's blood going missing in Clerkenwell.'

'Christ's blood?' repeated May, more confused than ever.

Bryant irritably waved the thought aside. 'He said something very odd, but I didn't think anything of it at the time. Masters thinks aloud, it's not always easy to follow what he's on about. With people like that, you let a certain amount of what they say slip by you. He said, "I lecture on ancient mythologies these days. I'm not in haematology any more, unless you count the Athenian." I knew he studied medicine, of course, he's a doctor, but I had no idea of the branch he specialized in. Haematology, the study of blood, blood-producing tissues and, more importantly in this case, sanguinary diseases. So why would he mention the Athenian? Well, to a lecturer in mythology there can only be one Athenian – the greatest king of Athens, Theseus. I think he was referring to the Theseus Research group euphemistically, one of those bright little remarks he can expect to toss out and have ignored by his acolytes.'

'Except that you didn't miss it,' said May, pleased. 'Let's search the place. You can explain the rest later.'

'Alas, it's unlikely I'll be able to do that. We need to find Mrs Quinten before we get any further answers.'

Asking the bar staff if any of them had noticed a tall, grey-haired academic in the saloon during the last few days merely started an argument between them about height, weight and hair colour, at which point the detectives realized they would not get any easy answers.

'She needed to seek him out,' said Bryant, 'but there's no record of her calling him from her house phone or her mobile, so she must have known where to go.'

'Either that, or she's somewhere else entirely.'

'I can't allow myself to think that, John. I need to be right about this. We've nothing else left.'

Colin Bimsley was too big for Jackie Quinten's home. Owing to his difficulties with space and balance, he had grown up in a house where the only ornaments were unbreakable and usually cemented down. Now he edged his way through rooms cluttered with pottery jugs, dainty china bowls, display glassware, antique violins, rare maps and fragile Edwardian dolls' furniture. 'I don't know where to begin looking with all this crap about,' he complained.

'She's a collector,' said Meera. 'I've already been here once today, I didn't need you to come back with me.'

'Maybe you missed something.'

Meera shot him a look that could have peeled wallpaper. 'Go and do the kitchen. I'll check the bedrooms. I don't trust you on the stairs. Wait.'

Bimsley's eyes widened in alarm. 'What?'

'That girl who dropped you off, have you seen her again?'

'Izabella? Not yet. I was going to give her a ring tonight, see if she was up for a beer and a curry, but now it looks like we'll be working late. At least we'll be together, eh?' Meera seemed to be immune to his smile, but he tried one hopefully.

'Yeah, great.' He feared she was being sarcastic.

With a sigh, Bimsley headed for the kitchen and went through all the drawers, even looking inside the microwave. There was nothing here that he would not have expected to find. He leaned back on the draining board, looking around the tiny galley, and knocked a cup into the sink. He was trying to fit the handle back on when he noticed the empty cardboard boxes in the small back yard.

The brand-new leaf incinerator seemed an odd thing to own, as there were no trees overhanging the property. Outside, he removed the steel lid and peered in at the charred remains of paperwork. He knew that burned pages could sometimes be deciphered if they were layered between sheets of cotton and sent to forensic document experts, but the rain had worked its way into the metal container and had soaked the remains. Reaching in, he dug his shovel-like hands into the soggy mess. The downpour had put the fire out, and only the top sheets had been burnt. Underneath, entire folders were wet but intact. He began to lift them out.

'Meera,' he called, 'give me a hand.'

Together they managed to bag half a dozen barely scorched folders of paper. 'Let's get this inside and read it,' he suggested.

'We should take it back.'

'No time for that, and no place to take it back to, remember? If there's something here that can tell us where Quinten went, we need to know right now.'

They started to sort through the documents. *You chase thieves and murderers through the city streets*, thought Bimsley with a sigh, *but somehow you always end up doing paperwork. That's how they caught Al Capone. That's what always gets the convictions in the end.*

42

BLOOD MONEY

Jackie Quinten had all but given up hope of finding Dr Harold Masters.

She had tried his darkened house in Spitalfields before heading back to the lecture hall in the British Museum, where an assistant had traced him to a rear section of the basement. Jackie was presented with instructions for finding Room 2135, but the building was a labyrinth of identical corridors and office doors. This was the backstage area of the British Museum that the public never saw: institutional, drab, unchanged in decades.

Overhead, neon strip-lights buzzed faintly behind dusty plastic panels. The last of the visitors had gone. Only the night guards and a few members of staff were left, but the museum was larger than a city block, and the handful who remained were hidden somewhere behind sound-deadening walls. The building that acted as a great repository of the past had defied many attempts to make it less oppressive, and only the dimpled glass roof of the new Great Court was truly capable of raising spirits. Elsewhere, in the narrow back channels, morgue-like chambers and suffocating windowless rooms, the weight of history bore down with a melancholy pressure that slowed movement and reduced all conversation to awed whispers.

Jackie had been feeling unsettled ever since she awoke that morning. She had discovered some days ago that Joanne Kellerman had died, and although it seemed a tragedy there was nothing to be done, for they had hardly been close friends. But in today's issue of *Hard News* she found two more names, Naomi Curtis and Carol Wynley, dead within a day of one another. She scoured the newspapers looking for further articles and found one small piece in the *Evening Standard*, another in a local free-sheet, but the rest of the news items were only concerned with a pretty young black girl who had died of unnatural causes in a pub she had never heard of.

She panicked. She could think of no one else but Dr Masters to discuss the matter with, but even he had proved elusive. Suddenly, it seemed, the events of the past had returned to disturb her sleep . . .

The person she should have called, she realized, was Arthur Bryant. The problem was that she liked him, and enlisting his aid meant revealing the full extent of her complicity.

The corridor seemed to lead nowhere. Its end wall was entirely blank, the skirting board merely running around it to connect two opposing doors. A marble bust of a forgotten plunderer of antiquities stood on a discoloured marble plinth. Jackie checked the number on the slip of paper in her hand and counted down the doors. She knocked on 2135 and waited, but there was no answer. The handle turned easily, so she entered.

The room was lined with plans chests, upon which were piled tagged sections of stone, statues patiently awaiting reassembly. Masters was seated beneath the single cone of light from his green enamel reading lamp, intently writing, his eyes so close to the page that his nose almost touched the paper.

'Harold?' She took a step further into the darkened room. 'I'm sorry, am I disturbing you?'

'No. I suppose I was half-expecting you.' He sounded confused, as if he had just woken up to find himself in a strange place. He sat back in his chair, stretching his spine. 'You lose track of time down here. It's terrible for the posture.' He did not rise to greet her. 'How are you, Jackie?'

'I expected to see you at the Yorkshire Grey this week.'

'Oh, the Immortals. It completely slipped my mind. I've had a lot to worry about lately. I suppose you've heard something. It was inevitable that you would.'

She came forward into the light, setting her handbag on the edge of the swamped desk. 'I haven't been able to concentrate on anything else all day. I don't know what to think. I tried calling Jocelyn, but I couldn't get any answer.'

'She's also dead.' Masters seemed to lose interest, and returned to his writing.

'That's absurd.'

'Absurd or not, it's a fact,' he said impatiently. 'She died in the Old Bell Tavern in Fleet Street. Rather, I should say she was killed, just like the others.'

'In another pub – it doesn't make sense.'

'Oh, I'm afraid it does.' Masters placed a ruler on the page and carefully drew a line in blue ink. 'That was the way he worked.'

'But that just leaves me, Mary and Jennifer. I mean, out of the mothers.'

'You weren't real mothers or even surrogate ones, you were little more than nurses.'

'We became attached to our charges – how could they have expected us not to?'

'Well, you shouldn't have. There's no room for sentiment where science is concerned. He would have come after the rest of you as well, but the police stopped him. He's dead.'

'My God.' Jackie drew out a chair opposite Masters and sat down heavily. 'I can't believe somebody would have done this. Was it really so important that we knew?'

'Don't be so naïve, of course it's important. You can't compromise in a situation like this.'

'Then I don't understand why the press aren't making more of it. Surely people want the facts?'

'Really?' He looked up at her now and slowly removed his reading glasses. 'Don't you think it's in the Ministry's interests not to let it get out?'

'We still live in a democracy, Harold, no matter how tainted it's become of late. Things like this can't—'

'Things like this,' he cut across her, 'happen all the time in places where the powerful gather. What about Litvinenko? His dinner at the Sheraton Park Lane was poisoned with Polonium-210, for God's sake. A series of government murder plots involving Russian spies, death and a trail of radioactive contamination? It sounds like the plot of a James Bond film, but it happened right here. Nobody cares about a relapsed psychotic putting a few alcoholic middle-aged legal secretaries to sleep. How many times have stories about reoffending "care-in-the-community" patients made the papers for a couple of days before being forgotten?'

'How do you know so much about it?' she asked, suddenly suspicious. She had once valued Masters' friendship, had comforted him during his wife's decline and death, but his defensive attitude was starting to disturb her.

'Porton Down re-hired me on a freelance contract.'

'I thought you said you would never go back there.'

'They had an academic problem that I found intriguing. I said I'd help them out.'

She glanced nervously back at the door, and he caught her looking. 'Why would you do that?' she asked. 'What happened to you?'

'You may ask what is the purpose of an academic? What are we for? I thought it was to make discoveries, to render visible the lines that bind civilizations. Then one day I made a discovery that called into question everything for which I thought I stood. It's not just about the slow accumulation of empirical data, you know. We are granted epiphanies occasionally. We may even pronounce them to the world, but like the Oracle, we are doomed never to be believed.'

'What did you do for Porton Down?' she persisted.

'There's such a thing as accountability, Jackie. The research teams there couldn't be seen to – they needed a solution to a thorny ethical problem. You must understand. I didn't know any of them except you, of course.' He pushed his writing pad back with careful deliberation.

She spoke in shocked gravity. 'What did you do?'

'Society must abide by the rules it creates, otherwise we descend into moral anarchy.' He spoke with the clarity of a man who had something to hide. 'You know how the law works in cases like this. You were sworn to secrecy, and now you're in breach of your contracts. The documents you signed – you *all* signed – are still legally binding. And you were paid well. Do you want to betray your country?'

'It was blood money, and you know it.'

Masters sighed. 'This is all water under the bridge. Everything has been cleared up now. There's no reason why any of it should ever get out.'

'It will get out, Harold. Mary and Jennifer are still here. *I'm* still here,' Jackie persisted. 'I'm still alive.'

'No, I'm afraid you're not,' said Masters, wearily rising from behind his desk.

43

BENEATH THE ANTIQUITIES

The British Museum was the oldest public museum on the planet.

It had been built to house the purchases and gifts collected from around the world by Sir Hans Sloane in 1753, items of such antiquity that appreciating the convoluted circumstances of their history had become a challenge in itself. Almost every exhibit told an extraordinary story, from the graceful Portland Vase, produced before the birth of Christ, only to be smashed into two hundred pieces by a drunken sailor in 1845 and then painstakingly reassembled, to the Lindow Man, a two-thousand-year-old peasant preserved in the acid of a Cheshire peat bog.

It was not a particularly friendly or accessible museum. Artefacts withheld their secrets, and the weight of lost empires hung heavily about the remains. A mere stroll through chambers of glass cabinets taught little, and left no impression; it worked best when no more than half a dozen objects were examined at one time.

Janice Longbright and Jack Renfield had managed to

get themselves admitted, but the girl who had opened the side door thought Masters had gone for the night, and went off to look for him in the direction of the Egyptian Hall.

'I'm not going to wait for her,' said Renfield. 'She could be up to something dodgy. He'll be out of the toilet window before we can grab hold of him.'

'He's a senior curator and lecturer at one of the world's most prestigious institutions,' said Longbright, studying the Grecian statues at the top of the stairs. 'He doesn't leap out of lavatory windows. You have a suspicious mind.'

'I'm a bloody copper. Come on, let's have a shufti. You're going to have trouble keeping up with me in those shoes. I can't believe they let you get away with a breach of uniform regulations like that.'

'I've always worn heels on duty, it's my look. Mr Bryant says he believes in the foolishness of consistency.' Longbright reluctantly followed her opposite number up the south staircase. Dominating the entire landing was a white marble discus-thrower, devoid of its correct setting, out of place and time.

'You don't have to get all toffee-nosed about it, Janice. I know where you come from, you're south London working class, just like me. Either you want to catch a law-breaker, in which case you do everything within your power to do so, or you're happy to let him get away.'

'We don't usually do a lot of running about,' she said lamely. Renfield made her realize how sheltered she had been at the PCU. There had been one hundred and eighty murders in the capital over the last year. Two and a half thousand reported rapes. Nearly two hundred thousand instances of violence against the person. And nearly one million men and women in the Met. Perhaps now she would have to go back into the force and deal with the crimes they faced every day of their working lives.

'Do you know what this bloke looks like, Janice?'

'I'd recognize him, but you're going the wrong way. He'll be at the back of the building, where the researchers' offices are.' She hunted about for the correct avenue. 'Down here.'

'This isn't the way my old squad would have gone about it,' grumbled Renfield. 'If she's with Masters, do we take them both in for questioning? As far as I know, they haven't broken any law.'

'We talk to them honestly, Renfield, that's what the PCU does best. It's not always about following rules.'

'Yeah, I figured that much out. This geezer's not dangerous, is he?' Renfield tried the door opposite, but it was locked. 'She's not at risk? Not that I'm bothered. If we find 'em and he cuts up rough we'll be all right, 'cause you're big, I'm heavy and he's just a bookworm. Now which way?'

'Turn left.' Hopping to pull her shoe strap back in place, she led them along a harshly lit passage painted in searing stripes of cadmium yellow.

'How do you know where to go?'

'Mr Bryant has a lot of friends who use these offices. Restorers, engravers, historians.' She tried a heavy oak door as they passed, but it failed to open. 'He sounded worried, and when he gets like that I know there's something going on in his head that he hasn't told us about. I think Masters should be in one of the chambers along here.'

'You all seem to have so much respect for him, but he doesn't do a lot, does he, your Mr Bryant?'

'People either get him or they don't, he's old school. He does things quietly, in his own way. Doesn't like to waste words or expend unnecessary energy. He believes in unfashionable concepts: grace, calm, honesty, understatement.'

'Then he's out of step with the world, and he'll get trodden on.'

'I thought you were going to try and understand.'

'I'm still biting my tongue sometimes, OK? What are you doing?'

'I'm calling him.' She pressed an ear hard against her mobile. 'Hardly any signal. Can you hear me? Yes, we're there now, Masters is supposed to be somewhere nearby. What? We'll try it, but you need to get here as soon as you can.'

'What did he say?' asked Renfield as Longbright closed her phone.

'He says we're to try rooms 2100 to 2140.' Longbright pointed to the corridor ahead. 'And he thinks Jackie Quinten's life is at risk.'

44

ACCOUNTABILITY

'Wait, we have to go back,' said Longbright. All the passages had begun to look the same. 'We're too far over.'

'Do you know where he is, or don't you?' Renfield looked around. The buzzing overhead panels bathed the halls in sea-green light.

'The corridors are meant to be painted differently in this section.' She turned round. 'We've gone wrong somewhere.'

'We need to go back to the big marble stairwell, where the bloke with the frisbee was. You can work it out again from there.'

Renfield broke into a run, forcing her to keep up. They reached a narrow staff staircase and he took the steps three at a time, as if he had finally come to terms with the idea that Bryant was not playing the fool, and that a murder could only be halted by their intervention. Longbright followed closely behind, almost slamming into him as he stopped dead and listened.

They both heard the voice, too loud for normal speech

in a museum. Renfield continued along the passageway, putting on an extra spurt of speed when he spotted something she had yet to see.

He knows something bad is about to happen, she thought. She had seen this instinctive talent, born of experience and an almost supernatural prescience, in just a handful of policemen. It was the last thing she had expected to encounter in a man like Renfield. *He's one of us*, she thought, surprised to recognize her own ability.

Jackie Quinten made a run for it but wasn't as agile as she thought, and her ankle twisted beneath her weight on the slippery tiled floor. She fell hard.

Masters didn't come after her. If anything, he seemed mortified at having to sort out the mess he now found himself in. He was fumbling about in his desk drawer, looking for something.

'Please,' he called after her. 'I just came up with the solution, it was a theoretical conundrum, that's all. I didn't want to be involved. I'm not cut out for this sort of thing. My career here is over, did I tell you? The museum is letting me go. Some new people have come in, and they don't approve of my lecture style. I'm too partisan. It seems you can't have opinions in public these days. And I don't get the audience figures they want. I have to do other things now in order to survive. But this is too much to expect of anyone, let alone me.' He found the object of his search and removed it from the drawer – a long red-and-green-tartan scarf. 'I've been looking for this everywhere. Please, you mustn't be frightened. It'll do neither of us any good.'

He watched as she climbed to her feet and hobbled to the door, then came around the desk to her, holding up the scarf.

'I'm afraid I don't have anything else I can use,' he

apologized, wrapping the scarf around her exposed throat and pulling it tight. 'I promise you, I've never done anything like this before. I don't want to do it now, but there's no other way out. Of course, I admit it's my fault. I didn't think the police would close in on Anthony so quickly, and I certainly never imagined he would start leaving them clues. Now I have to clear up the mess he's created or they'll deal with me, too. You do understand, don't you?'

With the fiery noose of the scarf across her throat, Jackie could only stare helplessly up at her captor. His height gave him an immense advantage; he was able to keep her off-balance as he dragged her back into the corridor towards the staircase.

'When you're young, you imagine rising to the top of your profession, but of course you never can.' He was almost talking to himself now, faltering in a plea to be understood. 'There's always someone above you, someone behind you, someone to watch out for, someone to answer to. Do you know how far up this chain goes? Further than you'd ever dream. There's no one who can help me, no sympathy for what I've done, and why should there be? We live in a society that can only function by finding someone to blame, and they will rightly blame me. My solution to their problem was brilliant in its simplicity, but of course things never stay simple. I found them a madman, and now that he has failed I am being forced to finish his work.'

The more she struggled, the tighter the noose grew. He yanked on the scarf, as one would pull on a dog's lead to rein it in. She fought to stay upright, knowing that if she fell she would be strangled to death.

'It's a matter of accountability. Contract out the work and it seems almost inevitable that the person you've entrusted it to will let you down. In the old days it was

"Never mind, old chap, you did your best." Now it's "Fix it yourself or be prepared to take the blame for everything." Are you familiar with George Orwell? You remember in *1984*, how Winston Smith tells Julia "We are the dead"? That's how I feel now.'

He yanked hard on the scarf, causing her to gasp in pain. Her heels left ragged black lines along the cream linoleum floor.

'Once I was a brilliant academic with a soaring future ahead of me. When you agree to do something you know to be wrong, you tell yourself it will just happen once. Then you find yourself doing it just to remain afloat. Finally you become just like them, one of the dead, a walking cadaver obeying orders to stay alive.'

He hauled her to the edge of the balustrade and kicked her legs out from under her, easily holding her squirming body against the stonework. Jackie felt her centre of gravity shifting as he pulled her over the edge. They were only two floors up, but he was tipping her upside-down to cause the maximum impact. She felt her stomach flop, as though she was boarding a funfair ride.

Her greying auburn hair fell over her face, obscuring her sight. His hand slipped between her thighs, sliding over her tights, so that he was holding her almost vertically. She knew that the fall could kill her. She could only fear that it would not be instant.

They were above Masters, Longbright saw that now. They had passed along the passage near the top of the building, aligned with the roof of the Great Court, to emerge in the service area at the top of the stairwell. The academic was diagonally below them, trying to unhook Mrs Quinten's legs from the balustrade, but now her right hand had gained purchase on the rail, so he was pummelling at her back and stomach in a desperate attempt to make her release her grip.

The impossibility of the situation was enough to paralyse Longbright. If they made their presence known to Masters he would either release her, allowing her to fall under her own weight, or attack her with greater violence.

She was still trying to reach a decision when Renfield shot down the stairs and threw his broad frame in a foolhardy but spectacular airborne rugby tackle that slammed Masters to the steps so hard that it cracked his ribs and punched the air from his lungs.

Renfield climbed to his feet, unfazed, and reached over the balcony just as Jackie Quinten's grip failed, dragging her back across the balustrade like a sack of flour. He fell on to the stairs beside Masters, with Quinten lying on top of him. It was undignified, but seemed to have done the trick.

'You make one sudden move, sunshine,' he told the inert doctor, 'and I'll tear your bleeding head off.' But with the scarf loosened from her throat, Mrs Quinten suddenly started to scream and thrash about in shock, and in the brief moments it took Renfield to quell the tangle of limbs, Masters had risen and run into the gallery straight ahead of them.

Renfield abandoned his charge and was following now, but Longbright had the lead and closed in behind Masters as he blundered past the Cetole, the only surviving English musical instrument of the Middle Ages, resplendent in its glass case.

He was limping, clutching at his cracked ribcage, and she caught up with him in the clock room, by Congreve's rolling-ball timepiece of 1810. He threw out his right arm with such suddenness that she was taken by surprise. The blow to her face knocked her head back, sending her to the floor, but she was up on her feet even before Renfield appeared in the doorway.

'No, Jack,' she told the sergeant. 'He's mine.'

Masters was more shocked than anyone when Longbright slammed into him, pressing down on the fractured ribs in his chest. He exhaled painfully and fell back, hitting the case behind with his full weight. Inside, the bulbous black-and-white vase tilted on to its rim.

Longbright stepped back in horror. 'Oh no,' she said quietly. 'The Portland Vase. Not again.' It had survived two millennia only to be shattered. In one of the greatest restoration feats ever attempted in modern times, it had been made whole once more. She watched the vase as it rolled around on the edge of its base, teetering on its plinth.

The priceless antique had passed its point of equilibrium, and tipped over.

The glass case was not wide enough to allow it to fall properly, and the vase was held at a forty-five-degree angle, settling safely as the wounded academic slid down to the floor and began to cry for his own fractured life.

45

THE METHOD

'It's all in here,' said April, tapping the rescued folders. 'And it's all about babies. Or rather, mothers and babies.'

Ye Olde Mitre tavern in Ely Court, Hatton Garden, was a godsend to the nine drenched, exhausted men and women who found themselves together on a miserably wet Saturday night. The members of the PCU had nowhere else to go. Alma Sorrowbridge had banned them from Bryant's house because Colin Bimsley had walked something nasty through the lounge on his boots before knocking over a jug less unique, but with more sentimental value, than the Portland Vase.

April, Meera and Colin might have uncovered the documentation needed to resolve the investigation, but Renfield was nonplussed to find himself the hero of the hour. Uncomfortable with the attention, he spent most of his time at the bar, returning with fresh drinks whenever he spotted an empty glass on the table. He had already bought Longbright three pints of Guinness. He liked a woman who could hold her stout.

'We're still piecing together a timeline of events,' April warned, spreading the print-outs and typed pages across the beer-stained table. The detective constables had elected her to translate their elements into something resembling a narrative. 'As far as we can tell, it begins with Dr Peter Jukes, chief scientist for chemical and biological defence at the MoD's Porton Down laboratory.'

'Jukes?' repeated Kershaw. 'What has he got to do with all this?'

'If you recall, Giles, we knew he was a colleague of Jocelyn Roquesby, and that he had drowned while he was still employed as a consultant for Porton Down. It made sense that she met him at work. She might even have had an affair with him.'

'But she wasn't at Porton Down – '

'No, like the others, Mrs Roquesby worked for Theseus Research in King's Cross, one of the companies to whom Porton Down outsourced contracts. The women were legal secretaries, nothing more than that. Jackie Quinten was formerly employed there. She'd retired, but had agreed to be pressed back into service on a part-time basis. Her security rating was still intact, after all, but what brought her back? Well, they were seven middle-aged women who all appeared to share something in common. None of them were able to have children of their own.'

'Wait,' said Banbury. 'Doesn't Mrs Roquesby have a daughter?'

'Eleanor Roquesby is adopted,' April corrected.

'And Jackie Quinten's child is her stepson,' Bryant pointed out.

'One of Porton Down's chief remits was – and no doubt still is – to prevent a chemical terrorist attack from occurring in London and the other major cities of Great Britain,' April continued. 'You remember the Aum Shinrikyo religious cult in Japan? In 1995, they attempted to hasten the apocalypse by carrying out five Sarin gas attacks on the Tokyo metro, killing twelve and injuring a thousand. It would appear from Mrs Quinten's unburned notes that Theseus had indeed developed a new vaccine. It had been tried on animals with a high level of success, but they needed to test it on humans, and in the light of increasing terrorist warnings that culminated in the 7/7 attacks, they had to act quickly.

'So, in the course of their experiments, Jukes discreetly asked around for volunteers to take part in an experiment. He needed to carry it out with unethical expediency. His brief was to administer a preventative vaccine to live subjects, humans less than eighteen months old. None of the infants are identified in Mrs Quinten's notes, but it seems at least two had been abandoned in Eastern European orphanages. To Joanne Kellerman and the others, it lessened the moral burden if they were assured that the babies had been given up for adoption in the direst of circumstances. It also seems clear the women were told that their charges faced absolutely no risk of infection. They agreed to foster them, taking care of the infants during their working hours at Theseus, some helping to monitor their well-being through the night. The babies were to be allowed medication for ten weeks, but at the end of this period they unexpectedly became sick, and one by one they died. All this we have from Mrs Quinten's notes.'

'What went wrong?' asked Kershaw.

'Jukes' drug proved to have unforeseen side effects. Perhaps the infants would have lived had they been older or healthier – but who would allow their children to undergo such testing, even given assurances that no possible harm could come to them? So the mortified women were paid off and sworn to secrecy. They left their jobs with good redundancy money – we have Mrs Quinten's old payslips

– and were reminded of their allegiance to the Official Secrets Act.

'What nobody counted on was the fact that Joanne Kellerman and the others felt increasingly uncomfortable with their own consciences, and were eventually unable to process the guilt surrounding their unwitting complicity. They agreed to meet up in a pub. Perhaps just two of them met at first, but the meetings clearly grew to involve five out of the seven women. They liked a drink and they were on safe neutral ground, away from loved ones. Their security was not seen to be compromised. They could talk freely without being watched. London is full of secrets, and they were dealing with theirs in the best way they knew how, by quietly and privately discussing it.'

'But secrets have a way of escaping.'

'Exactly. It was Jackie Quinten who remembered her colleague Masters, and went to him for advice. He didn't know the others and probably only knew Mrs Quinten slightly, but she trusted him.'

'No doubt she appealed to him as a humanitarian,' said Bryant. 'But he betrayed her by telling Theseus about the possible information leak. They, in return, hired him to come up with a foolproof way of containing the damage. Imagine the scandal if the matter got out to the press. It was an appealingly bizarre conjectural problem. And his solution was suitably peculiar to it.'

'That's right,' said April. 'Masters was intrigued by the proposition. He decided that in order to commit an undiscoverable crime an agent was needed, a fall guy. So he contacted various clinics and hospitals to ask them about the psychological profiles of their patients.'

'And he found someone made for the job,' Bryant explained. 'A man who would harm if carefully directed and provided with the correct means. It was Masters who placed the request to have Pellew released, with the weight of the MoD behind him. And armed with Pellew's confidential notes, it was he who gave him the syringes. Under those circumstances, how hard was it to get Pellew to fall back into his old habits, do you think? I mean, by pushing the right psychological buttons and supplying the method?'

'So Theseus got the poor, deranged Pellew released through Masters, who offered him easy victims?' asked Longbright.

'That's right,' Bryant agreed. 'All Pellew had to do was specify where and when he was prepared to commit the acts he had fantasized about for so long.'

'And he wanted to perform his little psychodramas in pubs,' said Kershaw.

'Of course, they were the only places in which he would operate. It was why he had kidnapped his girlfriend in the past, what had led to his original conviction. Masters would have known that.'

'Stranger things have happened,' said May. 'It could have been the perfect cover-up. With the deaths only traceable as far as a reoffending mental patient, there could be no sign of Theseus's involvement. The entire matter would have been sealed, and the plan wouldn't be able to be traced back. But no one considered the idea that their killer might want to be caught. He started leaving behind clues.'

'Funny how you only ever really find out what people are capable of when their plans go wrong,' said Longbright, thinking about the increasingly panicked Masters.

'I hate to say I told you so,' Bryant gleamed. 'Pellew knew he was being manipulated and hated it, so he set out to be caught. I can't imagine the mental turmoil he must have been going through. No wonder he ended up running into the traffic before he could be brought to justice. But his death left others who could still go public.'

'Masters had already gone to extraordinary lengths to comply with whatever Pellew said he needed to carry out Theseus's cover-up,' said April, 'and because he insisted on catching Carol Wynley on her way home, they were forced to fake up the front of a public house to lure her in.'

'I told you I hadn't imagined it,' Bryant interrupted. 'You all thought I was going barmy. Once Pellew had started, he couldn't be stopped without giving the game away. By this time, Theseus must have been so desperate for the rest of Masters' plan to work that they were prepared to hire a designer and a couple of scenery shifters to knock up a simple *trompe l'oeil*, a false pub front that would lead into the dressed and emptied shop. They bribed the owner to close down for the evening, then put everything back in place afterwards. They had even recorded the sound of pub chatter. But they messed up the authenticity by using a couple of conflicting photographic references for the building, and constructed a pub that could not possibly exist. The Victoria had been built in 1845 but the Victoria Cross wasn't awarded until 1857. They compounded the error by including the clock just as it had appeared in my photograph. Wonderful news to Pellew, of course, who continued to sabotage their plans by leaving us clues in the pubs he picked. "Doctor", "seven belles", "conspiracy", things that weren't as they seemed, even his own name. It was Pellew who left the photograph in the Exmouth Arms for us to find. Unfortunately, in keeping with the strange workings of his mind, these pointers proved so obscure that—'

'That no one but you could have found him, Arthur,' said May, sipping his bitter.

'I must admit, I do find myself intrigued by the strange

pairing of Pellew and Masters. Pellew's profile pegged him as an egotist unable to empathize with others. True to type, he appears to have been selfish, withdrawn, incapable of normal social interaction. How surprised must he have been by his sudden release? He was aware of the appalling nature of his actions – why else would he try to guarantee his own capture? But Masters' behaviour, supposedly acting for the greater good, must have puzzled him. And Pellew was on a roll. Part of him was addicted to the thrill of the hunt, part of him was abominably ashamed. Still, the aberrant behaviour patterns that had been reawoken in him were enough to drive him to attack a woman who wasn't on the list, purely out of desire.'

'Jasmina Sherwin, the girl who was assaulted in the Albion, Barnsbury,' said Bimsley, grasping the bigger picture.

'So, what happens now?' asked Longbright.

'We have to go after Theseus,' said Bryant, without pausing to think.

'We've got no status, no office, no dosh,' said Meera disconsolately. 'And we're working out of a pub.'

'Besides, Theseus is a government outsource,' May reminded him. 'How far do you honestly think you'll get?'

'When a democratic government is no longer accountable for its actions, it becomes a dictatorship. Besides, who says they even know what's been going on? The Ministry of Defence is a law unto itself. I wouldn't be surprised if they've hung Theseus out to dry.'

Behind them, the door banged open and Raymond Land burst in wearing a plastic mackintosh, spraying water around like a retriever emerging from a pond. 'Ah, here you all are. I've been looking for you everywhere.' He shook his umbrella violently, searching for somewhere to leave it.

'Get you a drink?' asked Renfield.

'No, no, can't stop, unfortunately, the wife will give me gyp. Purely a business call.' He turned to his detectives and saw the paperwork spread on the table 'Should you be examining evidence in a pub?'

'They're only copies,' April explained. 'Obviously the originals are safely stowed away.'

'Quite, understood. You should know that Leslie Faraday has promised to try and find you new accommodation as soon as possible. This won't be for ever, you know. You can't operate out of a boozer.'

'Come off it, Raymondo,' said Bryant. 'You know as well as I do that they've finally got us where they want us. What's the likelihood of them re-housing the unit somewhere else?'

'I do see your point, but I'm not here to discuss that. It's rather more serious, I'm afraid.' He drew a fortifying breath. 'To me has befallen the unpleasant task of placing you and Mr May under arrest.'

'What on earth for?' asked May, startled.

'Breach of the Official Secrets Act, I'm afraid.'

'But we don't operate under its jurisdiction.'

'Since the Peculiar Crimes Unit is answerable to the Home Office, you are government employees. You have knowingly disseminated information from protected Ministry of Defence sources.'

'I forwarded Jocelyn Roquesby's computer files to the office terminal,' April admitted. 'It never occurred to me that it was already in someone else's hands – '

'So you'll both have to come with me to West End Central and face charges.' Land's determination faded into sheepishness.

'We'd love to help you, *vieux haricot*, but I'm afraid it's quite impossible,' said Bryant with a smirk. 'You see, you're in Ye Old Mitre tavern.'

'What has that got to do with anything?' asked Land.

'Well, due to a mix-up with certain clauses in the Land Registry Act several centuries ago, Ye Old Mitre is not, technically speaking, part of London, but in ancient Cambridgeshire. The City of London police have no jurisdiction in here.'

'You're having a laugh, aren't you?' Land turned to the barman, dumbfounded. 'Is this true?'

'I'm afraid so, mate,' said the barman. 'No one can be arrested within the pub or in the immediate environs of Ely Court. This isn't London, it's Cambridge. Don't look at me, I'm Australian. You lot are the ones with the bloody silly laws.'

Bryant coaxed his distraught boss to a stool and helped him out of his mackintosh. 'And as we're not going to be leaving here until well after the last bell has sounded,' he said, 'you might as well get a round in for all of us.'

46

GUERRILLA TACTICS

'We unwittingly opposed a government project,' whispered May, waiting while the nurse finished attending to Mrs Quinten. 'What did you expect to happen?'

'I expected a desire to trace culpability,' snapped his partner, looking around at the sleeping hospital ward.

After a boozy night with his emphatic detectives, Land had agreed to try and have the charges against them temporarily suspended on cognizance of their exemplary records and their willingness to abide by instructions issued from HO Internal Security. It was nothing more than they expected and demanded, but while they were cooling their heels at home for the remainder of the night, scouring internet reports for any news of the case, they discovered that the managing director of Theseus Research had already been assigned to another post, this time in Atlanta, Georgia.

'There are others who know, you may be assured of that,' said Bryant, burying himself inside his tweed coat. 'Containment on this scale never works. I've no doubt both the birth mothers and the remaining fosterers would have their credibility destroyed should any choose to come forward, but there are others who must have seen what they saw.'

'Inadmissable hearsay, not empirical data. How thoroughly has all the proof been destroyed? Our one hope now is that Jackie – ah, Mrs Quinten.' May sat forward in his chair and studied her sleepy eyes. 'Not in too much pain, I hope?'

'Some bruising, a few scratches, nothing a child couldn't handle,' the nurse told them. 'But she'll have a very sore throat for a while. You shouldn't be here, you know. The other patients aren't awake yet.' She adjusted the curtains around them and left.

'I've been wondering about Harold Masters,' said Mrs Quinten softly. 'I thought I understood him. I can't imagine why any man would have done what he did. He wasn't interested in making money.'

'It was less about money than pride,' said Bryant. 'The museum had reduced his workload and was in the process of letting him go. He'd worked for Porton Down before, and knew how far Theseus would go to cover up a mistake, because at the end of the day that's all it was. Remember those British volunteers who participated in the anti-inflammatory drugs trial conducted by the German pharmaceutical company TeGenero AG? Their heads swelled up and they nearly died. The drug was designed to treat rheumatoid arthritis, leukaemia and multiple sclerosis. The Theseus drug trial was conducted for an even more altruistic reason: to prevent innocents from dying on the streets of London.'

'They showed us the paperwork,' said Jackie Quinten. 'All of the babies had been signed over to the state by their mothers. One was an orphan whose parents had died travelling to Britain from Ethiopia. Another was abandoned in a McDonald's bag by heroin addicts.

Everyone I spoke to at Theseus was committed to helping the children. They told us it would just be one safe short-term drug trial. I saw them every day. Harold Masters saw me with the little Ethiopian boy and said, "You could always adopt him when he leaves here." But I couldn't, you see. I'd been turned down before, after some trouble with my stepson. And Jocelyn had faced problems with alcoholism. None of us thought we could truly adopt, not for a minute, but we took the opportunity to look after the babies and were paid a little extra.

'It was Carol's baby that got sick first. He started crying and couldn't stop, until he could barely draw breath. It all happened so quickly, on the third and fourth days of the trial. One after the other they went blue – cyanosis, the doctor said – and their hearts stopped. They held a single funeral on the Friday, just hours after the last autopsy. A terrible afternoon. It didn't stop raining, and the graves couldn't be filled in because of flooding. We were never told what had gone wrong. We were paid our bonuses, reminded of our loyalties to the company and that was that.

'But I couldn't stop thinking about my little boy. I had to talk to someone, and so I called Jocelyn. One time we persuaded Carol and Joanne to join us, and shortly after that we began holding regular meetings in different pubs.'

'It got back to Theseus that you had re-formed your group of friends,' said May. 'It looks like Masters sold you out for a contract to fix the security leak.'

'But we wouldn't have gone to the press,' said Jackie miserably. 'We just needed the comfort of conversation, some assurance that we weren't responsible for what had happened. What I don't understand is, how could they take such drastic action against us?' asked Jackie.

'Well, I'm afraid even we can't tell you that,' said Bryant, rising to leave. 'I'll call on you again.'

'I'll be going home in a while,' said Jackie. 'If you like, I can cook you a meal and help you answer any other questions you might have.'

'Thank you, no.' Bryant smiled sadly. 'Our work is not quite finished.'

'She doesn't understand how anyone can conceive of killing witnesses to what was technically a humanitarian defence project,' said May as they left University College Hospital, 'because she doesn't know who commissioned it. Masters said it went all the way to the top. I can guess whose signature was on the order to test the antitoxin. Did you know Theseus is an Anglo-American operation? There's a chap called Senator Nathan Maddock who fits the bill very nicely. A hard-line right-winger with the ear of both the president and the prime minister, the man who tells British defence what to do. But I don't think even he would have agreed to act without Masters' assurance that the remedy was completely untraceable.'

'What level of panic would induce a company used to handling state defence contracts to hire the services of a mental patient?' Bryant wondered as they walked through falling rain towards May's car. 'Didn't they stop to consider how many things could go wrong in that scenario?'

'You can look at it this way,' said May. 'Theseus survives.'

'Only because we'll never be allowed to go public with the story. We don't even have a unit any more.'

'And we can't go public, Arthur, because nobody there will ever acknowledge what happened, even if any one person had possession of all the facts.'

'They know, John. And we could let them know that *we* know. We could get in there.'

'No, no, no.' May shook his head in vehemence. 'We have nothing left, Arthur. As of this minute, we have no official status. What are you going to do, kick the door down and blast everyone with a shotgun?'

'You just said we have no official status. We're off the radar.' Bryant was forced to shout in order to compete with the traffic on Euston Road. 'This may require guerrilla tactics.'

'Don't you think you're a little too old to be thinking about bringing down the government?' asked May.

'I've been thinking about it all my life,' said Bryant with a twinkle in his eye. 'Might as well go out with a bang.'

47

PANDORA'S BOX

Arthur Bryant passed two six-foot butterflies and a red-rubber nurse tottering on platform heels before he started to wonder if he really was hallucinating this time.

At eight o'clock on Sunday morning, the only people on the streets of King's Cross were backpackers leaving their hostels and thematically dressed denizens of a large nightclub, all of whom looked very much the worse for wear.

The courtyard door leading to the refurbished office complex behind York Way had been left discreetly ajar by the overqualified Polish cleaners who nightly restored workspaces to their functional glory. Slipping inside, Bryant crossed the new cobblestones and once more found himself before the gates of Theseus Research.

What an arrogant name, he thought, peering through the bars at the brushed-steel logo adorning the sea of darkened glass before him. *Theseus was both mortal and divine. His father, Poseidon, was the god of the ocean. Appropriate, considering that Dr Peter Jukes had been washed up on shore, a victim of its turbulent currents.*

Bryant had studied the tidal charts and suspected that, as much as he wanted to blame Theseus, suicide could not be ruled out. He supposed no one would ever get to the absolute truth surrounding Dr Jukes' death. *Such is the path of vigilance*, he thought. *Each single mystery precipitates a dozen more. Then again, Theseus was thrown off a cliff after losing his popularity, so perhaps the company directors might find it best not to behave too much like gods.*

Mandume was in his usual place. Providing twenty-four-hour security for Theseus Research required three men, but Bryant had calculated the shifts correctly. His obvious respect for the security officer and his performance of general doddery politeness stood him in good stead. Mandume saw him and smiled, happy to approach. He even opened the gate slightly to chat.

'Hi there. Any luck with your walking club?'

'We've decided to re-route our tour through another part of town, but thank you for asking. I missed you yesterday, when I came to visit my grandson.'

'My day off,' the guard told him. 'I went to visit my little boy. He lives with his mother.'

'It's difficult to know where to take the kids sometimes, isn't it?' said Bryant, as if he had any clue at all about children and divorced parents.

'He likes dinosaurs, so we went to the Natural History Museum. You know that place?'

'Certainly, I've been there many times. I daresay they will put me there when I retire. A joke.' The guard had looked blank, but now smiled. 'Why don't you bring your boy here to see where his father works? I'm sure he'd be interested.'

Mandume's smile vanished. 'No, no, not here.'

He's heard something, thought Bryant. *Secrets have a way of escaping.* 'When I came here yesterday I stupidly forgot to leave my grandson's christening gift. My son's wife gave birth to a baby boy. I wonder, could I go and leave it on his desk? It would only take a moment.'

'Where is your son today? Could you not give it to him yourself?'

'No, he has to visit his wife in hospital, and they're not allowed to use mobiles inside, so I can't call him.' *The lies*, he thought. *They trip from the tongue so easily I'm almost ashamed of myself.*

'Or if I can't leave it on his desk, perhaps you could. I'd be very grateful. No child's birth should go uncelebrated in the eyes of Our Lord, don't you agree?' For a fleeting moment, Bryant wondered if he was overdoing it.

Mandume looked so uncomfortable that Bryant felt bad about pushing him.

'I could leave it behind reception, in the janitor's room,' he said uncertainly.

'But he may not get it then. I believe he goes straight up to his desk from the car park. You know how things can go missing in a building this size.' *Time to show that you've got more front than Selfridges*, thought Bryant. 'Look, I know you're not allowed to go to the laboratories. They are underground, aren't they, and require security passes. But I'm also a government employee, and I'll be happy to take responsibility for the package myself.' He gave Mandume a fleeting glimpse of his police pass. 'You see, I'm actually a policeman. So surely you could go up to the second-floor reception desk and leave it there.'

The guard glanced back at the building nervously. Bryant knew it was bristling with cameras. 'Sure, I am allowed up there. I can go wherever I want.'

'Thank you, it's a small thing but he'll be so very pleased.' He passed the small, ribbon-tied box and card through the gate.

'Hey, no problem. You take care of yourself.'

He trusts me, Bryant thought guiltily as he turned away.

Paradoxically, the idea had come from Harold Masters himself, when he had revealed at the beginning of the week that a crystal vial containing the blood of Christ was liable to hold germs that would be dangerous in a modern environment. It had set Bryant thinking, and reminded him that they were employing a man with connections in such a field.

Dan Banbury had done a brilliant job at short notice. *If he ever goes to the bad we'll all be in danger, the lad has a terrible knack for such things*, he thought, eyeing the innocent package.

Going to the press about Theseus would require leaving a trail back to the PCU, so Dan had suggested that an appropriate way to deal with the company was to send them a message showing that their secret was out. Inside the chocolate box was a soluble membrane filled with a colourless, odourless fluid. Banbury had whipped it up in Kershaw's lab from ordinary household ingredients, using a recipe he had developed at college.

It would take approximately five hours for the membrane to dissolve at room temperature, releasing the chemical through the slotted plastic base of the box. As it evaporated, the exposed oily particles would be drawn into the working ventilation system and would cling to every surface inside the building.

The chemical components would induce mild nausea and vomiting, but would have no lasting effect. However, the offices would need to be evacuated and quarantined while everything was cleaned. In a nice touch, Banbury had thought to include the photographs of the four women who had died because of what they knew. Resignations would no doubt be tendered, questions would be asked, and new brooms would discreetly sweep clean, but ultimately the company would survive.

As he walked away, it occurred to Bryant that the only person to get hurt by his actions would be the guard. *They'll fire Mandume and remove his security status*, he thought gloomily.

48

THE LAST FAREWELL

On the following Wednesday morning, Arthur Bryant stood motionless in the rain on Gray's Inn Road, watching the iridescent carapaces of black taxis chug past King's Cross station.

Beyond the railway tracks, cranes were moving girders with regal slowness, replacing the demolished Victorian housing blocks with vast glass boxes. *London is becoming an alien place to me*, he thought, *polyglot, splintered and patchwork. But I think I'm actually learning to like it this way. Perhaps we can finally be whoever we want to be.*

Once there had been recognizable London types, ranks as distinct and separate as bird families were to twitchers. They had been replaced by fluctuating, instinctive tribes. Now, the city's occupants seemed united by tension and velocity.

We've traded away something precious, he realized. *This is no longer a city in which you can ever relax. I remember . . .*

He remembered empty wet streets where the sound

of clinking milk bottles acted as alarm clocks, where the clop of a carthorse was a call to bring out unwanted furniture. He remembered so much that the weight of it all made him tired.

A faint nightscape of stars like sugar grains in the smoky dusk above London Fields.

Ragged children running after a Bentley driven slowly through Bethnal Green, the same children who danced behind the trucks that sprayed water on roads during August scorchers.

The rickety Embankment tree-walk, illuminated with Chinese lanterns made of coloured paper.

Raucous chimps' tea parties at the London Zoological Gardens.

His mother swimming in the Thames, sunbathing on the sickly yellow artificial beach at Tower Bridge. Albert, his tragically short-lived brother, building sand-castles.

Thomas and Jack, his uncles, mending beehives behind Southwark Bridge, delivering sacks of root vegetables for illegal sale in the side streets of Bermondsey.

His crazy half-sister Alice, playing the untuneable piano in her dive bar in the basement of the Borough Corn Exchange, the same bar that had the channel of a forgotten underground river sluicing through the back of its gents' toilet.

Too much to remember. Time to let it go, he told himself.

Nothing had yet appeared in print about the contamination of a Defence Ministry outsource agency, but two days ago he had received notification from Leslie Faraday that the PCU had been officially disbanded owing to public-spending cuts.

The offices above Mornington Crescent Tube station had already been filled by a new department specializing in some kind of electronic fraud. Nobody had been told who comprised the new team, or what exactly they did. The old locks had already been replaced with a swipe-card system, and white shutters had been lowered over the arched windows. *At least we stayed true to ourselves,* he smiled. *Even if it did involve poisoning a government building in an act of revenge. A small subversion, perhaps, but a necessary one.*

The tall blue shape flapping through the downpour towards him coalesced into the figure of John May. 'Arthur, what are you doing here?' he demanded to know. 'I thought we were going to meet on Waterloo Bridge as usual. You'll catch your death of cold.'

'I wanted to be somewhere different today,' said Bryant. 'I'm very wet.'

'Is there a decent pub around here?'

The elderly detective swivelled himself about, checking in either direction. 'That way,' he pointed, peeping out above his scarf.

They went to the Water Rats on Gray's Inn Road. 'I know this place,' said May, pushing open the door. 'Bob Dylan performed here in 1962. And Oasis.'

'I suppose that's a pop group of some sort,' said Bryant, hauling himself on to a bar stool.

'More of a Beatles tribute band. I thought you were going to stay up to date with popular culture,' May admonished.

'Oh, I tried but it was so boring, just affairs and divorces and who's snubbing who. Like the 1950s, only more vulgar. I don't understand why the young admire celebrities who possess the charm of intestinal parasites. I saw that singer in the paper, the one with a face like a boiled owl, complaining about how she hated to be recognized. In the accompanying photograph she had chosen to reveal a substantial portion of her pubic bone below a black-leather corset. Within ten seconds of finishing the article I had already forgotten her name.'

'I thought you had got your memory back.'

'Mrs Mandeville's techniques worked wonders, I must say. I still tend to favour remembrance of the arcane over the relevant, but that's more to do with personal taste.' He held up his pint, waiting impatiently for it to settle. 'For example, do you know why this pub is associated with music, and how it got its name?'

May raised an eyebrow. 'I have a feeling you're going to tell me.'

'You'll like this one. I'm thinking of including it on my next guided tour of London. At the end of the nineteenth century, some music-hall performers purchased a puny little horse called Magpie, and used its race winnings to help the London poor and Eastern European refugees. One rainy day, a day not unlike this, a couple of the owners were returning the soaked Magpie to its stable when a passing bus-driver asked what it was. They replied that it was a trotting pony. 'Trotting pony?' mocked the driver. 'It looks more like a bleedin' water rat!' From that remark was born the Grand Order of the Water Rats, a showbusiness brotherhood presided over by Prince Philip and Prince Charles that performs charitable works irrespective of race, creed or colour. Not bad work for a run-down boozer behind a railway station.'

'Perhaps it's important that someone should remember things like that,' said May.

'Indeed. So long as somebody remembers, the city remains alive.'

'I've been thinking about the PCU all week,' May admitted with a sigh. 'It's the others I feel sorry for. Where will they go? I don't suppose the Met will want any of them back. Why are gifted individuals always forced out by the mediocracy?'

'True. If you're a woman, or senior, or Muslim, you'll only ever get so far. *They* make sure of that. But we've done all our best work in our later years. Men only come to their senses in their fifties, around about the time that most housewives go mad. They realize what they've lost and what they can still achieve.'

'On the way over here I was thinking about the years we spent in the rooms above Mornington Crescent Tube station.'

'I'm going to miss the place. We had some fun there, didn't we?'

'You mean when we weren't blowing it up, hiding wanted criminals in its cupboards, freeing groups of illegal immigrants, burying evidence, falsifying documents and telling dirty jokes to members of the royal family?'

'It was all for the public good.' Bryant was wide-eyed with innocence, but it was a look that would have fooled no one. 'Although I'll admit I'm quite surprised that the ministry didn't pay someone to knock us off, simply for being a constant source of embarrassment to them.'

'I heard you took Dan Banbury back to the supermarket in Whidbourne Street the other day.'

'Yes, I thought I'd search for signs that the pub had been installed there. He told me they were pretty easy to spot once he knew where to look. Screwdriver damage, scraps of tape and paint-stencil marks. Of course, the building had originally been converted from a pub to a shop, so it required very little effort to turn back time for an evening. They simply placed painted flats over the lower half of the extended shop windows and whacked some plant-holders on top. We can't press charges on the store owner, as it seems he was pressured into cooperation by people from Theseus. Some kind of bureaucratic error to do with his immigration visa. I'd love to have seen the look on Harold Masters' face when Pellew told him what he wanted next.

Masters was over a barrel by that time. What could he do but comply with Pellew's request?'

'He'll carry the can for all of this, you wait and see. He's the perfect scapegoat, a dazed, embittered academic, trapped into compounding a series of crimes by proxy. How convenient for everyone.'

'I can't feel too sorry for him, John. He chose his path long ago. I shall enjoy writing up the case for my memoirs.'

'And to think we would never have uncovered any of this if you hadn't decided to wander home half-cut,' said May.

'I just wish I could remember what happened to Oswald Finch's ashes,' said Bryant, 'because that was really where it all – oh my God.'

'What's the matter?'

'I've just remembered what I did with them.'

'What *you* did with them?'

'I'll admit I was a bit drunk. I was standing at the bar staring at that ghastly cheap urn, thinking about how much Oswald would have hated being in it, and decided he should have a better home.'

'Oh no.' May clenched his teeth, preparing for the worst.

'I unscrewed the lid and took out the contents. The ashes were in a plastic bag. I was going to transfer him to Alma's tulip vase. I thought he'd be happier in there.'

'Why didn't you just take the urn home with you?'

'I hated it. I threw it into the bin behind the bar.'

'What did you do with his ashes, Arthur?'

'I put them in the only bag I could find. The one Janice had bought for the office.' Bryant tried to suppress a laugh, but it escaped and grew until May, too, understood what had happened, and found himself joining in.

49

THE COLOUR OF BLOOD

Arthur Bryant stood before the illuminated glass case containing the holy relic, and knew that he had discovered the answer to an extraordinary conundrum.

His hands shook with the knowledge of something so incredible. 'I'm the only other one who knows,' he told May. 'The only other person to figure it out, and it's all because of something Harold Masters said.'

They were back in the British Museum, far beneath the sound of pattering rain, in chambers filled with artefacts few tourists bothered to examine.

'The mythic ancient pubs, like the Jerusalem in Britton Street and the Rose and Crown in Clerkenwell, they don't reveal the secret. What I'm looking for isn't hidden in either of them. The Crown isn't a crown of thorns, just regal adornment. The so-called clues are mere puzzle-games for students of folklore. Harold knew all along, you see.'

'No, I don't see at all,' May admitted. 'You're being a very confusing old man. You told me you saw him to ask about the blood of Christ. I knew the subject had been bothering you ever since we investigated that street gang, the Saladins. How – what – did he know? And why on earth would he agree to tell you?'

As Bryant had predicted, the bewildered academic now found himself in the dock for crimes he had not committed, but with the weight of Britain's security forces behind his prosecution, he did not stand a chance in hell of being vindicated. With the PCU closed down and disbanded, its investigating officers could give him no help.

Bryant turned his attention back to the glittering relic.

'Masters has probably known about this for quite a while, that's what started his extra-curricular research projects and brought him to the attention of Theseus in the first place. What a terrible burden of knowledge he faced. He'd discovered the fabled blood of Christ, and knew he could never bring it to anyone's attention. He told me why himself, only I was too stupid to understand at the time.'

'You mean that's it?' said May. 'That peculiar thing in the case? Why isn't it better protected? Why aren't there hordes of prostrate nuns around it?'

'Because nobody else knows it's here. They think it's something else entirely.'

The reliquary was bottle-shaped, elaborately jewelled and gilded, surrounded by enamelled angels, arches and sunbursts. May craned forward to study the inscription on the side that read ISTA EST UNA SPINA CORONA DOMINI NOSTRI IHESU XPISK. He noted the small plaque attached to the casing. 'It says this is the Holy Thorn reliquary belonging to Jean, Duc de Berry, created between 1400 and 1410. It was built to house Christ's crown of thorns from the Crucifixion.'

'Yes, but there's a mystery behind this strange object that has never been solved.' Bryant gave him a knowing look. He loved having the ability to enlighten others.

'It began with the construction of an imperial crown decorated with four of the original thorns from Christ's head, but some time later the crown was broken up and its component parts were re-used to make more treasures. The gifting and possession of such items was capable of wielding immense political influence. So four new separate reliquaries were assembled, but three of them were created by forgers. The only way to tell them apart was by looking at the enamelled backs of the doors, there, see? The fake versions don't have those.' He thumped a forefinger on the glass, indicating the centre of the jewelled reliquary.

'Here the story gets murky, because nobody knows what happened to this thing between the time it was constructed and when it came into the possession of the British Museum in 1898. Ignore the sapphires, pearls and rubies in the setting, ignore the trumpeting angels and the rather lurid scene of the Last Judgement which surrounds it, not to mention those gruesome cherubs raising the dead, and you'll see that there's a crystal window at its heart. Just in case you miss the point, there's an inscription that reads 'This is a thorn from the crown of Our Lord Jesus Christ'. *Xpisk?* Why not *Cristi*, the Latin for Christ? Well, there's certainly a thorn in there. Or is that what it is? Did you remember to bring your Valiant with you?'

May dug in his pocket and produced a huge red-topped cinema torch, while his partner kept an eye out for guards.

'Now, point it very carefully at the crystal.'

May shone the torch over the centre of the reliquary. The jewels responded to light by revealing a deep lustre of indigos, ivories, scarlets. 'What am I looking for?'

'Not the thorn itself, but the edges where it meets the surrounding encrustation of precious metals.'

Shining the Valiant at the centre of the reliquary, he opened up its dark heart. A glinting line appeared, like a fine molten seam. 'There's a defect,' he said. 'It looks like a very faint crack. Oh – I think I understand what you're getting at.'

'Yes,' said Bryant softly, crouching beside his partner. 'It's not a thorn at all, is it? It's oxidization. The air's got to it through a flaw in the crystal.'

'Oxidized blood,' said May, awed.

'Given its colour, you can see how easily the vial's contents were mistaken for something made of wood.'

'The blood of Christ. You really think that's what it is?'

'There's one man who might hold the answers, and now I don't suppose I'll be able to get anywhere near him,' replied Bryant. 'What if the flaw is so tiny that the vial's contents are only oxidized on its surface?'

May found himself sweating, despite the chill in the museum. 'My God, I see what you mean. It's an analysis sample. We'd be able to conduct the ultimate investigation. We'd have a direct line to the heart of the Christian faith.'

'Think of the uproar such a thing would create. Masters knew this, and it became his curse to know. He discovered Pandora's Box, and not only could he not open it, he would never be able to tell anyone of its existence without destroying his entire career. He's an expert on mythology, John. He's one of the most public atheists in the country.'

'And what do we do?' asked May. 'Secrets have a way of escaping, remember?'

'This is one that cannot be allowed to get out,' said Bryant, taking his partner's arm and leading him away, just as the guard returned to the chamber. 'We ignore it, and allow it to lie among the other treasures of confused provenance. Even as I speak, a team of very expensive lawyers is looking for ways to discredit Harold Masters. They can't silence him, but they can stop him from being believed. That's why you and I will escape any charges. Why would they risk having us reveal the things we know when they can simply throw the book at him?'

'Where are we going?' asked May as they headed towards the museum entrance.

'One last stop. I promised to meet Janice at the Pineapple pub in Kentish Town. She wants to tell us something.'

The pub was almost empty. Simon, the manager, was rinsing glasses and sending text messages while a handful of regulars stared grimly into their pints. Bimsley and Longbright were folded into a corner with the day's newspapers.

Bryant brought over beers and set them down. 'So what's this big announcement you feel you had to present to us in person?' he asked somewhat rudely.

'I don't know how true this is,' said Longbright, making room for them, 'but Gladys, my mother, once told me that when Betty Grable had her legs insured, all the girls went out and did the same thing. Sometimes it takes the action of someone you admire to make you follow suit.'

'This is all very interesting, but perhaps you could get to the point.'

'We all knew your big secret, Arthur, your planned resignation. You never adjusted to biros, did you? Still use that Waterman fountain pen – and blotting paper. The one thing you should have written in code, you couldn't because Raymond had to read it. So after deciphering your dreadful handwriting in a mirror, we took a vote on it and decided that if you were going to leave, the entire department would resign en masse.'

'I appreciate the gesture, Janice, but you have your own

careers to worry about.' Bryant was horrified. 'John, talk them out of this lunacy.'

'I can't,' May apologized. 'I joined them. Chucked in my lot as well.'

For one of the few times in his life, Bryant was speechless.

'You see, without you there's nothing left, old sprocket. You're the connection point between us all – and not just us; think of the hundreds of people you've helped in your life, all the people you've joined together. You've brought so many of London's outsiders inside, to become part of a wonderful – albeit somewhat alarming – community. You're at the top of our alternative family tree.'

Bryant shifted uncomfortably on his chair. 'Let's not get too sentimental, eh? We're all broke and out of work.'

'I haven't got enough money left to pay my rent,' said Bimsley gloomily.

'I feel a bit sorry for poor old Renfield. He only just joined us. The Met will never have him back.'

'At least we'll always remain friends,' said Longbright. 'Whatever happens, whatever the future holds. All ten of us. I'm including Raymond in this.'

'Oh, wonderful, the children I never wanted,' said Bryant. 'Whose round is it?'

50

ASHES TO ASHES

Raymond Land set down the food bowl and sneezed violently. 'What I want to know,' he demanded, 'is how come I end up having to look after Crippen when I'm the one who's allergic to cats. Are you listening to me, Leanne?'

'No, darling,' said his wife, who was licking a lipstick pencil and straightening her décolletage in the bathroom, readying herself for a night of sin and self-deception with a Spanish toyboy she had picked up in Castanets Tapas Bar, Streatham.

Land searched forlornly for the litter tray. 'You always seem to be refurbishing yourself these days. Where are you going?'

'I'm off to rumple some hotel sheets and have cheap champagne dribbled over my naked body,' she answered through mashing lips.

'I thought you were visiting your mother. It's raining so hard, the cat can't go out. What have you done with its litter?'

'I wouldn't touch the stuff, and if you knew what my

nails cost you wouldn't let me either. Don't you remember? Sergeant Longbright gave you the tray and the bag when she brought the cat over.'

Land located the litter bag, unfolded it and removed a clear plastic envelope filled with grey powder. Tearing the top with his teeth, he tipped it into the yellow plastic tray as a cloud of dust blossomed and assaulted his nasal membranes. 'This stuff is awful,' he complained. 'It smells like Oswald's mortuary.'

'The only thing Oswald's mortuary smelled of was Oswald,' said Leanne, pouting her lips in the mirror and wondering about their effect on Hispanic gentlemen under the age of twenty-five.

How could you begin to explain London?

A city once the colour of tobacco and carrots, now all chalky stone and angled steel, but vivid chimneypots can still be glimpsed between slivers of rain-specked glass. Nine billion pounds' worth of Christmas bonuses have just been spent in the City's square mile. In the great financial institutions, whirlpools of money are stirred until the ripples splash all but those on the farthest reaches of society. To accommodate this expenditure, the insurance offices and banks of Holborn have reopened as opulent restaurants and bars. At night, drunken merriment splits the capital's seams, and daybreak arrives more silently than midnight.

You can't explain London, of course. That is the root of its charm. A pair of elderly men, overlooked by the young, whittling their thoughts into bar banter, ensconced in run-down public houses in unalluring parts of the world's richest city, what could they know or hope to change?

For if they hoped that their actions might ultimately change the policies of the government, challenge public opinion, inspire the complacent, even alter the course of the city's history, they were wrong. London, a law unto itself, would continue quite happily without their interference. And yet, without them, it could only be a poorer place.

John May went into University College Hospital on March 3rd for his cancer operation. Arthur Bryant went with him, and stayed by his side until the orderly came to take his old friend down for surgery. As John May passed through the doors, he raised his head from the pillow and gave a look back at his great friend that said, *I know what you're about, and don't you ever forget it. Everything is understood between us.*

The framed photograph placed behind the bar of the Pineapple pub in Leverton Street, Kentish Town, shows a wrinkled tortoise sporting windowpane glasses and a frayed brown trilby, wrapped in a moss-green scarf like an unravelling knitted python. Close beside him, taller and just three years younger, is a ramrod-backed gentleman of debonair demeanour, dressed in a rather gaudy Savile Row suit and a scarlet silk tie.

They are smiling for the camera and for each other, as if they have finally come to understand all the secrets of the city.

APPENDIX

Mr Bryant's List of London Public Houses Consulted During the Course of His Investigation

The Devereux, 20 Devereux Court, WC2
The Seven Stars, 53 Carey Street, WC2
The Old Dr Butler's Head, 2 Mason's Avenue, EC2
The Albion, 10 Thornhill Road, N1
The Pineapple, 51 Leverton Street, NW5
Penderel's Oak, 283 High Holborn, WC1
The Old Mitre, 1 Ely Court, EC1
The Punch Tavern, 99 Fleet Street, EC4
The Crown and Sugarloaf, 26 Bride Lane, EC4
The Hand and Racquet, 48 Whitcomb Street, WC2
The Green Man and French Horn, 54 St Martin's Lane, WC2
The Jerusalem Tavern, Britton Street, EC1
The Skinner's Arms, 114 Judd Street, WC1
The Boot, 116 Cromer Street, WC1
Mabel's Tavern, 9 Mabledon Place, WC1
The Victoria Cross

The Victoria Park, 360 Victoria Park Road, E9
The Victoria and Albert, Marylebone Station, Melcombe Place, NW1
The Victoria Stakes, 1 Muswell Hill, N10
The Queen's Larder, 1 Queen Square, WC1N
The Angerstein Hotel, 108 Woolwich Road, SE10
The Old Bell Tavern, 95 Fleet Street, EC4
The Sutton Arms, 6 Carthusian Street, EC1
Williamson's Tavern, 1 Groveland Court, Bow Lane, EC4
The Viaduct Tavern, 126 Newgate Street, EC1
The Tipperary, 66 Fleet Street, EC4
The Red Lion, Waverton Street, W1
The White Hart, 89 Whitechapel High Street, E1
The Crown and Anchor, 137 Drummond Street, NW1
The Royal Oak, 73 Columbia Road, E2
The Coach and Horses, 29 Greek Street, W1
The Green Man, 383 Euston Road, NW1
The Sun in the Sands, 123 Shooters Hill Road, SE3
The Sherlock Holmes, 10–11 Northumberland Avenue, WC2
The Old Bank of England, 194 Fleet Street, EC4
The Old King Lud, 78 Ludgate Hill, EC4
The Nun and Broken Compass, 42 Warren Street, W1
The Apple Tree, 45 Mount Pleasant, WC1
The Museum Tavern, 49 Great Russell Street, WC1
The Betsey Trotwood, 56 Farringdon Road, EC1
The Ship and Shovell, 1–3 Craven Passage, WC2
The Yorkshire Grey, 29–33 Gray's Inn Road, WC1
The Plough, 27 Museum Street, WC1
The Water Rats, 328 Gray's Inn Road, WC1
The Queen's Head and Artichoke, 30–32 Albany Street, NW1
The Cross Keys, 31 Endell Street, WC2
The Bloomsbury Tavern, 236 Shaftesbury Avenue, WC2

The Exmouth Arms, 23 Exmouth Market, EC1
The Clock House, 82 Leather Lane, EC1
The Magpie and Stump, 18 Old Bailey, EC4
The White Lion, 24 James Street, WC2
The Hope and Anchor, 74 Crowndale Road, NW1
The Hope, 94 Cowcross Street, EC1